BONNIE ENGSTROM

BUTTERFLY DREAMS

Bonnie Engstrom

Copyright © 2015 Bonnie Engstrom

Forget Me Not Romances, a division of Winged Publications.

    All rights reserved as permitted under the U.S. Copyright Act of 1976. No part of the publication may be reproduced, distributed or transmitted in any form or by any means, or stored in a database or retrieval system, without prior permission of the publisher.

    All verses from NIV version

This book is a work of fiction. Names, characters, places, and incidents are the product of the author's imagination and are used fictitiously. Any resemblance to actual events, locales, or persons, living or dead, is coincidental, except for the instances where they were used in conjunction with a business on purpose.
All rights reserved.

ISBN-13: 979-8-8690-8021-9

DEDICATION

This book, as all future books by me, is dedicated first to my Lord and Savior, Jesus Christ. Also to my patient and supportive husband, Dave; to my Newport Beach, California Bible Study, my City of Grace Church Arizona Bible study and my online prayer warriors and old friends, women who have prayed for me faithfully. May God bless them all abundantly as He has blessed me with them..

ACKNOWLEDGMENTS

I could never have had the courage, the discipline and the skill to write this and my other books without the support and guidance of the members of American Christian Fiction Writers ~ Deb Raney, A. K. (Alice) Arenz, Diana Dilcher, Christina Tarabochia, Barbara Warren, Gayle Roper (who read this manuscript first at an ACFW conference and told me to "make a list for Betsy"), Cynthia Hickey (publisher extraordinaire and friend), and Ann Allen (MS Word guru), as well as members of the Orange County (CA) Christian Fiction Writers Fellowship ~ Kathi Macias, Peggy Matthews Rose, Joseph Bentz who encouraged me to attend Mt. Hermon, and Beverly Bush Smith (posthumously, my original mentor who dragged me to my first writing conference and insisted I never give up). I am indebted to my first, and only, critique group from the Mount Hermon Writers Conference, especially Kathryn Cushman and Mike Berrier who advised me with sensitivity and never gave up on me.

I never intended to deceive anyone, especially Betsy. She is the love of my life. But, it's gone on too long. Deception is not right. The truth must set me free, as well as all those I love.

BONNIE ENGSTROM

Happiness is like a butterfly; the more you chase it, the more it will elude you, but if you turn your attention to other things, it will come and sit softly on your shoulder ...

- Henry David Thoreau

Prologue

"You make the most unique salads. Heavens, Betsy, you should go into the business."

And that's how it all started.

Unfortunately, or maybe not, that comment was made by my mother. That's why my signature salad is dubbed "Heavenly Harriett."

Lists. My bane.

Grocery, shopping, cleaning, gifts to buy, bills to pay...hopes, dreams, a butterfly life.

I open my journal and write what to me seems obvious at my stage of life.

What I want:
1. A full-time live-in housekeeper. Nada on cooking. That's my department.
2. A come-to-the-house daily personal trainer to help me eliminate the love handles, protruding tum-tum and ballooning derriere.
3. A new catering van. Old Sassy is becoming very cantankerous. But, if I get wish #4, this is a moot wish.
4. A good, God-fearing, Bible-believing husband who is dripping in dough-the money kind.

Closing the book with a sigh and a snuffle, I start chopping.

ONE

I used to be skilled at multi-tasking.

It's starting to be a weird day. If I weren't a Christian woman I would use some expletives.

For starters the tomato is mushy. Now the phone is ringing. I grab it with a slippery hand.

I cut my finger trying to separate the plastic wrap from an English cucumber while holding the phone between my ear and shoulder.

"Yes, Bett, I'll try." I guess I was a bit curt, but this particular client always has last minute requests, especially since we've become friends. This time she wants an earlier delivery. At least she doesn't want to change the menu.

Suffering catfish! I'm out of E.V.O.O., FoodNetworkTV star Rachel Ray's acronym for olive oil, the extra virgin kind. This would never happen to Rache. Rolling my eyes way up I ask, "How many other hiccups am I going to have today?" No answer, just a crick in my neck and the realization that one of the fluorescent lights is blinking, almost out. Probably why I cut my finger. Seeing my hands in this business is important.

I'm a personal chef. I specialize in unique and exotic salads that feature dressings from family recipes passed down through four generations. I call them Heavenly Salade Presentations. They're gorgeous, healthy, opulent bowls of greens elaborately decorated with snippets and handfuls of seeds and berries, and, of course, the expected faire—tomatoes, cucumbers, onions, black olives. The tomatoes are Heirloom Princess Toms; the cucumbers, well you already know they're the variety from across The Pond; the onions—red, white and yellow are organic; and the noir olives are the Kalamata variety from the Never on Sunday land of Greece.

My client, the senescent owner of several impressive boutiques, doesn't give the simple hoot of a barn owl laying eggs. All she cares about is having her Salade Presentations delivered twenty minutes before her guests arrive so my van with Heavenly Catering emblazoned on the sides will have pulled out of her drive and be back on Shea Boulevard before her company comes. I also assume she will feign, in her ingenious ability to fabricate, to have concocted my creation.

Oh, forgot. Sorry. My name is Elizabeth Whatzit. That's the name most of my clients use when introducing me. Wysinotski is apparently too complicated for them to remember. I've gotten used to it. Really doesn't matter as long as they order and pay me on time.

The above mentioned "salade" is intended for Bettina Bethany, owner of the famed Bett's Boutiques, founded here in Scottsdale, Arizona and spread far and wide from Corona del Mar, California to Sewickly, Squirrel Hills and Shadyside, Pennsylvania. Why there? Who knows? Bett, as she prefers to be addressed, was raised in one of the environs of Pittsburgh. Maybe it's a roots thing. Maybe after she attended her fiftieth high school reunion in Penn Hills, a suburb just east of Pittsburgh, she found an old flame that agreed after several drinks of spiked punch to be an investor. Only Bett knows, and she isn't telling. As for the California connection, Bett loves the ocean and opulence, especially together. "It's only a one hour plane ride from Phoenix and gave me an excuse to buy a beach house."

I save the salad by substituting red bell pepper for the overly ripe tomatoes. Color is important.

I put hydrogen peroxide on the tiny cut on my finger and watch it bubble. After applying one of the many Band-aids I keep in a kitchen drawer, I don my disposable surgical gloves—a sous chef's backup for finger emergencies. Maybe next time I'll try using an onionskin on the cut the way my neighborhood butcher suggested. Seems a bit off the wall to me, but Tony swears by it. He brings the tips of his fingers together, kisses them and flings the kiss heavenward. "Stopsa the bleeding right away. Trusta me."

Today Ms. Bett will have a new creation, a "Boutique Salade" in honor of her Bett's Boutiques. As I sprinkle bits of feta cheese and whisk a combination of lemon infused oil (since there is no more E.V.O.O.) and balsamic vinegar with Elizabeth's Secret Spices (oo, la, la, Emeril, I have them, too), I am ready to roll. Bam!

I cradle the enormous, acacia wood bowl resting it above my tummy paunch. Did I mention I'm not a twenty-something entrepreneurial chef, but an almost sixty-something, post-menopausal, fully blossomed woman looking for another good man? I march and chant in cadence to a favorite childhood song. Marching to Pretoria palpitates silently in my brain.

We have food, the food is good, and
So let us eat together...
When we eat, it is a treat, and
So we will sing together,
As we march along.

Old Sassy, my supposed-to-be-white catering van is in need of a bath. The sliding side door is stuck, again. *Dear Lord, Would you be so kind to give me a clue what else is going to happen this afternoon. Should I just give it up? Or do you want me to persevere as Paul admonishes?*

When I'm really stressed to my personal limits I call on the Creator. *I can do all things through Christ who strengthens me.* Yeh! I truly believe that because He's gotten me through two marriages, three kids and a myriad of occupations. Still, when desperate, I cry, "Jesus, I need you NOW." Then I beg forgiveness for yelling at God. Filled with guilt and remorse I will go home this evening and kneel down at the side of my queen bed with the expensive hotel mattress and pray. God still answers knee prayer, doesn't He?

After the third try (why is everything in thirds?), Old Sassy's door slides open as if on E.V.O.O.-powered hydraulics.

I rest the gargantuan wooden bowl on the side runner of the van. The van bed is divided into twelve spaces, each with stretchy netting surrounding them. I don't know what that stuff is called, but a lot of people have it in the backs of their SUVs to keep groceries from sliding. Rolf, the guy I bought the van from, suggested it when I told him I'd be transporting lots of bowls and casseroles and didn't want them to slip en route. I remember he was kind of cute for a senior citizen. Lots of curly black hair, some of which needed a trim at his neckline. And he had a great smile. A little toothy, but very friendly.

The now accommodating side door of the van is opening wide, and I have this weird sensation that the squeal of its gears is really the sound of laughter. I wonder if a six thousand pound pile of twelve-year old metal can laugh? Anchoring the bowl with my knee to keep it from tipping, I pat the side of my dirty heap and whisper some kitschy words.

Clyde, my first husband, used to talk to his vehicles. I must have picked up the annoying habit from him. He vowed his vintage VW healed itself after a cooing pep talk. I, on the other hand, attributed the fact it started again for having sat three days in the coolness of the garage. Poor thing was probably lonely, wanting to go for a run.

I set down the mini-cooler holding perishable ingredients and deposit the heavy bowl of salad between two netting thingies. I check to be sure the bowl is tightly covered with plastic wrap, twice, and open the little cooler to drop about a dozen ice cubes on top of the plastic. Then I cover those with another layer of plastic from the giant industrial size roll I keep behind the driver's seat. The cooler finds a temporary home in another netted condo. I place the carafe of dressing on the passenger seat and strap it in with the seat belt—forbidding it to even jiggle. We're off. Onward and upward to Bett's. This is my mission. This is my gift. I am Boutique Salade in person. Heavenly Catering is my game.

Oh, my two marriages? They were wonderful—until Number One ended with death and Number Two ended with deception.

TWO

People tell me things.

I have one of those personalities that without trying attracts secrets, sort of like lights in the dark attract flitting moths. I guess that's a good analogy because sometimes my wings feel very fragile and transparent. And I'm so stupid I keep fluttering around the light.

I've tried to figure out why people share things that I don't want to know and have no clue how to help them with. Maybe it's the cross I wear at my throat, or the honesty of my prices, or my big baby blues.

It's not that I really want to know my clients' secrets. Sometimes their burdens are more than I can bear because I always feel led to pray for them. Then, if I forget, I'm consumed with guilt. Guilt leads to more prayer, only this time seeking forgiveness for having such a lousy memory. Sometimes I ask God to intervene in retrospect. I figure He can do anything. He created time, so why not? In truth, it's probably because I tuck my grizzled hair behind my overly large ears. I guess I've got the "big ear syndrome," always willing to listen and nod in sympathy. I suppose it doesn't hurt, either, that the first time a client confides in me I mumble, "I'll pray."

Bett tells me more than I want to know. Pulling into her impressive circular drive in Fountain Hills I remember I should have been praying for a difficult decision she has to make. I bonk my forehead with a fist and pull my catering cap low. *Did I forget again, Lord?"*

"No," a soft voice seems to whisper, "You prayed diligently for a week. You can't pray 24/7 for every need." *I did try, didn't I, Lord? I know you heard me. Well, let's see if it worked.*

It suddenly occurs to me I am sitting in my idling van having a conversation with Heaven when I should be standing at Bett's four by six foot granite kitchen island adding finishing touches to her Boutique Salad. Grabbing my purse from behind my left ankle and unbuckling the carafe of dressing, I slide out of the van and bump the door shut with my well-endowed derriere. I deposit the items on the sprawling flagstone veranda before going back for the bowl and cooler.

Just as a precaution, I gently pat the stubborn door and mumble a little prayer. I swear I'm not superstitious, but prayer never hurts in any situation. No amount of tugging or cooing makes that door open. I check my watch. Only fifteen minutes until Bett's guests arrive. Balancing on one foot and raising the other in my best soccer kick stance, I wallop the thing. "Open Sesame," I cry. It does, laughing again.

Pushing the over-sized front door with my foot I schlep everything onto the kitchen island of Bett's opulent home. The house is really a mini-mansion, and the kitchen has circular wraparound windows overlooking a negative edge lap pool perched on the precipice of a sliced- off hill. The effect is being on top of a mountain so high that angels might swoop down to check out what's cooking. Being a little acrophobic I try not to glance at the toy-sized houses scattered on the Monopoly board valley below. I'm sprinkling organic sunflower kernels and dried cranberries in elaborate patterns over the greens when the doorbell chimes.

"Honey, will you get that? Just pretend you're here to help serve." Bett often calls me Honey. She isn't real good with names. She pokes her carefully made-up face out the powder room door, and not waiting for a reply, retreats.

I scoop up all evidence of salad fixings, jam the bowl in the Sub-Zero fridge and straighten my starched white jacket. Grabbing a red tea towel I drape it over my forearm for effect, race to the foyer and tug open the heavy door.

"You must be one of Bettina's best kept secrets."

The deep, husky voice rumbles from a tan throat at my eye level. I tilt my head, find myself staring at an angular jaw, wide lips held captive between a cleft chin and a Romanesque nose sweeping down from between Crayola blue eyes. One of America's favorite original Crayon colors. I'd read that somewhere. Between the depth of their blueness and what I hope is a twinkle of humor, the eyes do it and I pull the door open wide.

"W – welcome. Please come in." I feel like a fool and surely sound the part. I cling to the elegant brass device that serves as a door handle and just stand there. The tall man leans forward a bit and takes a hesitant step toward me. That's when I notice the salt and pepper graying above his perfectly flat ears. "S-sorry," I mumble. My, I'm witty.

"Noel, dawling," Bett drawls behind me. "For heavens sake, don't just stand there. I see you've met Eleanor."

At least she gets the first letter right. "Elizabeth," I hiss.

"Oh, didn't I say that?" She also isn't good at taking responsibility. Which is why I'd been praying for her.

The Crayola eyes sparkle again, and the corners of the wide mouth twitch slightly. Is he smiling, or trying to control a laugh? At Bett, or at me?

"Nice to meet you," we say in unison. That gives us both license to laugh.

I retreat to the kitchen. Noel, huh? Cool name. Of course it might be Joel the way Bett messes up names. Still, Blue Eyes hadn't corrected her. The salad plates rattle and I almost drop one as I transfer them from the counter to the freezer to chill them. Why are my hands shaking? I can't afford to have arthritis in my business, or I'll be slicing off fingers instead of onion tops.

The repetitious chiming bell tells me other guests arrive, but it's only a guess as to who answered the door. Maybe Bett had her act together, or maybe she indentured Noel. At least it's not my problem.

Voices drift from a living room the size of a stadium. "Dawlings" and "Long times" bounce up to the twenty-two foot cantilevered ceiling. I hear the pop of corks and the distinctive clinking of glasses. "Cheers, salute, santé" echo around the huge room mingling with laughter. A celebratory toast? Maybe I don't know all of Bett's secrets. Yet.

Alone and cloistered in a kitchen the size of my condo community's clubhouse, I check my watch for possibly the twenty-third time. I start talking to myself, another bad habit. *Heavens, Betsy, what on God's green Earth is taking so long?* I check the salad in the fridge and give the bowl a gentle shake trying not to disturb the pattern of sunflower seeds adorning it. I twirl the carafe of dressing. Should I have added more garlic? I hate being *the server*. I'm a caterer for crying out loud, not the hired help. But, for Bett, for some reason I'm not sure of, I make exceptions. I vow this will be the last time.

"Oh, yoo-hoo, Sweetie." Bett's voice penetrates my daydreaming. No "Honey" this time. No Eliza, no Eleanor or Elaine. How hard I wonder is it for a mature successful businesswoman to remember "Elizabeth?"

No matter. I feel redeemed, saved from loneliness and banishment. I know she didn't mean to exclude me, so I make an effort to shove a tiny bit of resentment down in my protruding gut. When we're alone she calls me her best friend, her Christian confidante. Shouldn't someone like that be included in the festivities?

I reluctantly approach the huge dining room, and to my consternation I bow slightly. Eight people, three women and five men, are seated along both sides of a fake Tuscan table that could easily accommodate twenty. It looks a bit bizarre, but at least they're clustered at one end. After returning to the kitchen, I bring out the chilled plates and forks on an ebony tray laid with a cream-colored linen cloth. It matches the napkins tucked in ebony rings at each guest's place. Bett and Noel are filling stemmed glasses with icy water from the nearby bar's refrigerator. At least I'm spared that duty.

"Why don't you bring out my salade, dear?" Bett chirps. *Her salade!*

I stomp back to the kitchen and reappear to present the five-gallon bowl of greens, tilting it so all can see the intricate patterns of accoutrements laced over the top. I'll be hog washed if I'm going to walk around the table to show each person individually. Not in my lifetime.

"Ooo, sumptuous-looking. Beautiful," the voices exclaim.

Noel says, "You are so, so creative, Bett, even with something as simple as a salad."

"Thank you, Love."

Now that's over the top. Nothing is "simple" about this salad. I grip the sides of the bowl to resist dumping it on Noel's head. Even Bett should be offended by his remark, especially if the salad is supposed to be her concoction.

I make a flourish of dribbling dressing from the carafe and serving the salad, but refuse to carry each plate individually to every guest. I pass them down. Bett gives me a funny little squint I pretend not to see. I keep a smile pasted on my mouth, grit my teeth, grab the empty bowl and run back to the kitchen. Next time I will arrive thirty minutes ahead of schedule and leave ten minutes before any guests are due to arrive.

I quickly race the salad bowl, the cooler and carafe to my van. Thankfully, the door opens to my touch. Galloping guacamole, I forgot my purse. Slinking as quietly as a slightly overweight fifty-something chef can, I slither into the kitchen to retrieve it when Bett's thespian-tinny voice chirps from the swinging door.

"Evelyn, dear, would you mind awfully gathering up the plates and serving the dessert?" The sixth commandment comes to mind. God help me, please. I'm not really capable of murder, am I?

The cheesecake is from Cheesy Delights. No better, really, than Trader Joe's, and probably far more expensive. I divide it into eight wedges and drizzle a raspberry sauce that came with it over each slice. Feeling the need to enhance it, I locate a box of confectioners sugar in the walk-in pantry. I find a sifter and with a spoon scrape powdered sugar over each plate. Bett had the foresight to scoop coffee into the electronic coffee maker and even set the timer. Goodness, the woman is getting organized.

After serving the plates of cake on a tray the size of my buffet and placing a sterling silver carafe of coffee and cream on the large table, I retreat. Again. This time I hope it will last.

"Honey, we need to talk." Bett's moist hands enclose my still slightly shaking ones. She's left her guests, pursued me into the kitchen.

"Not now, I can't," I hear my trembling voice reply.

"When? Tomorrow? This is urgent."

I feel for Bett, but I do try to have a life. Tomorrow is Sunday, my day of rest. After church I try to go to a museum, a park with a sandwich in a plastic baggie, or even the lake with the ducks. Tomorrow is my day, and God's. Nothing, not even Bett, is going to disturb it.

"Please, Honey, I have a really BIG secret to share with you. And, I need your Christian advice."

Did I mention people tell me things?

I feel so guilty. But, I must protect myself, and especially Betsy. Yes, I know her name better than anyone, perhaps even better than her "mother." I pretend to be an airhead, to forget her name. Fifty-eight years is a long time to deny the truth. I want her to meet someone special, someone who I trust to love her the way she deserves to be loved. I hope I've made the right decision. I need to find a way to keep her here under my wing.

THREE

I heard a really good message in church. Funny, they don't call them sermons anymore. It was about being your brother's, or sister's, keeper. It had some relevance to Genesis 4:9 when Cain asked God the question about Abel. The parts I sort of half listened to I took to heart.

I want to reach out to others, to pray for them, even serve them. I belong to a community women's Bible study that meets every third Monday. One of the studies we had last year was how to be a woman of service. Pretty heavy. I volunteer every Thanksgiving to serve slop to the homeless. I even sort castoff clothes at the Salvation Army twice a year. That's serving, isn't it?

I see God on his throne shaking his head. "Not exactly what I had in mind, Lizzy." Can't the Almighty at least get my name right?

I ignore my cell phone playing Amazing Grace. I check the messages. It's Bett sobbing and begging me to hear her latest trauma. It's 9:15, on the cusp of going to bed. I decide I can't deal with Bett tonight. Sorry, God. I slip into my fuzzy slippers and clomp into my bedroom. Maybe tomorrow when I'm not so tired.

Then the LORD said to Cain, "Where is your brother Abel?"

"I don't know," he replied. "Am I my brother's keeper?"

It's three-thirty a.m. I'm rubbing my eyes. Did I really dream that verse of Scripture? I climb out of bed, fussing with the sheet tangled around my big toe.

Bett doesn't get it. Maybe she never will. I believe she thinks my faith will rub off on her by association. I wish that were true, but I worry. She's probably pushing eighty, so she'd better hurry.

I remember a conversation we had the other day.

"Honey, the Good Lord doesn't need to deal with my troubles. The man's too busy with real pain and suffering to worry about old Bettina Bethany. I caused my own pain, and I will deal with it in my own way. Besides, He gave me you for a friend, and you know how to talk to Him."

I try to explain, for the umpteenth time. He cares about her troubles, He cares about her. He is the best friend she'll ever have. One of my favorite praise songs bursts forth in my wobbly voice. "I am a friend of Jesus. He is my friend." Bett giggles. Of course she didn't know this was a real song, probably thought I made it up. Guess I didn't get my point across.

The next morning at 9 a.m., I flip my cell phone shut after reluctantly agreeing to meet her for lunch – at her house. Guess who's providing lunch? I did make her promise to dig the extra cheesecake out of the freezer. God wouldn't want me to have sugar withdrawals, would He?

I swing Old Sassy into the curved drive of the mini-mansion. Fountain Hills is especially beautiful this morning. The signature fountain off Shea Boulevard spouts high and clear reaching over three hundred feet toward the faded blue of the Arizona sky. Noted in the Guinness Book of Records as the highest fountain in the world, it sits in the middle of a thirty-acre lake and gushes for fifteen minutes every hour. I check my watch as I see the dramatic sight. Yep, a few minutes after eleven a.m.

It rained last night—not a pounding monsoon rain—more like a pitter-patter of angel wings. Or maybe the angels were flinging pebbles at my window. Plunk, ping, plunk, ping were the sounds I heard as I tried to untangle the sheet at 3:30 a.m. The roses are in full bloom next to Bett's veranda, seemingly unaffected by the blistering 102-degree heat. At least it's cooled off a bit, and there's a whisper of a breeze slightly ruffling my bangs. Two days ago it was a hundred and eleven in the shade, and last week the temperature topped out at 114. Fall, such as it is in Arizona, is definitely in the air. Next weekend will be Labor Day. I have half a dozen orders for side salads and an on-site barbeque to cater in person. No rest for this laborer.

I grab the small cooler holding just enough salad for Bett and me and slam Old Sassy's door. I'm feeling a bit sassy, myself, today. Swinging the cooler in one hand, and my fake designer purse in the other, I'm humming, "It's a beautiful day in Arizona today, it's a beautiful day in this neighborhood." Some childhood memories linger forever. I don't want to be a grownup today. But, Bett and God have other plans for me.

"Bessie, dear. Thank you so much for coming. You are a lifesaver." Bett is attired in a flowing, flowered purple caftan of silk. One of her designs for her Retro line now so popular in her boutiques. The delicate fabric clings to her as she swirls. The tinkling sound of her Capri shell jewelry, perhaps ten necklaces and twenty bracelets, catch me off guard. What is it with this woman, this teenage wannabe? The three-inch heels of her strappy sandals click on the tile floor as she drags me by the hand to the oversized kitchen. Weaving long manicured fingertips through her "she'll never tell" blonde nest of curls she faces me with misty eyes. "I so need your advice, and your prayers."

We both pick at the quickie version of the Chinese Chicken Salad I'd prepared. Bett's fork scrapes a piece of shredded lettuce around on her china plate. The screeching sound makes me shiver. But, I am hungry, so I dig in and carefully chew each bite twenty times as my father once taught me, and stab another piece of chicken. This is not going well.

"Bett, please get to the point. I have an appointment at two. A really important customer." I feel my teeth gritting, and I have a knot in my back. I love this woman, but right now she is driving me bonkers. What can possibly be such a big deal?

FOUR

"I have a child."

This is a revelation, of sorts. But, it's not the be all end all. Lots of people have children, even children they don't acknowledge. I sense Bett's announcement is more complicated. Her face scrunches up, possibly contorting in pain. A tear makes a little trace down her right cheek, carving an actual indentation in the heavy makeup. I resist the urge to smooth it with my finger.

"It seems like such a long time ago. I was only eighteen." She pauses to dab her eyes with a monogramed linen napkin. "I gave the child up for adoption, and I've regretted it ever since." I don't know what to say, so I say nothing. I'm sure you've heard of the pregnant pause. No pun intended. That's what it feels like. I don't want to remind her it was a long time ago, about fifty-seven years ago. And, math is not my strong point. My mom told me once that my birth mother was eighteen when I was born. She also told me she died during my birth. That leaves out Bett as a possibility. Not that I think of her. Well, maybe for a millisecond.

"You seem very burdened, Bett." Clever statement, Betsy. "I was adopted, and I had a wonderful life. Have you tried to find your child? Is it important?" I immediately think it could be if Bett has some disease that's passed down genetically. But, I don't want to pry. I don't even think to ask the child's sex.

I'd never been very curious about my birth parents. I was

adopted at less than a year and my parents gave me a great life. As far as they and I were concerned, I was their baby. Pure and simple. Maybe because I'm an only child I never questioned. True, my mother doted on me. Mom grew up pretty poor, the third and last child in her family. She spent most of her teen years wearing her older sister's hand-me-downs. She also loves to read, so she encouraged me in her favorite pastime.

I remember one Christmas getting forty-three books under the tree. To encourage my love for reading? And another Christmas when in eighth grade, and my figure was developing, getting thirty-two sweaters. Let's not go there. But, I never took any of this for granted. I felt secure and loved. When I was thirteen my mother and grandmother spent weeks (I found out later) designing and sewing a room ensemble in pink corduroy piped in green. I came home from school one day and found my room transformed. Curtains, bedspread, even pink carpeting and a pink telephone. What more could a girl ask? Bett's confession toys with my brain. Should I have asked about my so-called birth parents? Until now, I wasn't even curious. Is there something wrong, weird, lacking in me?

The other thing I remember, sitting across from Bett and her teary confession, is I look a lot, a whole lot, like my parents. We all have dimples in our cheeks in the same places, funny little dents in our left cheeks - more pronounced when we laugh. I'd never given it much thought until I notice a similar one in Bett's cheek. Must be a universal thing, common.

~

Back in my condo I stack and restack a leaning tower of ashtrays. As the one from Intercontinental Hotels leans, threatening to tumble the tower, I carefully remove it and place it on the coffee table starting the whole stacking process over. The ones from Marriott, Hilton and Westin are all about the same size, so they stabilize the others. The pièce de resistance is the small rectangular black glass one from The Meridian in Beverly Hills. I place it on top. This is what I do when I'm tempted to go back to smoking. The black, amber and clear class receptacles remind me what they smelled like when they were full. That does it. The precarious tower of glass and ceramic tumbles scattering across my coffee table. Nothing breaks. These suckers were made to last. Souvenirs of the past.

I'm troubled. I ruminate. I try to remember Bett's every word. Why don't I have more empathy for her? Lord, help me understand. Her "secret" is not a subject of ostracism nowadays. It's actually become politically correct to have, and admit to having had, children out of wedlock, even giving them up for adoption. Isn't it that famous female psychologist on talk radio who encourages adoption versus keeping the child as a single parent?

I know Bett's in emotional pain and agonizes over a decision she made decades ago. But, why now? That's what I need to find out, and I intend to. Dimpled cheek jutting forward. I call Mom.

~

"Hi, Mom, it's your born troublemaker."

She snickers. "What did you do now, dear, put hot sauce in Grandma's secret dressing by mistake?"

I chuckle back, and it all drips out like a leaky hose. I explain a friend confessed her guilt to me about giving a child up for adoption years ago. And how I wasn't all that empathetic. And, how I'm now having guilt pangs about actually loving her and Dad and my crazy cousins and never feeling the need to find my birth parents. The sound of her indrawn breath doesn't tell me much. After all, she's of Swedish heritage, and Scandinavian women are noted for little gasps as a natural part of their conversation.

"Mom?"

"Well, Elizabeth Alice Emma, you know what I always say."

"You think too much for your own good," we both say in unison. I almost reach to hook pinkies with her and make a wish. It crosses my mind that when Mom uses my full given name she's serious. No "Betsy" for her.

Sigh.

"I hope you realize I never *felt* adopted. It really wasn't a big thing with me to know who my birth parents are. If you'd never told me, what the heck! It's just that since this came up, I wonder should I have questioned more? Am I weird this way?"

"Bits (that's her nickname for me), you've just given me the greatest compliment ever." I hear a papery sound and sense she's reached for a tissue. "You always were, and always will be, my Baby Bits." Another pause, another tissue? "To be honest with you (one of Mom's favorite phrases, as if she was seldom honest!), I've almost never thought about it, too." There is that pregnant pause again that keeps cropping up in my conversations. "Do you want to?"

The tremor in her voice creeps hesitantly through the airwaves, or whatever those things are called that connect telephone lines between a cell phone and a landline. *Oh, Lord, I didn't want to hurt Mom.* "Mom, you okay? I shouldn't have brought this up." I feel like I've been digging up old garbage to see what's moldy underneath. My mind sees a landfill of broken bodies and grinning skeletons with left cheek dimples. Agh! Tonight for sure I'll have bad dreams.

"Frankly, Bits, it was a bit of a shock. You really aren't curious? It's okay if you are." I can almost see her clamping her jaw in a reassuring grin, eyes closed. "Seems strange to me that you would suddenly wonder about the need to know at your age."

She is right. How does one live almost six decades without caring, without wanting to know one's ancestral roots, then in the blink of an eye wonder? Something ancient and forbidden stirs in my soul. Not a happy feeling. I make a mental folder, file it and catalogue it to the back of my brain. That takes about three seconds.

I apologize, and she invites me for dinner Sunday. I accept, glad to get off the parental hook for my faux pas.

FIVE

Sunday is my only free day. Friday and Saturday I delivered bacon and cheese potato salads, fruit compotes and coleslaw to eight clients having early Labor Day celebrations. Monday, officially Labor Day, I am scheduled to be the chef-on-site for a corporate barbeque, one hundred fifty people. I usually don't do these things alone without an assistant. But, since it's only a barbeque I figure I can handle it. Flip burgers, put out bowls of pre-made side dishes. Bigga deal.

For Sunday dinner Mom cooks a pork roast, my favorite and about the only thing I haven't mastered as a chef. Mine never gets crusty on the outside, or it's stringy, or hard and overdone, or way too rare for the Other White Meat. Dad quips about a former patient who's called. He's a retired shrink, but old patients still call him. Still bound by confidentiality, he shares stories, not names. Some of his patients must be older than he. We laugh and chew. I think what a gift it is to be in this family.

Monday is the Apostle Paul's version of hell in Second Peter. "In their greed these teachers will exploit you with stories they have made up. Their condemnation has long been hanging over them, and their destruction has not been sleeping. For if God did not spare angels when they sinned, but sent them to hell, putting them into gloomy dungeon to be held for judgment…"

I'm in an earthly gloomy dungeon. Nancy Faraday, my client

for the day, and spouse of the renowned Lester, is freaking out. Lester is CEO of Faraday Financials, a huge mortgage lending company throughout the Valley of the Sun and environs. His influence is felt in many venues – fundraisers, business ventures, nonprofit organizations and, yes, even churches. Lester is a do-all, be-all sort of man. And he drives poor Nancy over the edge.

"Lizbeth, I can't seem to get these napkins folded right. Help, please." At least Nancy came close to my real name.

"Nancy." I bite my lip and try not to shake her by the shoulders. "This is supposed to be fun, relaxing. It's a barbeque, not a prom."

"I need to be the perfect hostess. Les is counting on me," says married for only nine months Nancy.

I take a big gulp from my handy water bottle, bite my tongue and give it to her straight. "Marriage is not about performing!"

Nancy's huge mahogany brown eyes form soup tureen proportions. And get moist. She turns aside and makes an effort to fuss with napkins. Why, I wonder, would anyone use linen napkins for a barbeque? White, yet!

I tuck my errant tongue back in its place. "I'm pretty good at napkin folding. I'll teach you a trick."

"It's not just the napkins, Beth, but I've never had formal training." I must have given her a dumb look. "You know, schooling for the elite. How to be a lady, how to entertain. Charm school." The look of defeat on her pretty face tugs at my heart. I open my big mouth again.

"Nancy, charm is what God gives you. It's not something you learn or go to school for. YOU have charm. You are a lovely warm person who has a big smile. You've got charm, honey. Have you ever read Proverbs 31?"

"You mean in…the Bible?"

"Yep. Best description of the perfect woman."

"I'm…Les and I aren't very religious." If possible, her eyes got more huge.

"Well, it's just a suggestion." I start forming the meat patties and chopping onions and red peppers for the salad. Nancy goes back to fussing with the perfect napkin design using my trick.

Just before the first guest rings the bell, I sense it's about time to give her a big bear hug. She seems startled; then hugs back, her tiny arms around my ample waist. "Thanks, Beth, I needed that." So much for remembering my name.

The barbeque is turning out perfect. Guests are laughing and I'm flipping burgers. I'm actually having a good time, until…"I like mine killed, barely."

Smoldering Crayon blue eyes. I know Crayons can melt if heated, but can they smolder and twinkle? I flip another burger and it lands on the patio. Heavens, Betsy, what could be worse? Using my handy chef's towel I scoop it up and deposit it in the trash. Maybe Nancy and Les have a dog.

I glance his direction and pray the beads of sweat on my brow don't show beneath my bangs. I slide a fresh burger patty onto the grill. "Killed, huh? Have you ever heard of salmonella, mad cow's disease?" I hope I sound funny, but doubt it. Noel locks his Crayon eyes somewhere between my collar and my waist. I feel like he's chatting with two of the most prominent parts of my body.

"Yeh, I like my meat really rare." He emphasizes the last three words. I stare at his bolo tie. What is it with men who wear strings around their necks? Only in Arizona! Maybe Texas, too.

My confrontational mouth leaps ahead of my common sense. "I have a problem relating to men who wear nooses around their necks." I want to add, "Especially cute men," but common sense throws itself in my path for once. Thanks, mouth, now I endure the embarrassment of heat searing my neck and face, and hands trembling. When I try to take Noel's burger off the grill it flies dramatically through the tepid air and lands with a splat on his left Topsider. Red cow blood from the perfectly cooked patty oozes beneath the shoe's tongue and soaks his no longer oatmeal-colored sock. The hem of his khakis has a creeping pink stain. He gazes for a moment at the mess, somehow locks his eyes with mine and grins.

"Great flip! Let's repeat that. This time I'll hold the bun and catch it."

What a guy! A real forgiver. Who knows where this relationship will go. If there is one.

"Oh, Noel, are you okay? Here, let me wipe." Nancy, the hesitant hostess, appears with a roll of paper towels. She swipes and mops and sends me a glare while squishing the lost patty in her hand. She doesn't get it, but she is trying. She doesn't have a clue about the chemistry between Noel and me. He snickers, and I blush. I know I do because my post-menopausal body starts to drip with perspiration. I push my bangs off my forehead and flip another burger, this time onto the bun. He smiles, thanks me and moves to the buffet table to scoop up a huge mound of Aunt Lorrie's chicken salad. Good choice Noel. It's the best.

Maybe it's me with the chemistry problem.

~

Chronicles 10: *"Now Jabez called on the God of Israel, saying, 'Oh that You would bless me indeed and enlarge my border, and that Your hand might be with me, and that You would keep me from harm that it may not pain me!' And God granted him what he requested."*

It's my morning mantra, before I even tumble out of bed. I know, Christians don't believe in mantras, but I've never found another word that describes a repetitious prayer. Maybe I should stop asking God to enlarge my border. According to the Bible scholars I've read, enlarging borders can mean expanding our relationships by witnessing for God, even just meeting other people in unusual circumstances, often non-believers on whom we have an influence.

I shove off the aromatic eye pillow and claw at my puffy eyes. Could we get a little more concrete here, God? A bit more definitive? What exactly are borders? Never mind. I will trust the Holy Spirit to direct me. He always seems to have the answer I need.

That brings to my soggy mind a sermon, oops, message, I heard recently in church. Pastor gave a long discourse on how the Holy Spirit is a "Him." Not a ghost or ethereal being, but an actual being like Christ. The gist was we need to call on him specifically, not just ask Christ to send him, but treat him as we do Jesus in our prayers and supplications. A new concept for me.

Struggling with this idea, I fling my ham-like legs into the air one at a time, carefully pointing my toes toward the ceiling fan wobbling above. Then I do my version of my former trainer's pelvic tilt, lifting my ample bottom off the mattress with feet firmly planted and knees locked. This is the sum total of my morning workout. Feeling the crunching in my knees and the tightness in my hips, I succumb again to the hotel-quality mattress, my one personal extravagance. Could heaven on earth get any better? Eyes closed, I pray for all my loved ones, as well as those I've blatantly promised to pray for in weaker moments of empathy.

The day begins with, unfortunately, a look in the mirror. Alice in Wonderland I'm not. A shower, a dusting of makeup, tousling of hair locks does wonders. A new woman emerges—bright and confident.

Yep, I asked God to enlarge my border again today. My request either shows how dumb I am or how much I trust him. Maybe the word is not trust, but vulnerable. I do trust God. He's stood by me in the worst of times, and cheered with me in the best of times—to paraphrase Chuck Dickens. Now comes the big question.

Do I meet Noel for lattes at Starbucks as he suggested, or pretend to forget? My day is basically free since it's the day after Labor Day. No clients, no obligations, except Noel. Why me? Why him? The chemistry seemed to be there, but he's a movie star handsome Cary Grant type, and I'm me. He's so attractive I imagine women swooning over him in line at the market, grabbing his pre-packaged pork chop meal and insisting on paying for it. Then casually leaving their business cards next to the thingy we all slide our debit cards through.

I talk to myself a few minutes in the mirror then pull on a pair of black capris and a black jersey with a high collar to hide the birthmark at the base of my neck. Black is good. Slimming, sophisticated. I slip into sling-back two inch sandals, plunk a pair of dangling silver earrings in the tiny little holes in my lobes, wet my lips with my tongue as models are instructed to do before being photographed and check my gold watch, a gift from Uncle Albert before he died. The letch. It's nine-twenty-five. Fifteen minutes to get to Starbuck's on Frank Lloyd Wright Boulevard.

~

Oh, but for the grace of our good Lord, there might go me. I slide down from Old Sassy's high seat and land with a thud on the blacktop, twisting my ankle. As I give the dented front door a masterful kick with my modest sling back sandal, I stupidly spin around on the other foot. Now two ankles are aching. *Good, show, Betsy. Nosiness is not your forté.* My eyes can't help themselves, poor dears. A voluptuous upper body prances past me followed immediately by a bobbing derriere. Frizzy, bleached white hair bounces tickling bare shoulders that display clear plastic bra straps under a halter top. That's what I said, plastic straps. As if we observers couldn't tell they're there. Duh. Mind you, this woman looks about my age. Her makeup must have been applied three times to get that depth of caking. Lips so puffy and eyes so uplifted, only her cosmetic surgeon knows for sure. And only he or she knows about the taut derriere and those two protrusions between her armpits. My attitude is one of...well, we won't go there with that thought.

I smooth my jersey over my hips and feel a lot better. At least I'm me, not a phony wannabe. My hips have history—spread lovingly by the births of three children. Although I don't know the genetic reason for them, I suspect my birth mother also had Aphrodite-ish hips. Aw, Aphro, the Goddess of Love and Beauty.

I spy Noel sitting outside under the so-common-in-Arizona-to-beat-the-heat overhead misters at a small table. His gray speckled head is lowered over a large paper cup. Eyes squished closed, he seems to be praying. I try to approach quietly on tiptoe, but my sandals farrumph, and their hiccupping sounds give me away. His head jerks up and he grins. I'm sure my heart thumps louder than my sandals. Goose prickles sneak up my arms, and I feel beads of moisture forming a mini Niagara Falls down my back. Must be the heat, even though I've been impervious to it for years.

"Hi. Hot today, huh?" *Another clever intro, Betsy.*

To his credit, Noel rises and pulls out a chair for me. Wow, a gentleman in the twenty-first century. Who would have thought? I preen a little, fussing with my hair and setting my voluptuous fake designer purse on an adjacent chair. I stare at it; delighted the turquoise scrollwork matches my shoes perfectly.

Noel returns with the decaf fat-free hazelnut Frappuccino I requested. I take a sip and smile. He forgot the light whipped cream on top, but who cares. The man is gorgeous. Did I mention his eyes? The Crayon blue-colored orbs above cheeks that must have been carved by a Renaissance sculpture are riveted on moi. I try to think of something clever to say when he preempts me.

"Who woulda thunk it?" He grins mischievously using my Nana's old phrase. "Two kindred souls." Are we? I wonder. I rack my brain about what "kindred" means. Are we bonded, bound, in the same spirit? Hopefully, in the Holy Spirit. I want to question what he means. Instead, I grin back, wimp that I am.

"We are?"

"Sure, brought together by fate and Bett."

"What about Nancy and Les?"

"Oh, that was a coincidence."

"Really? And meeting at Bett's wasn't?"

"Preordained, planned."

This conversation is getting way beyond my sanity level. I cross my painfully twisted ankles and shift my now squashed bottom in the plastic chair. Wetness, from heat in the one hundred plus degree air and my body, is seeping through my black linen cropped pants. I think I'm sticking to the dirty white plastic chair. I gather my scattered thoughts and pose a brilliant question.

"What does that mean? Explain, please."

He looks at me like I'm not quite all there. I feel dense. Am I so clueless I can't figure out what this man means? I don't believe in fate, or preordination. And, I certainly didn't plan our initial meeting. Did someone else?

"Thanks, Noel, for the coffee." I rise gracelessly, stumbling over my own feet hampered by two twisted ankles. Grabbing my purse I skitter toward Old Sassy. I ignore the slapping of leather soles behind me. As I slide into the worn leather seat, the feeling is good and familiar, like an old friend. We exchange smells—my Estée Lauder Pleasures Intense and Sassy's Turtle Wax from her recent detailing, both luxuries.

"Elizabeth, what's wrong?"

Noel is banging on my car window with his fist. I try to pretend I can't hear him over Old Sassy's rumbling, but my "honesty is the best policy" nature kicks in. Since the car window won't open more than an inch, (gotta get that fixed sometime when I have an extra hundred fifty), I'm compelled to open the door. Noel reaches a hand toward me and clasps mine. Is he being forward, or just kind?

"I guess we're not on the same wavelength, Noel. I don't believe in fate. I do believe God sometimes orchestrates things, like friendships. But, fate, no. And, what's that comment mean about us meeting at Bett's was planned? Was I set up?"

He gives my hand a little squeeze and shuffles in his now

clean Topsiders. A rosy flush illuminates his nose and creeps across his cheekbones. The man stares at his shoes for a full thirty seconds. "I guess I should have told you. I'm Bett's chiropractor. If you know anything about how long it takes to loosen the tension in a stiff neck, it's—well, chiropractors and patients establish a relationship, chat a lot. I suppose you could equate it to chatting with your hair stylist or manicurist." He swipes a fist of knuckles across the bridge of his nose.

"I'm telling this badly. Bett knows I've been lonely since my wife died several years ago. She suggested I attend her little soirée, as she called it. Said she had someone special she wanted me to meet." He squeezes my hand again, and a shiver slides up my arm like a nylon zipper. I think he must be a good chiropractor, with a masterful touch. I space out, wondering how his long fingers would feel on my tense neck. And, why did Bett think I was "someone special"?

I yank my hand back and glare. "Me? She wanted you to meet me?" My voice rose several octaves above its normal squeal.

So, that's why she conned me into opening the door and serving the salad that afternoon. To "present" me to Noel, like a goose on a platter.

I deliberate about Bett's possible agenda being Ms. Matchmaker. I can't think of anything it would get her personally. Bett is a bit egocentric, but she's not the kind of person to use others deliberately for her own gain. She's not unkind, not money-grubbing, not seeking stardom; she's just semi-crazy Bett. A nice woman who started a small boutique business with a unique idea that grew by leaps and bounds.

I've known Bett for about five years, since I started Heavenly Catering. She'd called me from a Yellow Pages ad—she claimed. She actually interviewed me asking all kinds of questions, some personal about my character and background. I was so green, a real novice in entrepreneurship, so I revealed a lot about myself. But, to her credit, she never brought anything personal up again, just ordered. Bett became my best client.

I literally shake the one hundred degree heat cobwebs from my brain to concentrate on what Noel is saying. My thighs are starting to sweat, and I can feel my bare feet sticking to my shoes. So much for Weight Watchers, Jenny Craig and Body for Life.

I've tried them all. Mr. Crayon Blue Eyes finally speaks. "It's all my fault." Wow, not a bad line, but much overused.

"Yeh? How's that?" Another great Betsy comeback.

"I was scared. Should have been honest from the get go."

No kidding.

Maybe I was wrong. Introducing them, I mean. I just want Betsy to be happy, finally. Noel is such a good, decent man. Someday, I will have to confess, to tell Betsy the part I played in their romance. That thought hangs heavy on my heart.

SIX

Back in my condo, I peel off my sticky clothes and stand naked in front of the full-length mirror, adorned only by the silver cross at my throat. I grab my love handles and squeeze. I can actually shake them up and down. Agh. I experiment pulling them toward my back to tighten my tummy. Maybe I should check out that full-page ad for liposuction in the Sunday paper. Naw. Too scary, too expensive.

I'm sure there must be some book written about loving the body God gave you. I think of the old adage "God doesn't make mistakes." Maybe He's trying to tell me something. Like "Cut out the chocolate, Betsy."

A passage from Proverbs 31 comes to mind about the "perfect woman." Something about beauty is fleeting, but a woman who loves the Lord is adored. I haven't read it since 1990, the dissolution year of my unfortunate second marriage. I haven't really felt beautiful since, and I know I wasn't adored then. I felt more like Jonah in the whale then, clambering to get out. Now, I just feel like the whale.

I hike up the sweats I've grabbed from the closet, sans undies. Tugging the ASU sweatshirt over my expanding shoulders, the one I bought when my daughter Brie was studying there, the one that says "L" for large and is snug, I run my fingers through my mousy gray-brown hair trying to tangle it in the latest yuppie style. Maybe a dye job? At least I feel free and unencumbered by constricting undergarments. I have work to do, work that won't wait.

Tomorrow Bett's giving a "small dinner soirée"—ahem, for twenty. At least her table will be full. She did ask me ahead of time to stay and plate the food and serve it. Tomorrow is Wednesday, not usually a busy day for caterers, so I agree. She also requested I wear "nice street clothes, not that silly uniform. And ditch the hat." Wouldn't want to spoil her fun, so I will bring my over-sized apron to catch any spills. Guess she is in her "no servants in my house" mood. Probably pandering to the Scottsdale nouveau riche. I've heard they disdain servants, prefer hired help instead. That's me!

Since she left the menu up to me ("You have such good taste, dawling"), I opt for squab, braised, and then baked, in a black olive, Vidalia onion sauce with lots of garlic. And tarragon; and a sprinkling of cumin. I will stuff the little beasties with fresh tarragon and more garlic. Yum. The risotto must be made on site in Bett's magnificent kitchen. Hopefully, I will be able to keep my eyes from straying to the zero gravity pool that drops off over the mountainside while I carefully stir spoonfuls of chicken broth and sautéed mushrooms into the concoction. Fresh asparagus, baby stalks, complete the entrée. Mango sorbet balls floating on raspberry sauce will be the grandé finale. Fortunately, I found a use for my old martini glasses.

I scoop out the sorbet balls to freeze. They will survive well in my portable cooler with ice bags. I wash and dry each pigeon (yes, that's really what squab are – pigeons – not the garden variety, but pigeons, nonetheless) and pat each individually in damp paper towels. I can brown them tonight in E.V.O.O., and then bake them tomorrow in Bett's oven. I'm flipping the little devils in my red Le Creuset roaster when the phone rings.

The caller ID tells me it's Noel. I have a mini conversation with myself about whether to answer, or not. Myself wins. His deep voice thunders through the telecommunication airwaves. My name hasn't sounded this pretty or so important in years. "Betsy, you there?" Another clever Noel come on. The man is amazing.

We apologize in tandem for our "little misunderstanding" this morning. "I'm sorry; I'm sorry, too" becomes an echo. I pace through the dining room to the side patio door to unlock it while hugging the portable phone between my ear and shoulder. A sudden gusty wind is blowing the fronds of my neighbor's palm tree. Bougainvillea petals make pink mini-whirlwinds across the pebblestone terrace. The outdoor thermometer reads 98 degrees; a hopeful sign that fall is close.

I agree to "try a movie" when my stovetop explodes. Noel doesn't know what's happening, but he hears the boom and yells, "Call 911, call 911."

I race to the console in the entry to dig in my purse for my cell and dial 911 still clutching the kitchen phone in my other shaking hand. Noel sounds frantic, but not nearly as frantic as I feel. "Get out, Betsy. Now," he screams.

Did I mention I am stubborn?

Seven minutes later, or so I'm told, a "to die for" thirty-something firefighter swoops me off my front porch into his arms. He smells faintly of smoke and pungent aftershave. Maybe a new designer scent. I wiggle frantically to be released, although I admit it was nice to be rescued like a damsel in despair. "You all right, ma'am?" He sets me down by a huge hook and ladder truck. "You have someplace to stay tonight, 'cause you're not going back in there?"

If only I'd known. But, how could I have guessed fate intervening? Sorry, Lord. I know I'm not supposed to believe in fate, but I'm a new believer. These things take time. Maybe someone, hopefully You, gave me the opportunity to have Betsy in my house. Oh, God, I'm still learning.

SEVEN

My feet are tangled in satin. Strains of "My Girl" from The Temptations fifty's recording drift into my room. Wait. My room? This isn't my room. I don't have surround sound, and my own comforter is encased in a beige striped Calvin Klein duvet – bought on sale. Not a burgundy and loden green velvet so heavy I can't kick it off.

I push hard with my toes and hear a snuffle. Comforters don't make sounds, do they? I kick both feet, and a lump like a wet sand-filled pillow gets heavier, if possible. I'm not exactly afraid because I feel safe, but some things don't compute in my muddled mind. I'm starting to remember. Noel. Boom! Noel yelling on the phone. The bougainvillea blossoms twirling on my patio, the aromatic smell of garlic, then the nauseating smell of melting paint and burnt wood. Aw, and the strong arms of Mr. Rescue, so young, so handsome, smelled so good. I use the edge of the satin sheet to wipe my eyes. Did you know satin isn't absorbent? I try the back of my hand. How come skin wipes away the residue of sleep when satin just smears it? Must have forgotten to take my eye drops again. Oh, couldn't. Didn't have them.

This time I kick hard and raise my head over the smooth fabric cradling my chin to see what's hampering me. The lump is white, fluffy, and furry, and has topaz eyes. It must weigh at least twenty pounds. "Meow." Do cats really say that?

"Where'd you come from, Beautiful?" The answer is a slow,

distaining blink. Eyes filled with contempt for interrupting its beauty sleep, the creature stretches and extends its long heavy body across my ankles. It clearly only cares about the comfort of the comforter, not moi.

Okay, Betsy, figure this out. You are lying in a luxurious bed in an opulent room with burgundy velvet walls (yes, velvet walls—I swear), *and a giant feline is stretched across your legs. Hey, let's not fight it. Go for the gusto.* A verse from Second Samuel comes to mind. "He brought me out into a spacious place; he rescued me because he delighted in me."

In truth, I realize I'm in one of Bett's guest rooms. How did I guess? The velvet walls. Bett is the only person I know who would have velvet-paneled walls. So seventies. After crawling out from between the satiny layers, I brush my teeth with the silver handled guest toothbrush in the marble clad bathroom. I glance at the bed and recognize Snoopy.

"Hey, Snoop, have a good night?" Now I'm talking to an animal, and I'm still not sure how I got here. I think I know why—boom! But, how? Oh, strong arms, masculine scent—forgot. I just finished explaining to myself when Bett bursts into my room like a Nascar driver rounding the last lap.

"Dawling, how are you feeling this morning? So much to deal with. You must be exhausted. Did you sleep well? Did Snoops bother you?" She pauses to catch a breath. "Oh, my, your face is a mess. So much soot. What an awful time you've had."

I want to scream, "Bett, shut up!" I want to tell her I'm fine, but I'm not. Instead, I say, "How *did* I get here?"

"Honey, you forgot?" She raises her hands heavenward in mock amazement. "The hunk, don't you remember the hunk?" Her overly made up face scans my apparently sooty one. "Such a nice young man. Oh, that I were you! No, I don't mean that. So insensitive of me." She squeezes her eyes closed and jiggles her golden tresses, as if to shake away her remarks. She's close enough for me to see moisture on her eyelashes and hear her murmur.

"You almost died."

What if she had died? I can hardly bear it, thinking about it. I know it was a silly accident, but she was on the phone with Noel, bonding. I feel responsible for their relationship. I hate myself.

EIGHT

"You could have died."

Noel's matter of fact statement gives me little bumps up my arms, and I shiver. Perhaps I owe him a thank you. It was, after all, he who insisted, screaming, that I call nine-one-one. Not that I wouldn't have figured that out, in time. "I wish I could have been the hunk." Even though he couldn't see it, the look of puzzlement I feel on my face probably led to his next remark. "Do you remember anything, Betsy? The explosion, the fire, my phone call?" He hesitates. "Not even the hunk?"

I feel heat creeping up my face from jaw to forehead. Have I offended this man, this nice man with the salt and pepper hair and Crayon blue eyes, this man who is about my age and seems to like me, a lot? I shake my head and feel my unruly madwoman hair flouncing. I am so irreverent, but I ask God, in a brief silent prayer, to make it curly—and blonde. *Zap me, Lord, please. I need some sign of relief, some tangible sign that I'm okay and changed.*

"I'm sorry, Noel. It's still all a blur. Can you help me go over it again, bit by bit?"

This man is patient. It's late afternoon, and he sits by Bett's play pool on a chaise that probably cost the same as my entire living room furniture. Actually, we sit on the same piece of furniture, him leaning against the back cushion, coaxing me closer to him with gently wrapped arms. His little nudges feel good, and I wiggle my bottom to scoot back, then his arms envelope me.

"Let's start at the beginning," clever man says. "What were you doing when I called you?"

"I was doing the pre-prep for tomorrow's, oops today's, Bett dinner party."

"Tell me every step you went through." Did I mention the man is patient? I get antsy trying to recapture and explain every moment.

"I changed clothes after our meeting for coffee." No way was I going to call it a date, nor would I mention our parking lot confrontation. Certainly not my episode in front of the mirror. "I came down to the kitchen and did a basic mis en place, setting out all the ingredients for the recipe. I always create better with soothing sounds and aromas, so I turned on the radio to KJZZ and lit a vanilla candle. Then I answered your phone call." I pause for a breath and blow it out. Rather dramatically.

"Oh, I remember. I walked to the patio door to open it. It was such a lovely night, breezy, almost tropical. The latch stuck. It's an old door and that often happens. I was fussing with it when I heard the boom."

Noel's Romanesque nose nuzzles the back of my ear. Mmm, nice feeling. Why am I trembling? "What happened then?" he asks.

"You know. You screamed."

He chuckles and squeezes his arms around me tighter. I almost can't breathe. "I told you to call 911, right?"

I sigh loudly and take a mini-break here to, hopefully, compose myself. I'm no longer trembling, but my legs and arms are sprouting pin-prickling goose bumps. Now I'm shivering, in the oppressing Arizona heat. I feel fingers lightly drumming on my spine. Rubbing the drips of sweat off my forehead backhand, I half turn to Noel's shoulder.

"Yeh, but I would have done it anyway." Did I mention I am stubborn?

"Sure, when you were fried to a crisp."

My patronizing nature kicks in. "Noel, you saved my life." That wasn't so hard.

Another nuzzle, followed this time by a major body squeeze. Is Noel a hero? I have to decide.

Suddenly, he becomes analytical. "You do understand why your kitchen exploded, don't you?"

I roll my eyes and manage a mini-shake of my head.

"The candle, Bitsy, the candle." Now Noel's getting my name wrong. What is wrong with this picture? "It had to be the flame from the candle that ignited the gas. Did you notice if your burner hadn't ignited? How close was the candle to the stovetop? How long was it between lighting the candle and turning on the burner? Were you paying attention? Did you watch?"

Cheesh, Noel. I'm not used to being interrogated. Suddenly, I feel like a criminal. It's on the tip of my tongue to say this when he drums his fingertips down my leg. The sensation crawls up slowly to the base of my neck, and I slump back in his arms on the chaise. I'm foie gras, goose paste, mush.

Noel's strong arms twist me around so our noses touch. I smell wintergreen on his breath and feel the heat of his body. He rubs noses with me, like fairy tale Eskimos do, and chuckles softly. "Funny girl. You really don't remember, do you?"

I'm fighting the sensation to fight. Surely, if I'd remembered, I'd say so. Honesty is a biggie with me. Maybe Noel didn't get that from our conversation in the parking lot. Not to slur the male species, but some men can be so dense sometimes. I give him the benefit of my doubt and shake my head hard this time. Can he hear it rattle? He lays an oversized palm on my jaw and turns my head further toward him. A kiss—he's going to kiss me! Yikes! Do I want this, or should I resist? Before I can, he does. Firm and hard on the lips.

Thank goodness I cleaned up when Bett told me Noel was coming to call, actually on his way. Bett gave me fifteen minutes notice, not much for a sooty-faced gal whose hair smelled of burnt wood. Fortunately, the guest bathroom attached to the velvet-clad bedroom was well stocked. I slathered with Jessica McKlintock shower gel and made do with the myriad of cosmetics in the sectioned off vanity drawer. Minty mouthwash provided the finale.

His lips taste spicy against my minty ones. I haven't been kissed this way in more years than I can remember. I feel like a teenage girl, spinning with glee and a little woozy. I don't want this to stop, so I cling to the Hawaiian shirt on his brick-like chest and suction my lips to his. I am the vacuum cleaner, and he is the dust.

"Ee-yow." Twenty-plus pounds of white fur lands on my legs. Snoopy drapes himself across my ankles. I'm doubly captive.

NINE

"Did you and Noel have a nice talk, Becka?" (At least she got my name closer this time, and started it with a "B".) Bett sets a cup of herb tea in front of me at the kitchen table. We have to sit close just to see each other because Bett's kitchen table is eighty inches in circumference. If we sat across from each other, like I do at Mom's kitchen table, we'd be in two different galaxies. Everything in Bett's house is super-sized. I stir the brew in the tall Bernardaud cup with a vintage Wallace Grande Baroque silver spoon and wonder why a single woman would buy a cup for $145 to serve tea in.

I debate how to answer. Is Bett being nosey or concerned? I decide on the middle ground. "Yes, very nice talk."

Bett's forehead crinkles and her eyes narrow. Fine lines in her caked-on makeup form around her lips and on her cheeks. Maybe I should have said more. I couldn't bear it if her face collapsed now. Suddenly she laughs. A real deep belly laugh laced with a tinkling sound. She slaps her hand on the table's glass top. The metal and precious stones of her charm bracelet clatter. "You got 'im, Honey. He's yours. Congratulations."

Now what in blazes does that mean?

I'm stuck here in Bett's house. I can't afford a motel, and even if I could, I'd be crazy to go to one. Motels don't have velvet walls and a housekeeper named Consuela serving me breakfast in bed.

Even though I declined, then decided with a burst of energy to visit Bett's in-house gym, when I returned from my twenty minutes on the treadmill (hey, that's a start), a tray of coffee and fruit waited for me in my room. No donuts. Phooey!

Going back to my condo isn't an option yet. I checked it out yesterday when I met with the insurance company adjuster. He held a handkerchief to his nose, and I cried. The paint on my formerly refinished fake maple cabinets hung in strands and globs. The smell, well I won't go there. Because my living room, dining area and kitchen all blend into one space (the real estate agent called it a "great room"—yeh), my discount sofa that was once ivory is now charcoal gray, and the glass tops on the coffee and end tables are laden with layers of soot. The carpet looked like gremlins spread a layer of grime on it. As Glen, the insurance adjuster (who was young, but not really that cute) and I tiptoed gingerly on it, our footprint indentations cried, "Big Foot was here." I wanted to plop down in the middle of this mess and emit a primal scream.

Instead, I touched this nice young man's arm and said, "Well?" One of my more profound questions.

Glen shook his head vigorously. I couldn't tell if his eyes watered with tears or from the dense haze hanging in the air. At the time, I didn't care. Now I do.

I have to get out of Bett's. The woman is suffocating me with her fondling and concern. Snoopy is giving me arthritis of the ankles. Consuela, the housekeeper, is feeding me too much of all the wrong things. Comfort food to her is sweet rolls, pasta and anything else laden with carbs. Although she still hasn't given me donuts, I miss my salads.

Come to think of it, in the week I've been here, Bett hasn't once asked me to cook. I don't know whether to be grateful or offended.

"Bett?" I twist my linen napkin into a curlicue and bury it on my lap. The remnants of a delivered pizza are scattered across my china luncheon plate. Bits of lettuce drenched in an oily dressing mix with soggy crust and stringy mozzarella cheese. I ate it only for sustenance. Bett delicately sips tea from her expensive cup.

"Yeh?" No Bitsy, Bethany or even Betsy this time. She's allowing herself to be more familiar. Just "yeh?"

"I—I was wondering how you'd feel about me cooking a few meals. I feel so bad you had to cancel your dinner soiree the night I had the fire. Consuela has been great, but I'd like to contribute somehow."

"You sure?"

"Yep." I nod for emphasis. I hope my serious look convinces her.

"You really sure?"

"Yep, really sure." This time I grin.

She skitters across the built-in bench and flings her arms around me. I try to extract myself from her crush. "Honey, I thought you'd never ask. I didn't want to put you on the spot with your trauma and all. I was afraid you'd want to give up cooking forever after what you've been through. It will be like getting on a horse after being thrown off."

No, Bett, it will be like playing human again. "Do you think Consuela will be offended?" I wiggle out of her arms as she explodes into mirth.

Bett's hearty laugh is infectious and I join her. We both cackle so hard we're crying. I can personally attest that fine linen napkins do absorb tears.

~

Other than tossing a salad, I've never worked in a kitchen like this from scratch to completion. I'm used to prepping on a narrow counter, small glass mis en place bowls fighting each other for space. The utensils in my tiny kitchen were contained in several crockery pots. Here, in Bett's kitchen, I look up and choose what I need from the stainless steel rack hanging above the six-burner professional range. Instead of the two sizes of spoons and spatulas I'm used to, I have a choice of four or five. I feel like I'm on a network television cooking show. I feel intimidated. The huge island gives me plenty of space to prepare, but I need special running shoes to navigate it.

I'm nervous about making dinner. It's only for Bett and me. Consuela has gone home for the night. Still, it's my debut cooking a full meal in this gargantuan kitchen. Bett insists I "get back on the horse" and make the same meal I planned for her soiree when I had the unfortunate fire. She'd called around and ordered a trio of the tiny poultry to be delivered from a local upscale market. "Make three squab, Honey, so we can eat the leftovers for lunch tomorrow."

I'm plating two pigeons, tiny feet pointing to heaven, Italian parsley frilled under them, when the doorbell chimes. "Beth, can you get that, please?"

I answer the door reluctantly. There are so many interruptions at Bett's. Deliveries, Fed-ex and UPS, old friends invited impromptu for tea, her accountant, and…

"Noel. What are you doing here?" *That was clever and inviting, Betsy. What happened to your manners?*

"Uh. Bett invited me for dinner?" His handsome face crinkles, and that rosy thing creeps across his nose. The Crayon blue eyes bore right into my soul. I'm a dweep. Or, is it a dweeb? I just know my teenage cousin uses some word like that to describe idiots like me.

My turn to take his hand. I apologize, explaining I've been cooking and I'm distracted. It's not really a lie. *Sorry, Lord, but that's true. I am distracted by the sudden appearance of this man.* I lead him into the kitchen, of all places, and seat him at the eighty inch round table with a glass of iced tea. He sips and stares.

Nothing bothers me more than someone staring at me while I'm cooking. Noel's eyes, combined with my angst over why Bett pulled another caper on me, puts me in a dither. I vacillate between hating her and loving him. I pull out another plate and slap the third squab on it. Forget the leftovers for lunch tomorrow.

I hope my little suggestion about an excursion to Old Town Scottsdale won't be too obvious. I really want them to have a good time and to get to know each other better. I've never been a matchmaker before, but this is special. I trust Noel to make Betsy happy. I really want this to work. Please, God, forgive me if I'm interfering with Your plan.

TEN

Noel scrapes a last strand of meat from a miniature drumstick between his teeth and licks his fingertips. Bett and I follow suit. We agreed to eat at the kitchen table. "More intimate," Bett said.

As if a table the size of a small room can be intimate. I curl my tongue up against the roof of my mouth and keep the thought to myself. It turns out she was right. Formal dinner party manners are abandoned as we joke and laugh and pick at the little birds with our fingers.

The squabs are yummy, even though I had to use all dried herbs since Bett's fridge wasn't stocked with fresh tarragon and rosemary. Fortunately, she has a fondness for ethnic food, so her pantry is well stocked with black and green Greek olives (in cans!) and Basmati rice that I substituted for risotto. I'd found an unopened carton of free range chicken broth and some non-alcoholic white cooking wine waiting for me above two drawers of spices, including cumin. My debut meal in the palatial kitchen turned out okay.

Noel grins, and Bett smiles, rolling her eyes dreamily. I am pleased. We linger over coffee in the extravagant cups and Anna's Swedish Ginger Cookies from Ikea. Bett's pantry revealed an entire shelf of Scandinavian foods—lingonberries, packaged sauce mixtures for Swedish meatballs and salmon, Swedish pancake mix and syrup, flatbread and three different flavors of the Anna cookies. I bite into a crisp flower-shaped cookie and almost choke at Bett's next comment.

"So, what are you two lovebirds going to do this evening?"

"I thought maybe we'd run over to Old Town Scottsdale and do the Art Walk." Noel comments nonchalantly not missing a beat.

I try hard not to sputter, but I cough and a morsel of cookie flies into my coffee. How did we get from "Bett invited me" to "lovebirds" to him making a decision of how I'm going to spend my evening? In my most unassertive manner I smile and say, "That sounds like fun." Did I mention I'm a dweeb? Or is it dweep?

After minimal plate scraping on my part, Bett urges me to leave the dishes for Consuela to stack in the dishwasher the next morning. Instead, Noel insists on helping, and together we rinse, stack and wipe. A sort of rhythm, a camaraderie, develops between us, and I admit to myself it's nice.

I run to my velvet-clad room and grab a light jacket from the few items of clothing I managed to salvage from my condo before my eyes smarted shut from airborne soot. The weather's getting cooler, down in the fifties now in the evenings. Distinctively chilly for Arizona. After slipping into my favorite Clarke sandals, I meet Noel in the dome-shaped foyer. He steers me out the door by my elbow toward a red convertible PT Cruiser. "This is my fun car," he says. "And, yes, my other car really is a Mercedes." His deep laugh drifts in the night air elevating my mood. I plan to have fun.

Droves of pedestrians stroll along downtown Scottsdale's Main Street, lots of couples and some groups of friends, mostly women. By sheer luck we spot a parking spot in front of one of my favorite galleries and mosey into it. I try to make time to visit it whenever errands take me to Main Street. I love its eclectic offerings ranging from very traditional Monet-style oils to Picasso-like contemporary paintings. But it's the sleek sculptures of cats and birds by Gene Guibord that intrigue me. Although most of his subjects are feline or aviary, there's one of a racing hound dog called Joie de Vivre that captures my heart. The little bronze dog looks intent and focused, his ears pinned back, running with the wind. Perhaps he's chasing a rabbit, or a stick his master threw. He really does express joy for life, the kind of joy we all wish to capture. I run my hand across his cool polished back and grin at Noel. "Isn't he adorable?"

For the next hour we wander hand in hand from galleries displaying ultra-contemporary sculptures of steel and glass to others overflowing with American Indian pottery. Suddenly, we both stop and stare across the street. The outrageously pink and white façade of The Sugar Bowl Ice Cream Parlor calls to us. Well over forty years old, it's retro décor beckons, as well as its promise of old-fashioned sodas with huge globs of ice cream and seltzer laced with foamy froth. Mom and I used to indulge in gooey sundaes after exploring Main Street when it's trendy boutiques were the chic places to shop, years before huge Fashion Square was built.

Noel grins at me. "Ready for a sugar break?"

"You betcha." I grin back mischievously and let go his hand. "Last one in buys!"

I race across the street and beat him to the door. As I dash inside I collide with a vintage pink bubble gum machine almost knocking it over. Noel brings up the rear panting.

"Heavens to betsy!" The scrawny, all bones seventy-ish waitress arches her penciled eyebrows at our flushed faces. "You kids okay?"

We nod in unison as she leads us to a little round table with two metal scroll back chairs. She plops pink menus in front of us as we settle on pink vinyl seats that whoosh like whoopee cushions under our weight. I laugh inwardly at Scrawny's choice of words. Even though it was a colloquial expletive, she got my name right.

I order a double chocolate shake, extra thick, with two scoops of chocolate chip ice cream, whipped cream and a cherry. If you're gonna go, I always say, go for broke. Thank heavens the only thing lacking in my borrowed Bett bathroom is a scale.

Noel looks a little flushed and hesitates with his order. "I'm feeling a bit squeamish. Guess that run did me in. Think I'll just have a root beer float." I study his face and worry a little. The Noel crimson blush is there, accentuating his aquiline nose. But, unlike the rosy one in the parking lot, the blush I mean, it's sort of blotchy.

Scrawny, our server, plunks old-fashioned fluted soda fountain glasses in front of us with straws and long-handled spoons. Yum. I swirl a taste of the thick luxurious semi-liquid around in my mouth to savor its flavor. Can't get much more chocolatey than this. I hope there's chocolate, dark and extra rich, in heaven.

Noel hesitates again, bends forward over his float, sucks through his straw and throws up.

Bubbles escape from his now redder nose spraying droplets all over the cute round table. He's coughing hard and pounding his chest. When I scoot my chair back to pound on his back, it flips and lands with a thud. Scrawny rushes over, a cell phone in her hand. Noel gasps, "Can't breathe." When his right hand grips his left shoulder I yell to Scrawny. "Call 9-1-1, NOW!" Noel, who has now become "my Noel," is having a heart attack. *Sheesh, Betsy, you're so perceptive.*

I can't believe it. The Hunk loads Noel onto a gurney and shoves it and him into the back of the EMT van that followed the fire truck to the restaurant. This is surreal. Am I in some kind of déjà vue time warp?

Noel is stabilized now with plastic tubes in his arm and a mask over his face. I jump in the ambulance, planning to ride with him, when he reaches in a pocket and hands me the keys to his Cruiser. Such trust. What a guy. I squeeze his hand and nod. "I'll be right behind you, praying all the way. Praying," I add, "is what I do best. Better than cooking." His head moves slightly, indicating he understands.

Jumping out of the ambulance I search for the Hunk.

When I heard what happened, never mind how, I almost fainted. I felt so helpless. I had no idea where they'd taken Noel, nor how Betsy was handling this. My only option was to pray. This was a sure test of my new faith. Please, Lord, don't let me down.

ELEVEN

I expect to see Hunk in a putrid gray Mr. Doughboy uniform of thick pants and cumbersome looking jacket. Then I realize that garb is only for fighting fires, not heart attacks. Instead, he's sporting the new navy blue preppy uniform with button down collar I recently read about in the Scottsdale section of the paper. I must have been so discombobulated by Noel's attack I didn't notice his attire.

He's bent over carefully placing vials into compartments of a suitcase type box. Probably restocking for the next emergency. His head is bare, no hat, except for random tufts of bleached blonde. I have an "only her hairdresser knows for sure" moment of envy before I come to my senses. I touch his shoulder, lightly, I think, but he jumps, spins around and says, "Yes?"

"Sorry." Goodness, what reflexes. Glad he's on my team. "I—was wondering if you knew what hospital they took my friend to. I couldn't go with him in the ambulance 'cause I have to drive his car. I didn't think to ask before they took off." I bat my eyes and combine a prayer for Noel with a short one hoping Hunk will know the answer. HonorHealth Osborne is fairly close, but then so is HonorHealth Shea. Then there's Banner and several others. I could be driving around all night, and I promised Noel I'd be with him. Silly goose for giving me his keys.

"Say, you look familiar." Hunk squints his eyes and scrutinizes my face. "You the lady who had a fire in her condo last week?"

I nod.

"On Raintree, off 94th?"

I nod again. I'm losing my edge. Why is this man so persistent?

"The cook lady, chef. Right?"

I finally muster my courage and practically yell at the man. "Look. I'm that lady. What does it matter? My friend is dying and I just want to know what hospital they took him to. I need to be there."

Have you ever seen the face of a firefighter com-paramedic emotionally wounded? Let me tell you, it's not a pretty sight. His eyes get huge and his face blanks, then turns to stone. I notice subliminally Hunk is older than I thought. Probably fifty-ish. The irritation in his face reveals the true age of his sun-tanned features.

"Sorry, lady." He sounds contrite. "I didn't realize it was your friend in the ambulance." Remember the pregnant pause? "I've been worrying about you all week. He's gonna be okay, though. I'm pretty sure it was just a TIA, a little pre-warning. I hope he lays off the rich foods and exercises." His fingertips touch my sleeve. "You sure you're okay? That was a pretty bad fire."

I stifle the urge to ask if his soliloquy is over. I smile. "Thanks for your concern. I'm really okay. Where did you say my friend was taken?"

By the time I find the PT Cruiser and try to insert the key in the ignition my hand is shaking badly. It's almost ten, late for me, and I don't want to be stopped by the inveterate Scottsdale Police for speeding, even on a Thursday night. The pubs and clubs in Old Town, especially in tourist season, hop all week long. So, I drive slowly north on Scottsdale Road and turn on Indian School Road. I almost freak when an emaciated coyote runs lickety-split across the road in front of my car from a golf course. A sigh of relief whistles through my lips as I navigate onto the 101 Loop toward the hospital on Shea. So far the evening has been interesting, and it threatens to be a long one.

The hospital is just a block and a half off the freeway exit, and I have to cross over three lanes on Shea Boulevard to turn right onto 92nd Street where the emergency entrance is. It can be a bit tricky. Traffic is pretty light, being it's so late, but night drivers in Arizona don't pay attention, as they should. Not to mention the snowbirds, the Midwesterners and Easterners, many of them elderly, who live in Scottsdale only during Fall and Winter. People working a long day who are tired, and partygoers are more lax than usual in their driving habits. I creep slowly and weasel my way over lane by lane amid honking and horn blasts.

The next nerve wracking part will be finding a parking spot near the Emergency Entrance. *Oh, that you would bless me, indeed.* Ah, God is in my corner. I maneuver the Cruiser into a spot opposite the entrance and fiddle with how the remote locking system works. Old Sassy doesn't have any locking system that works, much less a remote one. Hands quivering and feet rushing toward the automatic doors, I almost pass a shadowy figure huddled on a stone bench. The Emergency Room doors have just glided open making their wheee noise when recognition hits my brain. "Noel? That you?"

His head lifts up from bent shoulders and sad eyes search my face. I plop my ample derriere next to him and take his hand. "Wha—why are you here? What happened, why aren't they treating you?" *Shut up, Betsy. Give the man a chance to talk.*

"Betsy, I'm so embarrassed" He looks down at his Docksider loafers, a habit I'm getting used to. "My heart is fine, I wasn't choking. I had an anxiety attack."

"A what?" I scream so loudly in his ear that I'm probably giving him another one. "What were you anxious about?" Noel is the epitome, or is it epitomy, of *in control*. Anyway, he's the example.

He turns his handsome salt and pepper head toward mine, and I notice moist eyes. "You, Betsy."

An anxiety attack because of moi? That sounds very

romantic. Me, Elizabeth (a.k.a. Betsy) Wysinotski, caused a grown man to be anxious. I must write this in my diary, a.k.a. journal. When I get back to wherever it is I live now. Oops, back to Noel.

"Do these…attacks…happen often?"

"Nope. Haven't had one for forty years when I met Maizie at our high school prom. I had to go outside and barf. The principal thought I'd been drinking, so he sent me home. I hadn't been, just really nervous about courting Maizie." The Crayon blue eyes search my face, then dip to focus on his knees. "She was my wife."

Noel, friend, you just dropped a bomb here. I don't know how to respond to this confession. So, I let it go and reply, "Noel, I'm so glad you got a clean bill of health. Can you drive me home now?"

Okay, I'm insensitive. I didn't respond with a hug and teary-eyed kiss. I was flabbergasted. After thirty years of widowhood and twenty-five of loneliness from being dumped, I'm not used to being the focus of a man's affections. And especially not the reason for an anxiety attack.

Truman, my latest former husband, wasn't exactly Mr. Romantic. Even though his name meant a faithful, loyal man. Right! I'd gotten used to the obligatory peck on the cheek before bedtime. Truman was an honest, dear and loving person. Just not to me.

But, that's another story for another time.

I drive the Cruiser, still worried about Noel's state of health. He seems fine to me blabbering the entire twenty-minute trip. If he apologizes one more time I may slap him. I sense there's some issue with his masculinity about anxiety attacks. So, I open my big mouth and spew.

"Noel, I'm just grateful you are healthy and fine. I know I'm dense, but I don't understand the problem. I'm flattered that if you did have an anxiety attack it was because of me. I'm sorry you had one because of Maizie. I'm not an anxiety attack kind of person, so this whole idea is foreign to me. What exactly is an anxiety attack, and why does it happen? Especially to you."

"Betsy, I know this isn't the best time or the right

place…I think I'm falling in love with you." Noel touches my right arm from the passenger seat, and I almost miss the turn to Bett's street. Wow, heavy stuff.

I screech into the long curved drive as the photosensitive lights come on. Bett flings open the door, if one can fling a three hundred pound door, and rushes to the Cruiser in a purple nightgown. She resembles a butterfly in flight.

"Dawlings!" *'Nuff said, Bett. Now, shut up.* "What a stressful evening." How'd she know? She wasn't there. I bite my lip, my tongue and the inside of my cheek. Tonight I will need to rinse out my mouth with hydrogen peroxide.

She gives a half wave to me through the driver's window and makes a beeline for Noel's door on the passenger side. So much for being the rescue hero.

"Noel, precious man, what happened? How are you? Are you in pain? Should I call Consuela to come sit by you during the night? We must take care of you."

Noel looks embarrassed, but I also detect a tiny bit of self-importance in his demeanor. He allows himself to be assisted out of the car by Bett who fondles his arm by rubbing her palm up and down its lightly tanned skin. I know she has no romantic feelings toward him. She's almost twenty years his senior. Maybe it's a motherly thing. So, why do I feel envious of her and protective of Noel?

TWELVE

"Mom, I'm such a ditz."

I curl my toes under my crisscrossed legs on my parent's red sofa and sip decaf Hazelnut coffee in a mug purchased from Target. "I can't, can't, be falling in love again. I'm fifty-eight years old. I don't want to make another relationship mistake."

The wise woman sitting across from me just smiles. She adjusts the cuff of her chartreuse sweatpants and reaches for her coffee mug. Pushing her Kate Spade glasses up on her nose, she finally replies. "What's wrong with falling in love? Love is a gift at any age."

Yeh, right, a gift to get hurt again. I look at this amazing woman and blink back tears. Why am I so negative? Mom taught me to be brave, self-sufficient, my own person.

"Here." She hands me a tissue from an onyx box on the end table. I'm still surprised after five years at the way my parents decorated their townhome. Yellow walls ("I want to bring the sunshine in"), carpet with the cutesy loom name Daffodil, glass and chrome tables and a fifty-two inch flat screen television mounted over the fireplace. Retro contemporary, and definitely eclectic. Did I mention the antique sideboard of Grandma's hosting the antique sterling silver tea set? ("Been in the family for eighty years.")

"Yeh, Mom, but..." My voice trails off and I whisper, "He's

really nice, and cute."

I wonder who's more insane, me or Mom. Love doesn't happen late in life, or does it? I'm questioning myself again. I know Mom isn't insane. She's the most sane person I know. Well, next to Dad who's very analytical. Mom's practical, down to earth. Maybe I should ask Dad about falling in love at fifty-eight. Mom's talking again, so I look up and search her face.

"Bits, did you hear me?"

"Sorry, I was ruminating."

"I *said* . . ." She pauses for emphasis, and probably to make sure I'm listening this time. "God is a God of second chances. Well, maybe third chances." She grins realizing her mistake about the number of my chances. "He may know all the hairs on your head, but He doesn't keep track of how many times you screwed up. It's called grace, Bits."

"Okay, explain to me. I know He wants happiness for me, but I thought I was very happy with life until Noel came along with his salt and pepper hair. I love my catering business – it's even starting to break even. Why would God want to change this?" I sip from my coffee mug and whisper again. "He's really cute, Mom." *Dead giveaway, Betsy.*

I rinse out my mug and put it in the stainless steel dishwasher. Mom has the most upgraded appliances, even a trash compactor. Her kitchen gleams, shiny with brushed chrome and silver. Maybe when I'm pushing eighty I'll have that, too. And a full head of salon blonde hair like Mom.

On the drive back to my temporary home at Bett's I decide to stop off at my barbequed condo. The few times I've returned I try to sneak in when no neighbors are outdoors. Surely they must be out of sorts about the yellow tape across the door and the still lingering odor. I'd rather not have nosey neighbors asking about when I'm going to clean it up, and what will my insurance pay, and how long do they have to deal with this travesty.

Taking a lined pad from my purse I decide to make notes for the three contractors I'm interviewing tomorrow. Maybe focusing on the sooty, smelly mess will help me forget Noel. I step over the yellow plastic tape that bears the word "condemned" and march with purpose into the living room. Soot stings my eyes, and nausea overcomes me from the putrid smell. I can't do it, I just can't. In a moment of desperation I call Noel on my cell phone. Did I tell you I have him on speed dial now? It was a concession after his "attack." My idea.

"I'll be right there. Go on the porch and wait for me. Give me ten minutes." What a guy! Did I mention that before?

Noel pulls up, this time in a sleek black Mercedes. I'm scrunched over on the top porch step fiddling with my mousy hair. I hear the subtle click of his car lock and look up.

"I'm here, Bits, to give you whatever help you need." Bits again! Has he been talking to Mom, or is it a common nickname for Elizabeth?

Noel sits beside me on the step and inches close. One big hand attached to his right arm squeezes my shoulder while the other envelopes both of my hands clasped between my knees. He pulls me close. "Did I tell you my dad was a contractor? I learned a lot from him working on his job sites during summer breaks from college."

My personal earthly savior has arrived. "You did?"

He nods. "I can tell you what you need to have done, what questions you need to ask a contractor, how much is a fair cost, and, if you want, I will interview them with you."

"What about your work? You have patients, a life beyond helping me."

"I can schedule my patients around my personal life. What time did you agree to meet the contractors?"

"All tomorrow. One at ten in the morning, the second at noon, and the third at two p.m. I didn't know how long each would take, so I left time in between and time for me to make notes about each of them. Seem okay?"

"Perfect. You're very organized. I admire that."

Yeh, sure. If only he knew.

After Noel leaves, I decide to go to Sprouts for fresh veggies. I haven't done a real grocery shopping in over a week, and I feel shopping deprived. Bett's been ordering from the upscale market, but she forgets to order the most ordinary, but basic things. Like cucumbers, red and green peppers, yams, onions and even lettuce. My culinary talents have been stretched using up canned goods in her cupboard and the few frozen vegetables she keeps in the freezer.

I pull out a cart and wipe it's handle and my hands with the new politically correct amenity offered at most markets—a wet disinfectant cloth. I savor the clean smell from it and cast my eyes on veggie nirvana. Mounds of fresh greens and reds and all colors of the rainbow are piled high, and at far lower prices than the chain markets. I make an effort to control myself, but I'm like a kid in a candy store with a dollar bill from a doting grandparent. I calculate how many ways and how many meals I can use asparagus at $1.99 a pound. Sole wrapped around it, Béarnaise sauce over it, stir-fried with shrimp, used as a bed under chicken. The list goes on. I control myself to buying three pounds. I pause to stare at an old lady in red velour sweats and drab gray hair who is talking to the bananas. Her hands flutter over them in cadence with her whispered words. I can't hear what she's saying, and I'm not sure I want to. But, she does make me wonder if I'm not putting my whole heart into choosing my produce.

The woman in front of me at the checkout counter looks from my cart to me and raises her eyebrows. The checkout guy does the same. "I have a big refrigerator," I say. "Lots of mouths to feed." They both shrug. Who cares what they think. I hate waste, but if I waste one green pepper, I still got a deal.

I'm whistling when I unload Old Sassy. I swear she is, too. Hefting six plastic bags, three on each hand, dangling from two fingers and my purse on a shoulder, I push open the heavy door to Bett's enclave. I haven't felt this free and happy in weeks. Loose as a goose, that's me. "Yoo-hoo, Bett, it's me—Elizabeth, Betsy." I make a point to enunciate both versions of my name clearly. They say repetition is the best teacher.

Bett swoops down the winding marble stairs and skids on her satin mules almost landing at my feet. She clutches both my arms digging into my flesh with talon-like nails so hard I winch and drop my grocery bags. For once her face is devoid of caked makeup. Its absence makes her look almost childlike. Her voice matches her appearance, tiny.

"It's Noel. He's had another attack."

THIRTEEN

The first question I ask myself is why did he call Bett instead of me? I dig in my purse for my cell phone, then remember I'd left it in the cup holder of Old Sassy. That was the beep, beep I'd heard on the way home from the market. I thought it was Old Sassy singing again, or that the "door open" chime was working overtime. I've had a lot of issues with Old Sassy's electrical system.

If slapping myself would help, I would. Instead, I get Bett to tell me what she knows. This is not an easy task since the woman is a stress case extraordinaire. I'm tempted to slap her to stop her incomprehensible blabbering, but I grab her hard by the shoulders as an alternative to violence. I play investigative reporter. The "who" I already know, so I eliminate that part.

"Bett, let's start with when."

Her dazed expression must mean she doesn't understand my obvious question. I try again. "When did Noel have the attack?"

"Oh. About half an hour ago."

I nod. So far, so good. "Where is he? Now," I add, because Bett isn't good at sequence.

"I—think—at the hospital?" She makes it a question.

"The same one? Scottsdale Shea?"

Her head bobs up and down, making her loopy curls flutter.

"Was he taken by ambulance? Or did he drive himself there? Do you know?"

Shrug.

"Bett, can you please put these groceries away. I need to go to Noel."

Another nod.

I make a quick decision and take the bags to the kitchen, then return to grab Bett by the wrist. She is still standing in the foyer like a clay statue, or maybe a child waiting for the next Mother May I announcement in the ancient game. Being the organized person I am (guess I am organized as Noel said), I had my groceries separated on the check out conveyor belt. Per my request, the goofy looking teenage boy put all the fresh vegetables in three bags and the few cold items—cream, butter and eggs—in another bag. Bread, nuts, rice and baking chocolate are in the last bag. I put that one still filled in the pantry.

"Please put all this in the fridge," I say pointing to the remaining bags.

"Okay, will do. Go to Noel." Suddenly, Bett has come alive.

~

This time I have trouble finding a parking spot near the emergency entrance. After I circle around twice, a young couple carrying a baby goes to their monstrous SUV. I wait patiently while they buckle the child into its car seat, put the diaper bag in and finally back out. I scoot in and flinging the door shut I almost forget to lock Old Sassy.

The pudgy-faced receptionist looks up from his novel. I talk over his "Can I help you?" and tell him my friend is supposed to be here, with an attack of some kind. I don't want to make a medical diagnosis, so I avoid the words "heart" and "anxiety."

"We got somebody name of Noel?" he asks the male nurse beside him. The other man does some playing on a computer and nods.

"Three A. You a relative?"

I'm tempted to say "sister," but that old honesty thing kicks in. "A very good friend." I underline the word *good* with my voice. "I know he wants to see me. He asked me to come." Well, not exactly, but he probably should have. The silly goose. I still haven't checked my cell phone messages, so he probably did ask for me.

Pudgy Face nods, and his partner gestures to me with a crooked finger. I follow him through a door marked No Admittance—Hospital Personnel Only to a room with a privacy curtain pulled around the bed. Noel is propped up on numerous pillows watching television. A game show. "T. T, idiot. Ask for a T. The word is theater." Wow, he must be really sick. Sorry, judgmental of me.

"Noel?" Why do we humans always form questions of a person's name when we catch them off-guard? His head snaps toward me to reveal a "being caught" expression on his handsome face.

"Betsy?" See, he does it, too.

"None other. How're you feeling?"

"Much better. Now that you're here," he has the grace to add.

"I'm glad." This conversation is not only going nowhere, but it's boring. I'm glad, truly glad, Noel seems fine, but this scenario is getting a bit old, too. I muster up my muster again to ask, "Noel, what's going on?"

He fusses with the sheets and pushes the mattress with his palms to scoot up on the pillows. Clicks off the TV remote, takes a sip of water from the plastic cup and straw on the nightstand.

I'm sure you've heard of the pregnant pause. Oh, yeh, from moi. Well, you just witnessed it again.

"Hi," he says as if he hadn't acknowledged me two minutes ago. An embarrassed blush spreads across his face making his Romanesque nose look larger.

I feel anger creeping up the backs of my legs to my neck. What is the deal with this man? I've heard of mountains and molehills, but this is bordering on the ridiculous. I repeat my question.

He looks at me sheepishly. I almost expect him to "Baa."

"Sorry. I seem to have this thing, this problem, when I get too close to you." What? Confession time? Am I supposed to feel guilty about this?

"Noel, you were fine this afternoon. In fact, you were my hero."

A look of pure puzzlement comes over his continence. "Me, a hero?"

"Yes. When I was at my wit's end I called you, and you came right over."

"I'm counting on you for tomorrow. I really need you and your expertise to deal with the contractors. Please don't let me down." I plant a perfunctory kiss on his brow and head out, hopefully leaving a scented trail of Jessica McKlintock perfume behind to entice him.

~

Back in the driver's seat of Old Sassy I try to control my emotions. I decide the only way to deal with them is a conversation with the Creator. "Dear Heavenly Father, First, thank you for Noel being all right, or at least he seems so. Thank you for being able to come to You with my petitions as petty as they are. I'm confused, God. I feel angry and a bit deceived. I don't want to feel either, but You made me human, so I have human emotions. I know, I'm not taking responsibility for something I should be able to control. Please help me understand how to control my frailties. I'm confused. Oh, did I say that?

"You may know the desires of my heart, but I'm not sure I do. I know it's too soon to think about a future with Noel, but our friendship seems to be developing into more. Please help me figure it out. I guess I'm scared. Burn me once, maybe even twice, it's my fault. Burn me three times, it certainly is mine.

"Thank you for the wisdom I know You will give me, and thank you in advance for bringing Noel's body and emotions in line with Your Word. In Jesus' Precious Name, Amen."

I sit for a few minutes feeling drained and feeling the peace of God's presence. I feel especially close to Him, and a Scripture about trusting and letting go of the past comes to mind. I'm not sure, but I think it's from Isaiah. "Forget the former things; don't dwell on the past. See, I'm doing a new thing!" I've probably messed it up by paraphrasing it, but it speaks to my heart. I'm encouraged about my relationship with Noel. Surely, God put that passage on my heart. Surely, God put Noel in my life.

My cell phone still beeps in the cup holder, so I flip it open to voicemail expecting to hear a plea from Noel to come rescue him at the hospital. Rats! The only message is from contractor number two who wants to change our meeting time tomorrow. Suddenly, I'm deflated like a punctured balloon. Noel never called me. He called Bett instead. I spew nasty names at him in absentia. "You ingrate. You shallow man. You phony."

Oops. What happened Betsy to "forget the former things" and seeking God's wisdom?

Old Sassy coughs when I turn the key, then she rumbles into a roar. As I back out of my parking space I notice angry faces in other car windows waiting for the precious commodity. Maybe I should have gone somewhere else to pray. I wave and smile and say a prayer for those needing to get to the emergency room. "Bless them, Lord, and bless the health of those they are going to see."

As I pull out of the parking lot onto 90th Street, my mind spins with guilty thoughts about Noel and what's on my plate, a.k.a. calendar. Realization hits and I suck in breath.

Tomorrow is Meet the Contractors' day.

FOURTEEN

I arrive, notebook in hand, at my smelly, sooty condo at nine forty-five. It's one of those Arizona mornings that fool you into thinking Fall really has come. The sun overhead is just as brilliant as it was in July when the temperature was one hundred fourteen degrees. But, it's blessedly cool this morning at ninety-two. Birds chirp oblivious to my morbid mood. A mockingbird taunts me when I repeat his sound. His whistles are so much better than mine, so much more authentic. I look up seeing him perched like a miniature king on the frond of a palm, just on the tip with his feathered chest puffed out as if to say I can do this, you can't. He ignores my squinty glare and stooped shoulders. I stick my tongue out at him, blah! I pull a tissue from my bag to wipe the moisture forming on my forehead under my yellow visor and plop down gracelessly on the step of my front porch. I'm weary.

Weary of no resolution about renovating my home, weary of Bett's silliness and cooking for her, weary of Noel's antics, I need answers. I need someone to say this is what's going to happen and this is when. At this point I'd take a definitive answer for almost anything, like why my chocolate soufflé fizzled last night. Maybe I beat the egg whites too long. I'm grabbing my bangs between my fingers and tugging so hard it hurts when I hear the purr of an engine.

The cute little red PT Cruiser zips up beside Old Sassy making her look like an overweight elephant without a trunk. Well, she has one, sort of, but not in the front. I laugh at the image. Thanks, God, I needed that.

Noel steps out lightly and flings a red door closed not bothering to use his remote to lock it. His stature is tall enough he can grin over the roof. What a guy! Have I said that before? This morning he wears leather thong sandals, generically know as flip-flops, a loose Hawaiian shirt, probably from Tommy Bahama, and khaki shorts with too many pockets. He looks spiffy, and, to boot, he's carrying a clipboard. I am impressed, although I'm not sure why. Maybe because he showed up.

He stretches out one hand, palm up, as he approaches me. "Betsy." This time he doesn't form a question of my name. Maybe we're getting somewhere, socially at least. I give him my most musical "Hi", rise to meet him, trip on the toe of my sandal and land in his arms. *Rotten eggs! Betsy, you are such a klutz.*

His strong arms save me from more mortification and hold me tight. "Your hero has arrived," he announces in a confident voice.

What? Oh, my flip comment to him last night in the hospital. Or, was it flip? I try to muddle through that in my mind, but his masculine smell and the muscles in his chest that my face is against confuse me. I think of extraditing myself from his grip when some primal emotion takes over. This feels good, so why would I want it to end? Maybe Mom is right, love at any age is a gift. The man at least deserves a thank you for rescuing me from farther embarrassment. Besides, I need his advice and support with the contractors. I touch his chin with my forefinger and stare straight into those Crayon blue, America's favorite color, eyes. "My hero."

We have no time to explore this intimate moment because Skip Schilling, contractor number one, arrives. He parks his long-bed pick-up next to Old Sassy making her look pretty sleek. I swear the old girl preens and starts to flirt with it.

"That there's Sam." He gestures toward the black vehicle whose flanks are caked with dust. "And I'm Skip,

Mrs....Waz..." He pushes the peaked cap up a bit on his forehead and frowns.

"Wysinotski," I offer. "And it's Miss." I can see the confusion on his face. Should he call me miss or ms.? How politically correct should he be? Just as I think he's about to crumble with uncertainty, he notices Noel and extends his hand in a manly gesture. I catch a slight glimmer crossing Noel's face, but hero that he is, he reaches back to take the overly large calloused hand with dirt under the fingernails in his carefully manicured one. They exchange shakes and howdys, and the beat moves on.

"You folks sure had a mess of a fire," Skip says. Noel and I fail to correct him about the "us" part. "You know what started it?"

"The fire department thinks it was a candle I was burning while cooking. And that maybe the gas flame hadn't ignited," I added. It is a little embarrassing to admit I'd been so dumb.

"Happens all the time," Skip says. "Makes a mess, but correctable."

"That's what the fire captain said," I feel compelled to add in my defense. "I got distracted by a phone call, and all the sudden—boom!"

"No need to explain, little lady. The missus almost did the same thing one time. 'Course she was twenty and a newlywed." He guffaws slapping a big hand on his thigh.

The three of us climb over the yellow tape and trek into the mess. Skip's head bobbles and twirls like that poor child in The Exorcist movie. Then he sucks in a whistle.

"Looks bad, but not a big project. Rip out the cabinets, replace them, paint them, clean up all the soot, maybe replace the kitchen vinyl floor. Replacing the appliances, if they need to be, and getting the carpet and upholstery cleaned is up to you. Oh, you might want to think about tearing out the false ceiling and installing recessed lighting. Lots better than that dated fluorescent fixture."

Skip made some notes on his clipboard, and Noel made some on his. We shook hands all around, and when Old Sassy's new beau roared out of the parking place, Noel and I looked at each other and in unison said, "Well?"

"Noel," I complained, "You didn't ask him a single question."

"Didn't need to. The man knows what he's doing. My only concern is the price, but I want to hear what the other guys say and compare."

Oh, right. I nod. Makes sense. He takes my hand and pulls me up from the porch step. "How about a coffee break? We have two hours until number two shows up."

~

Koffee Klatch is a little hole in the wall off Shea Boulevard near Albertson's market on Frank Lloyd Wright Boulevard. It's actually cuter, or is it more cutesy?, than the corporate versions of most Starbucks. Mitch, the owner, serves you himself, and always with a pearl of wisdom as he hands over the steaming cups. "Today is the first day of your life, so take advantage, capture your dreams and enjoy."

Okay, Mitch, got it. Could you try to be a little more original next time?

I admit to loving the ambiance. The tables are tiny and round, like the ones in the Sugar Bowl, inviting intimacy. No huge tables for parties of eight. The thick paper cups all have sayings on them, and the chairs all have arms. I settle in to the plastic-covered seat of one and smile at Noel. "I love this place. Mitch has rescued me several times with carafes of coffee when a client has forgotten to both buy it and make it."

"Yeh, he's a good guy. Actually, one of my patients. I know I shouldn't be sharing that, but I don't think he'd mind. Standing all day wrecks havoc with one's back."

I give Noel an absent smile. I twist the cardboard sleeve around my cup and trace a squiggly line of spilled coffee on the resin-topped table with a finger. Something's been worrying me and I think maybe now's the time to bring it up. Should I boldly take his hand, maybe give it a little squeeze, or should I bat the mascara enhanced lashes of my baby blues, or just blurt it out? I opt for the latter. It takes less energy.

"Noel, I've been meaning to discuss something with you. I'm pretty sure from some things I've said you know I'm a Christian and I really shouldn't date men who don't share my faith and I didn't mean to lead you on, and as much as I like you, I can't have a relationship, particularly a lasting one, with a man who doesn't share my faith, and because we've never talked about it before I don't know if you believe in God, or Christ, or even have faith of any kind." Whew. Got that out in one long babble.

I'm still looking down at my coffee artwork on the table, but I sense Noel reaching in his pocket. He pulls something out and slaps it on the table right in my wet artwork. It's a business card. It says Noel Sheppard, D.O., D.C. with his office address, phone number and a small Christian symbol bottom left, the Ichtus in the shape of a fish. My gaze drifts up to his face. "Why haven't you said? You know how important that is to me."

"It's important to me, too, Betsy. I thought you knew, that Bett told you. Thought that's why she introduced us. I didn't mean to deceive you. I'm kind of a private person. Turn the card over, please."

I flip the now soggy card and read the slightly blurred words. *But for you who revere my name, the sun of righteousness will rise with healing in its wings. And you will go out and leap like calves released from the stall. Malachi 4:2*

"It's not a promise of mine. I don't promise my patients will leave my office leaping like calves, but I do promise I will try." He stares intently at me with those Crayon blue eyes, now my favorite color. Finally, he says, "Well?"

For once I don't know what to say. I shake my head and notice tears dropping on Noel's card and my tabletop coffee artwork. Using the absorbent back of my hand to wipe them away, I look up and give him a Cheshire cat grin. Be still my heart.

"That's quite a statement of faith. Why didn't you tell me?"

He shrugs and reaches for my hand. "I don't announce my faith because I don't want to alienate someone who should, need to, come to me. But, I should have told you. I'm sorry."

"'S, okay. I'm really very glad. Thrilled in fact." My turn for a sheepish grin. Baa.

"We can talk some more later, but right now it's almost

time for contractor number two to show up. Ready?" Noel rises and tugs me by the hand. I hope my smile says it all. Yes, Noel, I am more than ready.

FIFTEEN

We pull up in the PT Cruiser next to a grimy white elongated pickup with Stan the Man emblazoned on its doors. It must make Old Sassy proud of her new bath. She sparkles next to Stan's vehicle. Even the words Heavenly Catering embellished on her sides shine, the metallic lettering glittering in the noon sun. I feel a little shiver from her and maybe a quick song as I open the sliding door and pull out my purse where I left it behind the driver's seat for safekeeping.

I extend my hand to Stan the Man and introduce myself. "Gotcha." His reply is less than professional, but I try to ignore that. He came highly recommended with five stars from an Internet site. I intend to keep an open mind. "So, Stan," I say after I introduce Noel, "Here's what we have to deal with." Stan leads the way stepping over the yellow tape, and Noel and I follow.

"Gotta do this, gotta do that, rip out here, replace that…big project." He pauses for breath and looks at us as if we should accept his assessment without question.

I thank him as he hands his estimate to Noel, passing the yellow-lined handwritten paper in front of me. What is it with these macho manual labor guys? Obviously, I am not intelligent enough to understand what he proposes for my kitchen, nor make a decision about how to fix it.

After Mr. Macho, Stan the Man, revs noisily out of the parking lot, Noel grabs my hand and leads me to the stoop on my front porch. He locks his Crayon eyes with mine. "He means well. Just ignorant. But, probably competent." I nod, frustrated about this whole interviewing contractors situation and my naiveté, but grateful Noel is here to help. "Let's see what Luke Samson the next guy has to say. He has a biblical name. That's encouraging. How'd you find him?"

I roll my eyes and make a face, not a pretty one. "Bett."

"Bett? She knows a contractor?"

"She insisted I contact Luke. Said he did a lot of stuff for her. Landscaping around her pool, replaced windows, that sort of stuff. He's a general contractor, so she swears he can do anything." Noel nods, but it's not one of those positive nods. I sense reservation on his part. After all, Bett is not the best reference for services. Except for me and Heavenly Salades.

I'm tired, and I need emotional support. I inch closer to Noel and rest my head on his shoulder. He puts a reassuring arm around me and rests his cheek on my hair. We both sigh.

"Noel."

"Betsy."

I sense a romantic breakthrough when a soft purr interrupts our reverie. A bright yellow Volkswagen bug chugs up the drive to the parking lot. A short stalky man with cropped brown hair moves with deliberate grace out of the VW's driver's seat. "Good afternoon," he says tucking a clipboard under his arm and extending a business card to me. "You must be Ms. Wysinotski." He pronounces it perfectly. I like him already.

I introduce Noel, and Luke follows us over the yellow tape. He stands in the kitchen looking at each cabinet individually. He sniffs the putrid air, opens cabinet doors and turns on the stove, having to light one burner with a match from his pocket. His "Mmm" comment isn't earth shaking, but it's somehow reassuring. No rash judgements here.

"Ms. Wysinotski," he begins. (Oh, I love this man already. He actually pronounced my name correctly twice.) "I know this looks horrible, and you probably feel devastated." He turns to me for affirmation. I nod and feel like a parrot.

"Unless I'm missing something, from the inside of your cabinets, since you still have dishes in them untouched by the fire, I think all you need is come refacing. And, a plumber to set your stove right."

"You mean I don't need to rip out the cabinets and replace the stove?"

"Nope. All the damage seems to be on the surface. You will have to air the place out and scrub everything with a disinfectant." He pauses to look in my direction. I look at Noel. Noel nods affirmatively and asks, "How long and how much." Cuts right to the chase that Noel. What a guy!

"Probably two days, maybe three. If I can get the cabinet refinishing guys in here tomorrow, two. You need to call the gas company and the company who made the stove. Get them out here as soon as possible. The scrubbing part is up to you." His grin threatens to stretch from ear to ear on his round face. He hands me, moi, a business card and a written estimate on an official invoice, not lined paper. I almost hug the man.

Instead, as the little yellow car chugs away, I hug Noel. "I guess you liked him," he says with an impish grin.

"You bet. He seemed sincere, knew what needed to be done and his estimate is within reason. Insurance probably won't pay for all of it, but I can eke the rest out of my savings. I'm so relieved." I glance at Luke Samson's card. "Noel, did you notice this? The name of his company is Dove Renovations, and there's a Christian dove symbol in the corner." I give Noel a wink and say, "Betcha Bett doesn't even know he's a Christian. She probably thinks the dove means he works swift as a bird flies, or something like that." We both chuckle and hug some more.

I pull back and take his hands in mine. Tilting my head back I whisper, "Thank you for being here."

"How about thanking me properly?" He wraps his strong chiropractor arms around me and lifts me to my toes. His breath is warm, I can feel it on my nose as he makes his way down my face to my lips. I close my eyes to better savor his masculine strength. Noel's kisses touch each of my cheeks then envelope my mouth. This time his breath is minty and his lips cling to mine for a long time. My legs start to shake from being on my tiptoes, so Noel lifts me higher, tighter. I don't want this to stop. It doesn't. His left hand is spread across my back rubbing lightly up and down, and his right hand is now on my neck making gentle massage motions. He eases me down slowly until I'm standing flat on my feet. He gives me a tender hug then disengages my clinging arms and makes an about face spin. Was I too forward, too needy? My knees feel as if they're about to collapse, but unable to move, I stand like a woman of salt. Oh, why do biblical references come to mind when I'm in the midst of a romance?

Noel is pacing the short length of my front porch, obviously a man disturbed. I keep standing there like an idiot, like the first time I saw him at Bett's front door. Except this time I cling to a wrought iron railing instead of a brass door handle. My hand is aching and my knuckles are turning white when he speaks.

"I—I'm sorry, Betsy. I just wanted you so much." His voice is shaky, and the rosy butterfly blush creeps across his face. He's studying his Topsiders again. Fists at his sides, he finally looks me full on in the face. "My feelings got out of control. You are so special, and I don't want to take advantage of you. Well, in truth, I'd love to, but it goes against our Christian beliefs. Even though we are over-the-hill Christians," he adds with a grin.

I loosen my grip on the railing and automatically flex my fingers. "Noel, you silly. I felt the same way, so don't apologize. If you hadn't stopped I'd probably be attacking you on the porch. You're a strong man, Noel, and I'm a weak woman who adores you." There, I said it.

"You do, really?" There goes that blush, or flush, or whatever it is, again. I bite the inside of my cheek and nod like a bobble head doll. Noel takes my hand and kisses the back of it gallant-like. What a guy! Did I mention that?

"We need to talk, Bitsy." My eyes widen and I put my fingertips on his lips to hush them.

"Noel." My voice is schoolmarm firm. Automatically, I stomp my foot. "Where did you get the idea to call me Bitsy?" I stare into the Crayon blue eyes with a heated glare. I hope I've made my point. "Where? From whom?"

Confusion clouds his face, and he shrugs his shoulders. "I guess it just seemed right. Isn't Bitsy a nickname for Betsy that's a nickname for Elizabeth?" He wrinkles his nose and cocks his head sideways. "Is something wrong? Does the name have a bad connotation for you? I think it's cute."

My turn to stare at my shoes. I wipe my hands on my denim skirt and shake my head. "Sorry. I over-reacted. It's just nobody ever called me Bitsy except my parents. Not even my friends growing up." The quizzical look is still on his face—like, "So?"

"This is going to sound silly and juvenile…but, I thought maybe you and Mom were in cahoots, romance cahoots."

Noel bursts into belly laughter and slaps his thighs. Then, seeing the devastation on my face, he turns serious. "Aw, Betsy, Bitsy, whatever you like to be called, or not, I'm sorry if I hurt you. I don't know your mom, but I'd love to meet her." He grins the Noel grin. "Can we arrange that sometime. Soon?"

Now I don't mind having Mom and Noel meet, but Mom would surely make more of our relationship than I'm ready for her to make. Especially since I'm not sure what our relationship is at this point. I know Noel was kidding, sort of, with his suggestion, but there was a glint of seriousness in his Crayon eyes. If possible, they got bluer.

I lace my fingers in front of me. Deep in thought, that's me. "You're right, Noel. We do need to talk—about a lot of things. How do you suggest we go about it?"

Why does his grin make me suspicious? "I find it's easier to talk freely when one is having fun. We both need to be at ease, with each other and our own emotions. I have an idea."

SIXTEEN

Thanks to Noel's idea I find myself sitting on a bench at the Phoenix Fairground eating kettle corn on Friday, October thirteenth. I haven't been superstitious since I was fifteen and accepted the Lord, so the date doesn't bother me. I was superstitious as a kid, even thought thirteen was my personal lucky number. Go figure.

It's the first day of The Arizona State Fair and the fairground is teaming with humanity in all sizes, shapes and colors. My chef-ness is appalled at the weird variety of foods for sale. Deep fried just about everything from brownies-on-a-stick and cookie dough and asparagus. I stick to the traditional popcorn ball. I read in the paper recently that last year over one hundred fifty gallons of the sticky concoction was consumed.

"Ith's fun." Between licking sticky goo from my fingers and picking bits of popcorn hulls from my teeth, my mouth isn't working right. Noel nods and smiles, revealing a brown chunk of the gooey corn stuck next to an eyetooth. We point to each other's mouths in sync. He laughs, I giggle. "Gotta wash up. Napkin's not doing it for me."

"Me, too."

We meet a few minutes later at the petting zoo, not at all surprised to find that adults are in the majority. True, some have toddlers in tow, but many are here like us on the senior discount. One little boy is obviously bored with the baby animals and tugs relentlessly on his father's hand. "Camel wide, camel. Pease."

"Did I tell you about the camel I saw one day in a backyard in Scottsdale?"

Noel's eyebrows arch, possibly questioning my sanity. "It's true. I was driving around one Sunday afternoon through the equestrian communities south of Cactus Road, the Cactus Corridor where so many barns and riding stables are. Taking a peek at how the other half lives. I'm toodling along in Sassy ooing and awing at the estates when something brown with a long neck catches in my peripheral vision. I swear Old Sassy slowed down on her own."

Now he rolls his eyes, and a "yeh, right" expression wrinkles his forehead.

"Well, maybe I took my foot off the pedal. Anyway, I spin Sassy around." I demonstrate making steering wheel turning motions with my hands. "...and pull up to a high fence. A droopy eye with long lashes that make me green with envy winks at me. It's a one-hump camel. He, it, whatever, slowly turns and ambles toward some kind of shelter. It was so cool."

Noel still looks skeptical, so I stick my tongue out and wave my fingers with thumbs stuck in my ears. "Oh, ye of little faith," I admonish him and playfully punch his arm.

I decide it's serious time. "Okay, Noel. This day has been fun, but we still haven't had our quote talk unquote. The only thing more I know about you is you don't like corn dogs, prefer spicy sausage, and you can suck down a bag of kettle corn faster than I. Oh, raspberry lemonade instead of plain. Also, you don't believe my camel story."

I admit I'm exasperated. Spending the day together really has been fun, but unproductive as far as the original intent. I'd hoped to find out about his deceased wife, his childhood and his dreams. I really wanted to know more about the anxiety attacks, too. Instead, I know never to make corn dogs for Noel. Or plain old lemonade.

"Well." He clears his throat and gives me a lopsided grin.

Agh. I hate it when he does that. Makes me all mushy. "I found out you look especially cute when you're mad. Like now. You've got spunk, Betsy. But, I knew that the night you raced me across the street to the Sugar Bowl. Or maybe you were just having a chocolate attack—that led up to my anxiety attack."

There it is, finally out in the open. Remember, he brought it up. "So, Noel my friend, tell me more about your anxiety attacks. How often, why, what do they feel like?"

We're walking hand in hand to the fairground's parking lot. I feel his big mitt tightening around my fingers. He's studying every step his Topsiders take. I make an effort to look straight ahead, no sneaking a peek for me.

"You know what they're like. My heart races, I get sweaty, sometimes shaky, I feel like I can't breathe, and sometimes throw up."

"That's it? You can't just go to the men's room and splash water on your face like women do when they have a hot flash?"

"Never thought about that. Guess I could try. Does it work for you?"

"It used to, but I haven't had a flash in five years, praise the Lord. I don't mean to sound flip, and I know the attacks have hospitalized you twice since I've known you. But, is it possible you are blowing them out of proportion? What does your shrink say?" I could cut the quiet with my boning knife. "You have seen a psychologist, haven't you?"

Slight shake of the head. Yes, I'm looking at him now. "You're telling me you have this problem that interferes with your life, our relationship, and you haven't consulted a professional?" I try to keep my voice even and calm, but calm is not in my vocabulary. I shake my own head in wonderment. I want to scream, "Men!" Or maybe just, "Man!"

We're almost at the car. Fortunately, the red Cruiser stands out in a sea of beige, black and silver vehicles. I'm sure neither of us would have remembered it was parked in aisle E23. We just honed in on it. Noel kicks his right Topsider toe in the dirt and takes both my hands. He's facing me with a look of anguish on his face. My heart starts to melt, but I keep it in check. I sense something important, some revelation, is going to be revealed.

"I'm a doctor. Doctors don't need other doctors. It's an unwritten code. Does that explain it?"

Yep. You're also a man. And the combination of man and doctor is telling, can be lethal. Just my womanly, girly opinion. "So, you're scared." The words shoot out of my mouth before my mind controls it. Noel looks ashamed, and scared.

"Guess you hit the nail on the head."

He leads me around to the passenger side of the car and opens the door for me. Always the gentleman. We make our way out of the parking lot , but I can't keep my errant mouth shut. It's not just curiosity, but I think I'm falling in love with this man. *Lord, help me say the right thing, please.*

"Noel, I know you've hinted at a future for us. I did, too. It's not that I'm not sympathetic, or empathetic, but I wouldn't want to spend my retirement years worrying about rescuing you from hospital emergency rooms because of anxiety attacks. Does that sound unfeeling, or cruel?"

He stares straight ahead, white knuckles gripping the steering wheel. I feel like a heel, then remember it was Noel who suggested "the talk." Not that much talking is happening. Suddenly, his fingers turn normal flesh color and his shoulders relax. I feel vindicated until he makes "the announcement."

"I did it, Betsy. I just got over an attack. Mind over matter." He lays a hand on my thigh and I shiver. *This can't be happening so fast, Lord. Or can it?*

I know my look is one of questioning. The "oh, ye, of little faith" scripture comes to mind again. This time slapping me in the face.

"I released it to God, Betsy. It started to happen again, so I just prayed and gave it to Him." He nods, affirming what took place. Another bobble head moment. "I know it can't happen that way for everyone, especially not for those who aren't God-centered. But, I vow it just happened to me."

"I'm so happy for you, Noel. And, I admit, selfishly for me. Are you sure?" What is it with me I can't keep my mouth shut?

"You don't believe me." It's a statement, not a question. I wring my hands praying for the right answer. God provides.

"I do believe you, Noel. Right now I'm praising God for this breakthrough for you." Now, honesty kicks in. "I confess I looked anxiety attacks up on the Internet. On my laptop I rescued from the condo," I add. "They don't seem all that easy to get rid of. They're also called panic attacks. And millions of Americans have them every year." I slap him playfully on the thigh. "But...the good statistic is they lessen in people over fifty-four."

"Really?"

"Yep. Seems when we mature, we become more immune to some psychological problems. Unless we're really old and senile." I slap his leg again feeling much better about Noel's prognosis and our possible future.

"Works for me," he says, and I notice his body relaxing more.

SEVENTEEN

"This is complicated, Noel. Can you help me understand?" I remember we've kissed coming close to devouring each other. We've shared laughter and come close to sharing secrets. We are not kids. Hopefully at heart, but not in years. Perhaps a better assessment is we have a shared relationship with Bett. That could unnerve anyone.

Noel parks in Bett's circular drive and comes around to help me out of the car. I'm getting weary of this being my temporary home. It's been over a month. Two or three more days and I can move back to my cozy condo. If Luke follows through.

Instead of answering me, he smiles. Holy cucumbers! The man drives me crazy when he smiles. It's one of those secret smiles that people who are close give to each other. I wonder, are we that close? I want to be.

"What?" My big mouth did it again, spoke before my brain kicked in.

"We are complicated, Betsy. You, me, us."

Gosh, how complicated can a friendship be between a chiropractor and a personal chef? Well, maybe if you throw in a matchmaker friend who owns glamorous boutiques.

I cock my head and get a crick in my neck. Luckily, I have an on-call chiropractor in attendance. "How so?" Another one of my witty, profound questions.

"To begin with we met through Bett." There goes that grin again. "Then after our initial attraction you had the fire, and I had an anxiety attack ruining our date. Then, I had another anxiety attack and called Bett instead of you. You got miffed about that and you found me in the hospital watching a game show. You forgave, and I helped you interview contractors. We made a decision—aw—together, about which one. That was a minor breakthrough."

The man is rambling. Does he keep a journal or is he a history buff? I recall every instance of which he speaks, but saints preserve me if I could keep it all in order. Maybe an obsessive compulsive? Naw—he doesn't pick his nails or run to the restroom every five minutes to wash his hands. He's thorough. That's it. I hate to break his bubble, but I must correct him.

"Noel. We made the decision about Luke being the contractor to hire based on his presentation and knowledge. It wasn't a breakthrough in our relationship. Our first kiss was." Oops. Did I really say that?

"And what in candied carrots does Bett have to do with this— our relationship? You scared again?" *Dear Lord, I will give you all power and glory if you keep my big foot out of my mouth. Please.*

The shuffling of Noel's Topsiders is getting a little old. So is passing the buck to Bett, although I do credit her with our initial introduction. Truth be told, though, it's entirely possible we wouldn't have given each other a turn of the head if we'd met in the supermarket.

"Yep, guess so." He shuffles some more. I try to remember what I asked. Oh, scared again? I pick up the beat.

"Why?" I know I'm not a raging beauty, but I don't think it's circumspect to remind him of that, coward that I am.

"Something is holding you back. Is it me? Or something buried in the past?" I decide to continue my soliloquy hoping to draw him out. I take a plunge.

"I know I'm not a gorgeous twenty-something trophy girl, but I am a sincere, loving, pushing sixty mature woman. I'm also a Christian who doesn't lie or cheat. Is that not enough?" He gives me a funny, quizzical look. "Did I forget steal?"

He mumbles something about not having this discussion standing in Bett's drive. We climb in the car and buckle up, click,

click.

~

"We are so rude." I glance at him and he nods his head, a quirk playing around his mouth. My announcement wasn't intended to be humorous, yet I start to laugh. Noel joins me until together we are a cacophony of glee. We even drown out the Cruiser's purring.

"No choice," he sputters, then coughs trying to contain his mirth. Oh, dear, is he going to throw up? "Slap me on the back, Betsy, please. Hard." I oblige and the coughing abates.

"Poor Bett. Do you think we gave her a migraine?" He shrugs at my fake innocent question and steers the little red car down Shea Boulevard—a man on a mission.

"Did you catch the hat? She was wearing a hat at night. Ha, ha, ha."

"Noel, that's cruel." I punch his arm lightly and hold my tummy. I'm having trouble composing myself thinking of Bett waving from her doorway. A fuchsia caftan draped her voluptuous frame; its folds billowing below the air conditioning vent above her gave her a surreal look. Snoopy was draped over her shoulder like a hunter's dead trophy. His two-foot long tail hung limply from his rump and dangled alongside her arm. But, what initiated our mirth was the hat. We only had a glance, but in retrospect we both agreed.

"It must have been three feet wide."

"And floppy."

"Did you get a load of the flowers?"

"Yep, and the lace and ruffles."

"Oh, Noel. We are so cruel. We are not behaving like good friends. She was waving to us and we ignored her."

"No, I waved back."

"You did? That's almost more cruel. You waved back, then zoomed away? I actually pretended not to see her."

"She looked right at me. What choice did I have?" I pray the frown on his forehead is telling me he feels bad. Hopefully worse than I do.

We pull into a parking spot in front of Mitch's Koffee Klatch and sit there in silence. If that old expression of twiddling one's thumbs applies, I guess that's what I'm doing. At least I'm not staring into space through the windshield like Noel is. My frustration's mounting, but I'll be boonswaggled if I'm going to make the first move. Just as my twiddling almost gets to Lady Mac Beth proportions, Noel blurts out, "We gotta talk."

Sheesh, call me dense, but I thought that was the idea. "Really?" I try hard to keep the sarcasm out of my voice, but the angry glare on Noel's face tells me I didn't succeed.

"Very funny, Betsy. Here I am ready to bare my soul to you and you make a sarcastic remark." He jumps out of the car, slams the door dramatically and yanks mine open. Good show, Noel. Now we know what kind of a mood you're in. I want to say it, but this time God helped me with the foot in mouth disease thing. I smile instead.

Noel glares again and plods ahead of me. Not his usual gentlemanly style. "Whatta you want? We're going to sit outside." Outside? How nice to be consulted. "More private," he adds as an explanation. I give him my order for an iced latté and pick a table in the corner of the tiny, empty outdoor patio. He pushes the glass door open with his shoulder while carrying our drinks and a wad of napkins. I help him wipe the Arizona dust off the table and park myself on a rickety chair. We settle and I wait. Gracious, I'm getting patient lately. I think of that song the famous female psychologist plays a lot on her radio show about having a new attitude. Actually, that was the subject of Pastor Kerry's message last Sunday. *Telling me something, are you, Lord?*

We sip drinks. I clear my throat, he clears his. This is getting downright boring. I hope God keeps the patient attitude thing going in me, because I'm having a problem with it. Just as I'm about to doze off or flip a gasket, Noel mumbles something like, "Have a performance problem."

What! I didn't know he performed. Is he an actor on the side? He's certainly handsome enough, sort of Michael Rennie style. Boy, does that show my age. Actually, one of my former mothers-in-law adored the man. Even made me get his autograph once when he was in town. After having embarrassed myself and her son at great emotional expense, when I gave her his photo with the autograph she merely said, "Thanks." I wanted to scream, "Do you realize what we had to go through to get this for you?" Even though I didn't do it then, I want to scream now.

Just as I'm about to let loose with a howl, Noel raises his head. "You understand, Betsy?"

"Not exactly." I wait, patiently. With a straight face.

Something stirs in me and I sense I should take his hand. I reach across the small table and lay my palm against the back of one of his cold hands gripping his drink. More than the chill of the iced coffee gives me shivers. He looks at me with sad blue eyes the color of a stormy sky. "I have trouble with intimate relationships."

"Oh."

"That's why I worry, why I have anxiety attacks. I have very strong feelings for you, but if we were to get married, I'd be a big disappointment as a husband."

Okay, now my head is spinning. I'm not sure if it's because of the "M" word or his confusing confession. I mentally and quickly explore my options. My mouth takes over again from my brain. But, I'm beginning to understand his performance euphemism.

"First, how do you know this? You've been widowed for what, five years? Second, how did marriage come into this conversation?" I can't help it, I giggle. Just saying the word marriage makes me do it. I guess that's good because Noel chuckles.

"Let's start with question number two," he says. For a fleeting moment I feel like I'm on that old game show where contestants choose between door number one and door number two. Is there a door number three for Noel and me? Maybe, if I can name the right price. Oops, that's a different show. I return to the moment, and I think I've missed what Noel said during my reverie.

"Betsy." His voice raises an octave. "Did you even hear what I said? You looked as if you were drifting off into La La Land." Got me there, Noel. I try to look contrite, but probably fail.

"Sorry. Can you please repeat your…comment?" I'm

trying to make my remark as innocuous as possible, but I think I almost heard a proposal while my mind was wandering.

He tries to conceal a sigh, but it escapes his lips. His shaking head and wan smile tell me I'd better start paying attention. After all, this is the man I love. Oops, did that thought really come from moi?

Now he grasps my hand firmly in his. "Back to question two. As I pointed out, apparently to the air, I have developed very strong feelings for you." He stops to make sure I'm focusing on him. "If these feelings continue to develop like I think they will, like I hope they will…" Long pause. "Aw, shucks, I love you, Betsy." My feeble heart does a pitter-patter thing, and I feel my face turning rasberry red. No male has professed love to me in such a sweet way since Bobby McNair did in the front seat of his Corvair in high school. No, if you're wondering, we never made it to the back seat.

"Oh, Noel." For once my mouth isn't working. My lips feel big and floppy, even though I've never had injections to make them puffy. My tongue isn't working too well, but I hope my misty eyes say how I feel. I squeeze his hand and nod.

"Is that a yes?" he asks. Polly Parrot takes over again and I nod, hoping I know what I've agreed to. Noel's fingers tickle the back of my hand and he kisses it. A real smooch, not some flitting touch of the lips. I'm amazed at how passionate a kiss on a hand can feel.

For a brief second reality takes over. "Could you answer question number one, please?" I feel like a heel, but it was, is, the most important question. Suddenly, I'm in an "I need to know" mode.

"It's a biggie. You think you can handle it?" He's staring at my hand still enclosed in his. This time Betsy Bobblehead takes over. What is it with my mute mouth? My neck, even with the crick in it, seems to work okay.

"When Maizie was ill, I was devastated, an emotional and psychological mess. I sought help from our church's pastor who has a certificate in counseling. But, I never could bring myself to tell him about my performance problem. I was so ashamed. Mostly for Maizie. I loved her very much, and," his voice catches here, "the one thing she wanted, a last request, was great sex." He releases my hand and wipes his brow with the wad of napkins. I think my puffy lips are hanging open. "She wanted to recreate our honeymoon."

I try to will my mouth to spurt out the expected words of sympathy and empathy. Instead, I squeeze his hand back and nod. Our relationship is becoming a lot of "instead" moments, but it can't be helped. Sometimes words aren't adequate. I nod, perhaps for the fifty-third time, but he gets the drift.

"Pastor was very kind. Said he understood and tried to reassure me. However, he was thirty-five at the time and wasn't dealing with a dying wife. To his credit he suggested I consult a psychiatrist who could write a prescription. I never did."

I try to process what Noel just told me. But, the ramifications are overwhelming. Finally, my courage comes through and my mouth works. "Are you saying IF we were to marry, it would be a celibate marriage?"

"Possibly."

"Noel, I know you're a Christian, but have you ever tested this problem – since Maizie died?" Frankly, I'm hoping he hasn't. But, even Christians ere.

"No."

"Are you willing to see a professional now? Mr. Doctor who doesn't believe in doctors." I can't help chiding him.

"Maybe."

Suddenly, my mind is made up. Noel needs to do something about this problem, if not for me or us, at least for himself and his worth as a man. God makes me bold, on the spot.

"I'm pretty sure you've read Song of Songs, one of the most beautiful books in the Bible." He nods. "And, no one knows just how old Adam and Eve were when she tasted the fruit and they succumbed to sin." He nods again. "They were both chastised by God and blessed by Him. Became our role models in some way, not only because of the sin, but because God granted them one of the most blessed roles in history—to procreate." Another nod. "Not that you or I at our age wants to, or should, procreate, but God provided us with complex emotions to share love." I stop here. This is exhausting me.

I admit I'm getting a little annoyed at Noel's nodding. Not that I can claim to be a non-nodder. Nodding seems to keep my head busy and my brain working. Maybe it does the same thing for Noel.

"Betsy, it's not that simple." Lids lower over the Crayon blue eyes, so I have to guess at their meaning. I'm guessing embarrassment—we already talked about that—and fear. An old, much discussed, subject. Yet, my tongue and lips don't obey my mind.

"Still afraid?"

"Sadly, yes."

For once my mind and mouth are at an impasse. "Noel, you have to deal with this *situation*. If not for us, for yourself."

Now he's nodding more than I ever did, and it's getting really annoying. I don't want to be insensitive, after all my future may be in jeopardy here, but we need to make progress. Or, should I say progress. I have a lightbulb moment. You know, the kind when some thought or idea zaps your brain?

"Noel." I wait until he gives me his full attention. "Have you mentioned your problem to Bett?"

"Sort of. Why?"

"Only 'cause she has a great shrink, probably even a whole address book full of them. I—uh—don't necessarily want you to share a lot with her. But, she might be a good resource for the right psychologist or psychiatrist or even, who knows, the right Christian counselor."

There is possibly about thirty seconds of silence before I have the courage to speak.

"Then, there's moi."

Noel's chin flips up like it's been hit with a stray bullet. His look says, "Whoa." I blink my feathery lashes and give him a brilliant smile. Oh, Girl, you are so good!

Noel gives me a slightly wicked look and winks.

"What exactly did you have in mind?"

I rub the crick in my neck. "An adjustment?"

EIGHTEEN

"I didn't mean *that*, exactly." Noel assumes a crestfallen demeanor, shoulders slouched and eyelids blinking as if he's going to cry.

"Silly, I meant…"

He interrupts my thought.

"I know. It's really a great idea, Betsy. You need an adjustment, and if while I'm doing it," he pauses, "I do the deep tissue and light massage, well – let's see if nature takes its course."

"Works for me, Big Man." Now, why did I call him that? Maybe to encourage him?

Noel grasps my hand and tugs me toward the little red car. I look back at our table mess of coffee cups and napkins. I'm such a cleanup person. But, Noel shakes his head and I acquiesce. Guess that's what Mitch does in his off time, clean tables.

During the ride to Noel's chiropractic office in Scottsdale I'm feeling a bit un-settled. After all, it's dark, past office hours. I'm surprised lights are on in the small complex of low offices. The women's health clinic is obviously still seeing patients since two very pregnant women toddle toward their doors and another lumbers out to her car. The veterinarian's office parking lot is busy with two green clad attendants walking dogs and four patients' "parents" loading carriers into their SUVs. I relax a bit more when I read the stenciled letters on Noel's door.

Noel Sheppard , CCRD, FICA
Board Certified
Hours: 10 a.m. to 8 p.m.
Monday – Friday
Saturdays by appointment only

Noel gives my arm a little love squeeze and grins. It's so good to see his face light up again, I almost forget why we're here. He flips on overhead lights and leads me to a dressing room. I give him a quizzical frown as he hands me a green hospital type gown.

"Everything except the underpants. Tie it in back."

"Yes, Sir!"

As I disrobe, I remember glimpsing an interesting waiting room. Eames chairs backed up to the colorful walls hung with lively contemporary paintings of stick-like figures running and leaping. Perhaps to encourage mobility. Magazines were scattered on low tables, and carafes of water with stacks of plastic cups nearby sat on a console. The whole effect was one of relaxation combined with rejuvenation.

I went to a chiropractor for a back injury many years ago. I remember feeling intimidated by his waiting area filled with shelves of ice packs and neck pillows for sale surrounded by putrid green walls. He adjusted me, then left me to a newbie chiro in training. It helped somewhat, but I never went back.

Noel tapped lightly on the dressing room door. "Ready?"

He leads me to a semi-darkened room with a low bed-like table. "Lie on your stomach, Betsy." His voice has that annoying doctor sound, like a recording.

"You're kidding. Right?"

"No, I need to massage your shoulders to loosen the tension." He waits patiently, hands on his hips. "You're not being a good patient, Betsy. You need to trust your doctor."

I sneer and flop onto my belly on the hard table. I don't like being told what to do by anyone, even a doctor, especially Noel. My face goes into a round thing like a hole in the table. I guess so I can breathe, and so women don't mess their makeup. I feel trapped. My hands flop at my sides and I find metal grips to grab. I cling to them for dear life.

"Relax your arms, Betsy. Drop them at your sides."

So much for hanging on. I feel like that old cliché of a drowned rat. I'm all floppy and have no control of my limbs. Just as I'm about to bolt, two thumbs penetrate the muscles between my shoulder blades. "Oh, ow, ooo!" This time, neither God, nor I, has any control over my mouth. The feeling is sheer pleasure and sheer pain. Great combo. I'm just getting into this when Noel tells me to flip over. Bummer.

I struggle resting my weight on my left hip and reminding myself about exercise classes available at the senior center. Finally, I collapse on my back and stare straight up into the Crayon blue eyes. Tonight they are clouded and intense. I close my own baby blues and fold my hands loosely across my belly feeling like a corpse. I'm just about as relaxed as one while Noel kneads my upper arms and my neck. His hands are gently grasping my jaws and he's rolling my head back and forth. I'm rocking on a boat in the ocean, gently rocking to the roll of the waves when suddenly—my neck cracks. My eyes flip open then flutter close in utter contentment. The man has the touch, no doubting it.

"Betsy?" His voice is a hoarse whisper in my ear. I don't want to respond and break into my feeling of euphoria. "Betsy, hurry, look. Please."

With immense effort I turn my head. Noel's waist is in line with my vision. I see a bulge below it.

"Oh."

"It's okay, Betsy. I'm okay. You were right. You are the best medicine for my problem."

I can't think of anything definitive to say, nothing clever. I just nod and grin, and I want to dance. In lieu of doing a jig, I sit up and hug him.

"You're fine, Noel. Just fine."

He lifts me and swings me around right there in the

examining room in my green gown. This may not be the answer for every man with Noel's problem, but it was for him, for us.

He sets me down, giving me another hug and says, "Get dressed, Betsy. Time to go home."

~

We giggle and sing on the way back to Bett's. We've come up with our own personal version of the kids' song Heads, Shoulders, Knees and Toes. We slap each other's knees and laugh so hard tears trickle down our faces. Mine just tickle, but I see Noel wiping the stubble of his five o'clock shadow furiously. Exhausted, and breathing heavily, we sigh in unison. I still have the big question to ask.

"Noel, what does this mean to our relationship? This quote, unquote, breakthrough?"

Something like a gurgle, followed by a chuckle, followed by another gurgle emits from his throat. He takes his hands from the steering wheel for just a second, and his arms fly up into the air. "Everything!"

Noticing my obvious silence he glances at my face. "I am a free man, Betsy. A free man." He places fingertips against my cheek, but keeps staring straight ahead. Turning off Ninety-sixth Street onto Via Linda Boulevard he heads west. Blocks of apartment complexes wiz by, and I wonder where we're headed.

"Noel, this is the opposite way to Bett's. What's up?"

"Going to celebrate, Betsy."

We pull into a small strip mall and park in the corner. I notice a furniture resale store named Re-create, a pancake parlor, a sushi restaurant and a tiny pizza place. The furniture store and pancake restaurant are dark. A few patrons sit at outside tables in front of the pizza parlor, and lights are blinking from the sushi restaurant as several Asian customers enter it. Did I mention I love sushi?

Noel is like a kid in a candy store grinning from ear to ear. He practically leaps from the driver's seat and races to open my door. "Pizza or sushi, milady?" he asks as he takes my hand in mock reverence. I admit I feel like royalty. Maybe Queen of Hearts admonishing Alice in Wonderland.

"No contest," I reply and grab his hand. We race together while I have a sense of déja vue remembering the ice cream parlor. The Japanese hostess looks askance at us, not sure if she really wants to seat this panting couple. She studies us for a moment, and after a polite pause followed by an obligatory bow, she asks, "Sushi bar or table?"

Noel points to a tiny table in the corner. "This reserved," Ms. Hostess replies. Her face is a composition in ivory. Not even a flutter of dark eyelashes. Noel nods and hands her a twenty. She leads us to the table. It's private and secluded, set off from the rest of the restaurant.

"What made you decide on sushi, on this place?" He looks a little disappointed, like a man deprived of his pizza. Still, he gave me the choice.

"Look around. Ninety percent of the diners are Asian, and most of them, if you listen, are speaking Japanese. That's a great restaurant review." I unfold my napkin and tear off the paper from the chopsticks. "Did you hear anyone speaking Italian at the pizza parlor?" His guffaw startled several patrons near us, and he covered his mouth with a hand, but his eyes still sparkled.

NINETEEN

The hour is late. I don't have a watch on, and I don't care what time it is. Probably only elevenish, maybe later. Maybe much later. Still, lights glimmer from numerous windows in Bett's expansive home. I feel like a schoolgirl with a curfew as we pull into the circular drive.

Noel and I squeeze hands and giggle. Yes, both of us. If you've never heard a grown man giggle with pleasure, you're missing something special. He plants a peck of a kiss on the tip of my nose—so cute—and leaps out of the car without closing his door. Trying to be quiet and not disturb Bett, I suppose. Opening my door, he bows with a flair and takes my hand to help me out. I feel like royalty. Maybe I should suggest an adjustment more often. I flatten my free hand in front of my mouth to suppress another giggle and bat my lashes.

"Shh, you'll wake her royal highness." Noel tries to look stern, but his Groucho Marx expression makes me giggle all the more. For the first time I notice how thick his eyebrows are when he wiggles them. Cary Grant, Michael Rennie and Groucho all rolled into one. Can I live with that? I remind myself those images are all surface. It's the man underneath, the soul of the man, that matters. Just as 1 Corinthians 13 comes to mind—"Love is patient, love is kind…"—a blinding light flashes and our heads jerk up.

"Yoo, hoo. You two okay?"

Bett. What on earth is she doing up? Spying on us? Waiting like a disconsolate parent? My latent teenage persona takes over, and I bristle.

Noel squeezes my hand so hard he almost crushes it. His wink gives me pause. Am I being too sensitive? He nods, then shakes his head ever so slightly. Is he reading my mind now? He winks again and does the Groucho eyebrow thing. "Isn't this fun? Between Bett and you, Betsy, I feel so young."

I take a deep cleansing breath. Maybe the man has something here. After all, we owe our meeting each other to Bett. And she is a sort of lonely mother wannabe. We both turn and wave, and for some unknown reason, even to me, I blow her a kiss. Suddenly, all the lights except the one on the porch go off. I turn to Noel and rest my head on his shoulder. "I feel young, too."

TWENTY

A month later.

I'm still at Bett's. Not officially, just for cooking. Luke did a super job renovating my condo from the fire damage. But, I was getting cramped in my little kitchen with all the orders coming in. Bett suggested I apply for a commercial health permit to use her kitchen for my larger orders. It was no problem getting one since her kitchen is larger than many restaurant ones, and all her appliances are labeled "commercial." As a bonus Consuela keeps it immaculate. I think it's a way for Bett to keep me close to her. She insists it is a wedding gift to me.

I'm mixing the batter for my wedding cake. I'm not a baker. But, this is something I've always dreamed of. Just the batter, not the decorations. I've hired Joseph and Joseph, decorators extreme and masters of fondant, to embellish it. They'll step in next month to create the cake of my dreams. Meanwhile, the five tiers of lemon and chocolate, alternating in size and flavor, will be double-wrapped in plastic and resting in Bett's monstrous freezer awaiting their masterful touch.

I'm licking the driblets of lemon batter off the spatula when my cell phone vibrates. The little window lights up, but not displaying a phone number. Odd, it's a "Restricted Number." Can't imagine, but since the cake layers are in the ovens—yes, two out of Bett's four ovens—I decide to answer with a cautious "hello."

"My aren't we the mousy-voiced thing? I might have expected that." The caller whose voice is definitely female, but marginally feminine, lets loose with a high-pitched cackle.

"Excuse me," I say as calmly as possible, "I believe you have the wrong number."

Another cackle, throaty this time. "If this is Betsy, Elizabeth, or whatever your name is, I've got it right." There's that pregnant pause again while I reflect, and she apparently waits for her words to sink in. "Lay off Noel you revolting snake, you wicked witch, you man hunter, you, you..." A stream of expletives, the ones that refer to me as a woman, drip like venomous E.V.O.O. from the raspy voice.

Of course any sensible person would hang up. One of my favorite childhood books was about an inquisitive and meddlesome little primate. His personality must have rubbed off on me. "WHO is this?" I hear myself screeching and bite my tongue. So much for my ladylike behavior.

"Don't get your (she uses a slang term to name a body part, actually two) in an uproar, Honey. You'll find out soon enough. Ask Noel." And with that, she hangs up leaving my shaking hand holding the phone.

Suffering shellfish, you betcha I'll ask Noel. If I let him live long enough.

"Who was that, dear? I thought I heard you screaming." Bett floats into the arena sized kitchen in a crimson lounge outfit—filmy pant legs each the width of most skirts topped by a tent-like overblouse with wing shaped sleeves that would make a butterfly envious. She looks like she is practicing to fly. Matching rouge highlights her cheekbones and puffy lips. In contrast, her blue eyes look troubled and center on the blush I feel creeping across my nose.

I shrug and busy myself with rinsing the batter bowls. Tears sting my eyes and I sense my shoulders trembling. I feel the gentle touch of her hand on my arm.

"Something's wrong," she states matter-of-factly. "What?"

The question hangs in the air while I try desperately to compose myself. As the tears start to stream down my cheeks, I realize composure is out of the question. I need to share. I really want to call Mom. But, Bett's right here standing six inches away from me, her hand softly caressing my arm. I can smell her perfume, and to distract myself, I try to figure out what scent it is. Shalimar? Channel Number Five? No, too plebeian for Bett. Probably some new designer scent, or one of those you create in that special little room at Nordstrom's. I've always been too intimidated to even step into it and approach the coiffed customer service associates (now that's a misnomer if ever there was one—what happened to sales ladies?) in their form-fitting black suits and tulip red lips.

I swing around dripping suds from my hands and grip Bett's arms. She tries valiantly not to cringe and shakes her head full of fluffy curls at my "Sorry." As I grab a towel, she takes my hand and leads me to the oversized round table in the equally oversized breakfast niche. The towel comes in handy to not only wipe my wet hands, but to blot the fountains running from my eyes.

She whispers, "Tell me about the call." How can she be so calm? Oh, she doesn't know yet. When I am upset I get so obtuse.

I relate the call. Not just the gist of it, but every nasty and unholy word. Unfortunately, one of my talents is total recall. I don't even like to say those words, but I think it's important Bett has a blow by blow description. That is if she's going to help me understand what's going on. Although it probably only took three minutes, I feel like I'd been venting for an hour. My throat is parched, and my voice sounds surreal. Still, I manage to blurt out, "I hate Noel. I hate him. I knew I shouldn't trust him."

"Monica." That's all Bett says. But, I notice she's wringing her clasped hands in front of her on the tabletop. Her eyes seem to be a bit glazed, too. Maybe it's an effect of the tears that are blurring mine.

"Monica? Who's Monica?" My question falls on deaf ears as Bett gets up to grab the portable phone.

Suddenly, I smell something like burning chocolate. Oh, my ripped knickers! My cake. Pulling open the oven door, I hear Bett punching in numbers on the phone. New tears fall on the deflated chocolate rounds. My beautiful cake layers are ruined.

"Monica." I hear Bett's hard voice in the background. "Lay off my friend. Noel never was yours. Grow up! Don't call me that, you infidel. I refuse to listen to that rubbish. I'm a God-fearing woman." I've turned around by this time and see Bett slam the handset down on the table. It bounces landing digits up and beeps. For just a second my mind leaps from pain and hurt to her declaration of being a "God-fearing woman."

"What in…?"

"I suppose you should know. Why Noel didn't expect this and warn you, I have no idea. Man's prerogative I guess. Or, maybe just the vain hope it wouldn't happen."

I sit down at the table again and search her eyes. "Explain, please."

"It started after his wife died—Maizie. When patients got word of it. Her death, I mean." She pauses to twist the enormous amethyst ring on her pinkie. "I recommended Noel to her when she came to work one day almost doubled over with back pain. Yes." She nods. Her eyes lock with mine, and I see pools of blue sadness. "She was one of my employees, bookkeeper, not a sales associate. I knew she was kind of loopy and needy. Craving male companionship. She'd begged me to set her up with someone. It never crossed my mind when I sent her to Noel. Just thought an adjustment of the back, not an invitation to romance." Bett's hands are now clasped together so tight her knuckles are Elmers Glue-white. I sense she regrets the decision to send Monica to Noel. I am so perceptive!

I glance up at the ceiling fan whirring above the table. I try to process this story in my muddled brain. I feel my chin quivering and give a little "chin up" in Bett's direction encouraging her to go on.

Sighing, she continues after relaxing her hands. "She became a real pain in the kazoo. Showed up when Noel stopped for a latte, even appeared in the grocery store behind him in line. Once she even pulled into the car wash right after him. Of course he was trapped talking to her while both of their cars went through the suds. After a year or so with no confrontations, we figured she'd given up." Bett pauses to blow out a breath, whoosh style. "To answer your unasked question, we both believed she was stalking him. For two years now, there's been no appearance or communication from Monica. She quit working for me about a month after I sent her to Noel for chiropractic help.

"I know she means nothing to Noel, except an unbidden thorn in his side. I'm so sorry."

I twist the towel I still hold in my hands. Could I believe Bett? Noel? What was his role in the Monica caper? Trust. I need trust. The only place I know for sure I can get it is from my Heavenly Father.

"Bett?" I reached across the table and grasped her hands. "Will you pray with me?"

~

"We prayed together, Mom. It was the most awesome thing."

Mom picks at her running socks and scratches her ankle exposing her seventy-eight year old veins. I look away.

"Awwww, Bits." She drags out the "aw." "What a blessing. Do you think she's actually accepted Christ?"

I don't know, and I can't say. I suspect on one plane Bett was just humoring me, but on another higher plane, I pray she was sincere. She never uttered a word when I prayed, just kept her head bowed and squeezed my hand. As far as I'm concerned, the rest is up to God. Instead of voicing my thoughts, I simply say, "Gosh, Mom. That's only for God to know." Yeh, opt out, Betsy. Did I mention I'm a dweeb, wimp, a sad example of a Christian?

Mom fiddles with the bracelet she inherited from Grandma. She seems to be studying the tiny glass ovals encased in gold. She's worn it on her wrist since about a week after Grandma died, when we cleaned out Grandma's effects—clothes, jewelry, baking pans (some of which I inherited), books and general stuff. I remember the smell in her bathroom. It was an old lady smell, but pleasant and heady. Soaps and perfumes and room deodorizers from another era.

"So," she holds me in her gaze twisting the bracelet around her wrist. "What do you plan to do?"

TWENTY ONE

The novel hits the wall with a splat. I'm sick of this author who used to thrill me with his mysteries that take place around Phoenix, places I know and can relate to. Now his characters spew out curses, and the settings are so surreal I don't recognize them.

I had hoped to distract myself from the latest Noel complication by reading a juicy novel. Obviously, it didn't work. This one was too juicy.

I'm lying on my bed, in my condo, not at Bett's. It was time to come home, if not to cook, to sleep. My digs aren't as luxurious as Bett's, but I need the secure feeling of my own simple surroundings. No fabric covered walls, just paint. No museum quality artwork, just prints—not even by anyone famous or renowned. Plastic handled toothbrush instead of silver-plated, a bathroom light I actually have to turn on manually by the wall switch, instead of one that glows instantly when I walk through the door. I am so bourgeois!

I snuggle under the down comforter I found at Macy's half-price sale last January and succumb to my version of heaven on earth with my ankles crossed and staring at the ceiling fan. Whir, whir. The twirl of the fan mimics my mind. Remembering how I once (make that twice) felt as a freshman in college, I know I'm not drunk. At least not with alcohol.

Still, my head spins. I click on my cell phone and notice Noel has called me four times today. Probably after the vicious call from Monica. Probably after Bett called Noel to inform him.

I feel lost. Swimming in an abyss. I remember looking the word abyss up once for a college paper. A "yawning gulf" was my favorite description. I surrender to the yawning part, uncross my ankles and pull up the comforter. My body is so tired my muscles ache, and I'm just drifting into dreamland when the doorbell rings.

I try to ignore the offending sound, but it repeats. Over and over again.

Still in my working attire sweatsuit, I stumble out from under the soft covers, again catching my toe. Shuffling for my fuzzy slippers I find them tucked under the bed. Why am I even doing this? I have no answer. At least none that makes sense.

The peephole in the door reveals a huge bouquet of roses. If I'd known Noel was hiding behind them, I might not have opened it. I guess curiosity got the best.

A hand waves, flutters, at the end of the hairy arm that isn't holding the bouquet. It retreats behind the mass of buds and two eyes peek out above an aquiline nose. Suddenly, the bouquet and its human holder drop to my waist level. Noel is on his knees. *Oh, dear Lord, what is going on here?*

"Betsy?" A whisper. "Please." Is he begging?

I refuse to acknowledge him other than, "Yes?"

He half rises abruptly and thrusts the flowers in my face. I don't know if it's because they're tickling my nose or the scent is overwhelming, but I sneeze—loudly.

The "sorrys" Noel's been whispering and babbling during the last sixty seconds escalate. Now, I'm feeling sorry for him. What is this world coming to?

"Come on, Noel. Off your knees," I say, grabbing his hand, but not taking the flowers. "You're going to need a chiropractor if you don't stand up soon."

He grins and shoves the roses at my chest. So romantic, but I still don't accept them. I admit I bury my face in the crimson blooms. There must be at least fifty of them, probably sixty if he bought them by dozens. Their scent is heady, reminds me of a perfume Mom sometimes wears. Maybe she wore it long ago when I was a toddler and she comforted me in the rocking chair. Anyway, it brings back memories that make my eyes tear. Noel, poor man, notices and mistakes my watery eyes for something else. Perhaps romantic interest and forgiveness.

The man is insufferable. Or at least our relationship is. I realize, being the realistic woman I am, he'd never thought about Monica calling me, nor even fathomed how a call from her could damage our love. Still, I stand the wounded warrior in this now love triangle. I manage to shove aside these nagging thoughts and search for a vase large enough to contain the massive bouquet.

"Friends?"

I turn to look at him and hope my scowl answers, but I'm guessing the quizzical look on his face says it doesn't. "Friends—friends," I scream. "What kind of friends treat friends this way? We, Noel, were supposed to be lovers, albeit Christian lovers. Two souls who share everything. No holds barred; no secrets; no skeletons buried—anywhere."

I'm exhausted from screeching. My throat is dry and parched. My diatribe is over. I pick at a bit of Snoopy fur on my sweats left over from Bett's. That dang-fangled cat's fur magnetizes to all surfaces, especially fabric. I'm waiting for Noel to touch my arm in apology, maybe in my dream of dreams crawl on the carpet and kowtow at my feet.

I look around in the silence. Noel is slumped on my sofa with the huge bouquet hanging limply in his arms. Am I seeing a wetness glistening on his cheeks? Aw, fiddlesticks, the man is weeping. I take a tentative step toward him and approach his humped over form just as he rubs a fist across his eyes with his free hand. I love it when a man cries. I hate it when a man cries. I feel so helpless.

When a woman cries in the presence of a manly man, she expects to be enfolded in his arms and given silent permission to slobber on his shoulder. A father, a brother, a husband or lover, or even a friend readily takes that role. It's a natural inclination for the male of the species to comfort and protect the female. But, turn the tables and it becomes a dilemma.

Few men are comfortable being the weeper, and most women are confused about how to react.

I make a decision, instantly, based on the knot in my gut. My occasionally logical mind tells me Noel never thought about the possibility of Monica learning about me, much less calling me. Isn't it a guy thing to not analyze romance? Seems they analyze just about everything else, but not love.

My heartstrings strum the song we sang to the other evening, something about two hearts entwined. I'm just about to make a beeline to the sofa and enfold Noel in my ample arms when he says, "Monica really called you the other night? How did you two hit it off?"

"Hit it off?" My screech owl voice takes over again. "Are you nuts? Crazy? You expected me to have an actual conversation with that witch, that home-wrecker?"

To his credit, Noel looks confused and lays the bouquet of roses on the coffee table. I stifle my concern about their blossoms leaving a permanent stain on the mahogany. His handsome gray-speckled head is bobbing from side to side. "I don't understand. Bett said Monica phoned you. She wasn't clear on the conversation. I guess I assumed after speaking with each other you'd had a good chat." He raises puppy dog eyes to me. "No?"

I nod Bobble head fashion. Does he get the inference, that I'm nodding to his "No?"

"I know Monica can be confrontational, but she's a pretty rational person." His eyes appeal to me for understanding. "She's not a bad person. I sensed she had an interest in me, but," he pauses for emphasis, "we never dated. Honest." His right hand crosses his heart in little boy Boy Scout fashion. "She was just a patient." He hangs his head looking exhausted. I'm still standing like Lot's wife, a pillar in stone, if not salt.

We both extend hands at the same time. His touch is warm as he pulls me down on the sofa next to him. His lips are fiery hot and taste of salt from his tears. His embrace is strong as one of those chiropractor hands caresses my back. I am mush. Did I mention I love this man, and would forgive him almost anything? "Almost" being the operative word.

~

"You made up."

It's a statement. Bett clasps my hands. We're munching on Swedish cookies and sipping hot herb tea in her so-called breakfast nook. This evening she's wearing a diaphanous sunflower yellow negligee and pegnoir. She's ready for bed, and so am I, emotionally. The filmy, see-through fabric clings to her and swooshes as she turns toward me. Her mop of curls spring up and down when she bobs her head waiting for confirmation. I don't want to go into minute detail about Noel and me making up, so I simply nod in the affirmative and smile at her questioning eyes.

I take a nibble of cinnamon cookie and let it melt on my tongue. "Yeh, it's okay. He explained."

"Praise the Lord," Bett exclaims and squeezes my hands again.

"Bett," I look her directly in the eyes. "I hope you aren't using that phrase lightly." I worry she's picked up some of my Christian jargon and either says it to impress me or doesn't realize what it really means.

The curls bounce again, and her eyes zero in on her teacup. "Nope. Know what it means."

I take a breath so deep I think I've sucked in all the air in the massive kitchen. *Lord, please guide my words.* "Bett, what exactly are you saying? Nonbelievers use that expression loosely, but so do believers. It's an expression of faith that we almost say without thinking." I pause and give her a significant look. "Tell me why you used it?"

Lady Mac Beth had nothing over Bett. I hope Bett's hand wringing isn't becoming an obsession. I reach for her hands. I clasp them tight, tilt her chin up with my forefinger and look at her face imploringly. She is shaking, her whole body quivering.

Her eyes are still downcast, and I can barely hear her whisper, "I did it."

"Did what?"

"Last night I was so upset about the rift between you and Noel I pleaded with God. I felt this tremor. It was almost like He spoke to me, me Bettina Bethany."

"Oh, Bett." My heart is swelling and my eyes are blurring. I touch her arm but have no more words.

"So, I spoke back. 'Why would you talk to me, Lord? I don't deserve your love or attention. Please, explain.' It was a very logical conversation. I really wanted to know."

Remember the pregnant pause? Focus on it again.

"So?" I've mentioned before how utterly brilliant my remarks are.

"Sooo…" She draws it out. "I had your Bible open to John 3:16. I read it over and over. 'For God so loved the world he gave his only begotten son that whoever believes in him will not perish.' Or, something like that." She loosens her grip on my hand and locks her eyes with mine.

"I'm getting older, Betty. I know my time will come someday soon, and I don't want to perish, to spend eternity without the comfort of God. Besides, I know you'll be up there with Him, and I want to be with you forever."

A chill creeps over my body, and I rub my arms feeling goose bumps. How do I explain to this dear woman she mustn't accept faith in God and Christ just because she wants to be with me forever? I want her need to be with the Lord forever and her relationship with Him now to be genuine. I blow a big breath, like when I've been exercising long and hard, and begin the lesson again.

I did it. I told Betsy I've accepted you, Lord. I'm not sure she believed me. What now, Jesus? I thought she'd be thrilled. I'm so confused.

TWENTY TWO

Ten years ago, when my stomach was flatter, I sometimes went without a bra. Not in public, mind you, just around the house. Although occasionally, like when I stepped out to retrieve the morning paper or take more garbage out to the can, a neighbor would see me. I felt pretty daring, even though I knew I blushed. Actually, I felt more daring than I did in the sixties and seventies during the "burn the bra" era. I guess my ego needed a little push up (no pun intended). I don't know what the flatter tummy had to do with this admission. Go figure. (Oops, no pun intended, again. Honest.)

Today, I need to get my thoughts together. I dwell on Bett's revelation of accepting Christ as her savior. Did I get through that curly skull last night? She claims I did, but she just kept nodding. Don't get me wrong, I'm thrilled Bett has made this life-changing decision. I keep raising my hands and shrilly claiming, "Praise the Lord." Now, who's the hypocrite?

I decide to do something practical for a change. Washing underwear, panties and bras counts, doesn't it? I reserved for doing laundry at my own digs. Bett's fancy washer and dryer were too complicated for me, and my learning curve isn't as quick as it used to be. I set the dial on wash and let it roll. Maybe Consuela has figured out the nuances of Bett's laundry appliances with porthole doors and sitting on risers. More power to her. At least she gets paid to do it.

Twiddling my thumbs is not my forté. Besides, I forget which direction I'm twiddling, then get all mixed up. I guess the old adage "all thumbs" applies aptly to me. I really should be cleaning my oven and scrubbing out the toilet. Instead, I opt for a more fun endeavor and convince myself I need to concoct a new recipe, something uniquely Betsy. I fantasize about one called "Noel's Nicoise", the perfect French inspired salad. Or, how about "Love on a Platter" or "Tryst?" Naw, too cutesy.

I'm just settling down at the kitchen table with my recipe journal and pen in hand when the annoying shrill of the phone interrupts my reverie. I haven't received a call on my home phone since the fire, so I'm a bit reluctant to answer. I did mention before that I'm not superstitious, but one can't take chances, can one? "Caller Unknown" displays on the ID window. I wait for the machine to kick in and hear Noel's shaky voice.

~

HonorHealth Shea Hospital is becoming my second home. Make that my third since Bett's is my second. Navigating to find a parking spot near the emergency entrance is second nature to me now. I salute the pudgy attendant in registration and he recognizes me. "Nell's friend, right?" He got it close, so I nod. "You're the *good friend*?" I nod again, feeling again like an imitation of that old Bobble head doll. "Right this way," he says nonchalantly leading me through the whooshing "Hospital Personnel Only" doors. I have a feeling of déja vue, but I plod obediently after Mr. Pudgy.

I open my mouth to ask, "What is it this time, Noel?" One glance at his face and I bite both my lip and my tongue. Not an easy feat.

He looks ghastly. Gray pallor spreads across his ashen face lying flat on a snowy white pillow. Noel's beautiful salt and pepper hair stands in stringy tufts emphasizing the tube sticking out of his nose. His eyes are closed, and he looks deathly pale. I notice another tube attached to his arm and leading to a see-through bag hanging precariously high above the bed. His cobalt blue eyes (yes, I found another color name for them) are hidden behind lids so tight I'd need a zipper to open them. I try to remain calm and try not to panic.

"Wha...what's wrong with him?" I hear my voice making sounds, but the sounds are echoes—like a child talking into a tin can. Pudgy touches my shoulder, and I notice for the first time his eyes are pools of sympathy. For a fleeting moment I wonder if he practices that look. Maybe he works on it in the hospital restroom during his breaks.

I know my meager attempt at internal levity is just to prolong the inevitable. I grip the side rail on Noel's bed for support and whisper, "Please, tell me."

~

Flu!

I'm fuming, stomping around my condo like a nervous, geeky kid auditioning for a high school marching band. What an idiot. Noel was the one who convinced me to go to Safeway last week for my flu shot. For the first time in several years, the flu vaccine is available everywhere—pharmacies, supermarkets, even (if you can believe it), doctor offices. No excuses. Nada. None. Me, I got mine between shopping for canned soup and mascara (not that I use much).

There'd be no use staying at the hospital. Besides, I am in a fowl, funky mood and fear I'll be confrontational when Noel wakes up. Yes, I was assured he would wake up—be achy and grumpy, but with the intravenous hydration he was being given, be fit as a fiddle in a few days. Grumpy isn't on my agenda right now, so I split.

I guess you could say I'm not the hand holding type. I do love Noel, very much. But, I have a problem with stubborn men, and dense men. Ego is a big thing with me. I believe I've mastered mine. After all, I've dealt with the love handles and big butt syndromes. I've accepted my body, even if others haven't. (An aside: Bett keeps hinting I should "work out" more, use her fitness room. I refrain from asking her why she wears those hideous caftans.) Again, I digress.

I'm having a hard time with the Noel illness situation. I don't mean to be insensitive, but our wedding is only a few months away. Cactus Community Church is booked; Mom is calling me daily with cute ideas and names of photographers, caterers and even a firm that provides real white cloth runners for the church aisle, not those disposable paper ones. Her latest suggestions are for favors—a tiny sauté pan holding a chocolate kiss with both of our names and saying "You light my fire"; candies with our names on the wrappers stuffed in miniature red convertibles; and the worst, two small teddy bears linked together with our names and wedding date on them. Hello, Mom, we are not in our twenties. I search Online for something more appropriate for our ages. Finding nothing, I design my own.

I ask you, what would you suggest for a chef and a chiropractor? Right. Something that has nothing to do with either of their professions, but has a lot to do with their love. Well, I haven't come up with it, either. Not yet. But, I will.

Right now I have to call the hospital and find out how "Mr. No Flu Shot" is doing.

~

I feel awful.

"Betsy." His weak voice whines over the phone. I try to ignore that. "I tried to get a flu shot. I was fifty-sixth in line, but the cut-off was fifty-five. I kept hoping someone would step out of line, but when the bent over gray-haired lady in front of me was called, well, that was it."

End of the line Noel. That will be my new teasing nickname for him.

"Oh, Noel, precious one." I'm being real syrupy here. "I didn't stay last night, because…" I have to make an instant decision. Do I lie, fib, fudge a little? Okay, you got me, tell the truth. You already know how I feel about lying. So, here goes.

"I'm sorry I didn't stay last night until you woke up. I didn't know how long that would be, or if you'd even know who I was. I guess I was having a problem with you having the flu when you said you'd be getting a shot. It's me, not you. I was the screw-up. I do love you. I'm so sorry."

I hang my head, hoping he can see it through the telephone lines. Guess not.

"Betsy, you mean you gave up on me?"

How could I explain that one of my former husbands pulled multiple sympathy tricks on me? How could I tell Noel, this paragon of senior virtue, this man I love more than earth, that I clung to the past when I should have been leaping with joy for the future? I ditch the nagging questions and take a deep breath, a very deep one.

"Noel, I want to explain. I will be there in ten minutes flat. I love you. Please don't stop loving me."

Hanging up the phone took a millisecond; grabbing my keys, my jacket and cell phone took maybe two minutes. I did the Betsy check—keys, cell, glasses, jacket. Got it. Aw, the chocolate chip cookies I'd baked earlier. From a mix. I won't tell. I stuff six of them in a plastic container, breeze out the door and do the Betsy flying leap into Old Sassy. I'm rolling.

~

I'm now an expert at parking in the emergency entrance parking lot of the hospital. But, I feel guilty. I'm actually supposed to go to the ICU, going through the main entrance. Since it's locked at night I'd have to find that special door that allows entrance. Trying not to look confused I stand soldier straight in front of Pudgy. Does the man ever have an evening off?

"Reporting for duty, SIR!"

His puff pastry cheeks and swollen eyes turn upward. "Nell, again, huh?" He ignores my sergeant act. So much for levity. Where has all the humor gone in this world? Seems to me that in all the pain and suffering in emergency rooms and ICUs, humor is very much needed. Not appreciated, I guess.

I ignore the "Nell" reference, believing he means Noel. Again, I follow him like an errant lamb. Noel's curtained off cubicle seems less frightening. The tube thingy is out of his nose and he is sitting up with two pillows behind him. He seems to be dozing, a feathery whisper blowing from his nostrils. I don't want to disturb him, so I ease myself into a Vinyl padded armchair near his bed.

"He's being moved to a room soon." Pudgy's whisper is loud and cuts through the quiet like a steak knife cutting through pasta and scraping on the plate. I wonder again where this man learned his "bedside manner," an anomaly if ever there was one.

"Good. Does that mean he's better?" I remember

belatedly to ask when. Before Pudgy can answer a nurse who brings to mind a lost species with wide, bony shoulders (Yes, I can actually see the protrusions popping out of her patterned smock. Which reminds me, what ever happened to starched white and perky caps?) and a face that could put Jack Nicholson over the edge again, bursts into the room with noisy purpose. The curtain whooshes behind her at about the same time she sets her hands on hips that are thankfully wider than mine. The face that I thought could sink a thousand ships broke into a grin that could melt an iceberg. I never was very good at reading people.

"Hi, Handsome. Guess you're out of the woods," she grins like a Cheshire. I think of pouffy Snoopy and how my affection for him has grown, albeit his cumbersome weight lying across my legs and numbing them. Despite her behemoth appearance, I decide I like the creases and wrinkles in her weather-beaten face that seem to light up the room now that she's smiling. Under this craggy appearance I sense a kind heart. So much for first impressions. Gotta work on that.

I've decided to call her (in my mind, of course) Nurse Fetchit, since she's coming to fetch Noel. Just then she notices moi sitting perched on the edge of the room's only chair. Turning, she gives me a full-face smile. "Nurse Ratchit, here. Good to meet you."

I just about lose it when she breaks into a guffaw. Her laughter starts out loud and boisterous, then decreases into a near whisper. Suddenly, her voice lifts somewhere between that whisper and a lilting melody into one of my favorite praise songs. "It's not about me, it's all about You." She winks, and I notice a twinkle in her eyes. Surely this woman is an angel, one of God's emissaries sent to earth to protect and encourage.

Turning to me after her brief vocal soliloquy, she walks around Noel's hospital bed and reaches for my hands. Her hands are tiny in comparison to the size of her body. They are warm, and her grasp is firm and comforting. Her eyes bubble with leftover humor from the Nurse Ratchit quip.

"I'm sorry. I hope I didn't frighten you, or put you off too much. Sometimes, I can't resist." She searches my face, her amber eyes wandering over my own obvious wrinkles and creases. "You are a believer." It's a statement, not a question.

"It's written on your face, it's demonstrated by the caring you have for Noel, and," she grins again, "the cross at your throat is a dead giveaway."

Not to mention the Bible resting on my lap I think. Nevertheless, I like this woman—a lot. She's genuine. How often does that happen? I trust her. That's another bordering on miracle incident.

Perhaps she senses the confusion in my eyes. Suddenly, she perks up and emits that melodic laugh again. "I'm sorry. I didn't properly introduce myself. I'm really, as unbelievable as it sounds, Nurse Jones, Netta Jones. God's servant." She pauses to let that sink in.

Seems to me it's time for my two cents worth to be inserted here. The tip of my tongue is almost raw from biting it, and the dry desert air isn't being kind to the skin on my constantly wrung knuckles. Besides, I have a lot invested in those two squabblers. Not financial—well, some—but mostly emotional.

History.

Although I'm not exactly ready for clumps of dirt to be dumped on me, I'm no spring chicken, either. I just feel the tick of time, the swing of the pendulum wearing a groove below the clock's face.

What to do? That's the big question, especially without giving away my secret. Yet.

TWENTY THREE

I'm trotting after Nurse Netta Jones and two orderlies who are wheeling Noel down a hall on a gurney. Nurse J. is silently directing traffic, hands flailing in gestures to put my Italian butcher, Tony, to shame. Netta, I now call her that at her request, started out behind the orderlies steadying Noel's IV bags attached to a tall skinny coat rack-type thing. By the time we reach the bank of elevators, she has abandoned the coat rack and is waving people away like a traffic officer at an accident scene. I wish I had an orange vest to give her. I also wish I had my digital camera in my purse. The Arizona Republic would probably have bought the photos of the outraged and frightened crowd trying to enter the elevator. So much for lost opportunities.

Alone together in the moving room, we ascend to floor three where she punches in a passcode for the glass double doors to swing open outward. We pass two nursing stations on our journey, both with three or four heads bowed down reading charts, until…

"Coming through here. Priority."

All the heads jerk up on internal neck springs, flop back and forth like Slinky coils and smile. Some grin. Gotta love this woman. She rules.

As she opens the door to 23B and gestures for me to

enter, I feel Netta and I have bonded. I'm helping her puff up pillows and straighten sheets, but I feel like she's helping me. She makes me feel needed and important, and as the orderlies shift Noel into his new hospital bed, Netta takes my hand and guides it into Noel's limp one. Then, after dismissing the two burly men with a curt nod, she places one of her tiny hands under our clasped ones and her other on top. "Let us pray."

~

It's raining. Drat.

I've decided to be a good girl and leave by the hospital's main entrance. Besides, Pudgy and I have been seeing a little too much of each other lately, and one of us will undoubtedly lose it soon. Probably me.

So, I trek along the curving balcony hallway to the elevator. I admit it's more scenic than shuffling through the ER waiting room filled with whining children and sneezing adults. And Pudgy.

The glass door swings open easily to my touch, and though sheltered by an overhang so no raindrops stain it, the watery deluge is coming down so hard I can hardly see beyond the sidewalk. I suppose I'll have to guess where I parked my car. Oh, emergency entrance, other side of hospital. Great.

I long for the umbrella I keep behind the driver's seat of Old Sassy, the one I have with me every sunny day and never have when I need it, and bury my hands deep in the pockets of my velour warm-ups. Might as well make a run for it. Head lowered, hands in pockets, elbows waving like the wings of a chicken whose eggs have just been snatched from under her, I trot along the sidewalk leading to the emergency parking lot. I start to count my blessings. Among them, top priority, is the fact that this hospital doesn't have a locked psych ward. Otherwise, anyone who might see me would surely call security. I think about how much easier it would have been to traipse through the endless corridors to the ER and wave to Pudgy on my way out. Oh, well, hindsight again.

The Fall raindrops, so unexpected (global warming? Maybe the worrywarts are right?), are so dense they're imitating Havasu Falls, or at least the pictures I've seen of it. I feel as if I could part them with my hands, like those beaded curtains that have made a design comeback as room dividers from the hippie era. Maybe I could step through and discover a rainbow and the proverbial pot of gold glistening at the end of the curved ribbons.

I plod on attempting to step over puddles, but discover miniature rivers crisscross the sidewalk spattering it with mud and loose gravel, those tiny stones my little granddaughter in California, who I haven't seen in six months, loved to pick up and examine. She actually talked to them, chattering away in unintelligible gibberish when she was a two year old. After the conversation ended, she'd replace each tiny stone back to its original spot with care. I wonder, albeit briefly, as I wipe rainwater from my face with my sleeve, was she too compulsive at two? Did she get that trait from me, her Grammy? Then, I wonder, how could I have let six months go by without holding that precious child in my arms.

I shake off the guilty thoughts and splat through the muddy waters. Wet foliage brushes my right arm and rain sloshes down my sleeve into my pocket. Yikes! I think of Shelley Bates novel, A Pocketful of Pearls. Why, I don't know. I just know I have a pocketful of raindrops. I slip a few times on wet leaves and almost lose my balance. This is no gentle rain. It's a full-blown monsoon type rain in November. Didn't that funny columnist in the Arizona Republic predict this? Or, was he being tongue in cheek?

I finally reach the wider, patio-type area close to the ER and realize I'm biting the inside of my cheek, hard. I guess I have a weird way of concentrating. Heading for the bench under the cover of the patio for a moment of dryness relief, my cell phone chimes. I'd planned to sit here and dig into my purse for my car keys anyway, so no big deal. Until, my purse slips off slippery knees and lands in a puddle in front of me. My beautiful fake designer purse is sitting in a small pond soaking up wetness. Bummer. The positive side is the purse really is genuine leather, so whatever unfortunate animal's hide it belonged to, I know somewhere in this world the poor thing was used to being rained on.

Suddenly, I'm very tired. My bones, even my various cartilages, ache and my muscles are limp. I'm barely standing thanks to worn out rubber band muscles. I try to focus on a Bible verse about someone Jesus touched who felt this way, this tired, this unable to walk. Instead, I find myself remembering Pastor's story about visiting homeless people living under a bridge. None of it computes, and my head is spinning. I lean forward to grab the straps of my now drowning purse. I must retrieve the cellphone. I miss the purse, but my hand digs in deep just before the beautiful tooled, oversized pouch is carried away on a small river of rainwater. I can hardly hold the slippery phone, but I manage to flip it open with a weak finger.

"Bethy, sweetie, how's our Noel? You still at the hospital? Inquiring Betts wants to know." She chuckles loudly and pauses, obviously waiting for a clever comeback.

I plan to give her one, update her on all the Noel latest. I have a habit of pacing while talking on the phone, actually fast pacing on a cell phone. Achy as I am, I'm forcing my weary body to move. I make it back to the bench and dispassionately watch my beautiful fake designer bag navigate the parking lot in a muddy gorge. It's making its way toward an Escalade, a huge SUV that costs big bucks. *Bag of mine, if you're going to be squashed, you have good taste.*

I get up to pace again, planning to give Bett a positive update on Noel. One of my knees makes a popping sound, and my thighs ache. Never mind, I tell myself, until my ankles start to crumble. I decide it's time to try to retrieve my purse. It's swirling lazily in a puddle next to the SUV, and it looks lonely.

I'm still listening to Bett's blabberings when I almost reach the purse. "Bett, dear, can I call you back in a few minutes? I'm outside in the rain trying to retrieve my purse."

"It's raining there? I didn't know. Why are you outside? What's with your purse?" she chirps. "I hope you haven't lost it. So many valuables to replace. Okay, call me back in a few."

I've almost reached the purse. Slapping the phone shut I take another step and lean over to grab the straps. Slam!

So much for careful planning.

Why is it, Lord, that my timing always seems bad? I did say a quick prayer before I called her. Now, I'm worried. The connection broke and when I call back no one answers. Maybe I should go to the hospital. But, I'm terrified of driving in the rain. Wonder if Consuela is home? I trust you to provide. Amazing, isn't it, that I'd never have said that a few months ago?

TWENTY FOUR

"Ankle. Sprained, maybe broken. Probably cast."

A nurse with short curly brown hair and a small tattoo of a heart on her forearm is talking as if I can't hear her. She asks a barrage of questions I try to answer through my pain.

"How did it happen? Does it hurt here? How about here? When's the last time you had a tetanus shot? Do you have someone to drive you home? What kind of insurance do you have?"

Biting my tongue, and the inside of my cheek again to prevent the words I'm tempted to say, I whisper one-word answers while grimacing with pain.

"Doctor will be here in a minute." Her no nonsense announcement doesn't relieve me. How am I to get home? And, if I do, how am I to manage? I remember her words. "Cast." Agh.

A light tap on the door, and a bespectacled man with thinning gray hair in a white lab coat enters. He pastes a narrow smile between his beaked nose and flat chin. "Doctor Janis, here." He reaches for my hand as if we are meeting at an obligatory social function, or a boring receiving line. I've already dubbed him Dr. No Nonsense, Not Particularly Interested, Just Doing His Job. "So, Ms..., how are you feeling?" He obviously can't pronounce my surname, so he lets it drift in the air.

If I had the energy, I would sit up and deck him one, maybe two. How the rudgyfudge does he think I'm feeling? Instead, I do the tongue-biting, cheek-biting thing again and nod. "Okay."

But, I am not okay. I know that, and I'm sure he does, too. If he's any kind of a doctor. I wonder where he got his medical degree. Funny, in the ER patients don't get to see all those framed diplomas docs have on the walls of private practice offices. Another "gotta trust" issue.

Before I can ask my own questions, Dr. Janis waves a bony hand toward the curly-haired nurse. "X-ray." It's a simple statement, a command, but it scares the bedoozle out of me. My mind had been clinging to "sprained." So much for fantasy.

"Doctor?" He pauses in the half-open door to look at me like I'm some sort of alien. I direct my soliloquy to half-raised bushy eyebrows.

"I live alone. I can't have a cast, or I can't work. I need to be able to drive my car. I'm a personal chef and deliver food to clients. I need to get around my kitchen and cook. That's how I make my income."

"I'm sorry." He turns to Nurse Curly Hair. "Take her to X-ray." Looking at me for perhaps a millisecond, his face softens. "Maybe it won't be as bad as I suspect. God sometimes gives us surprises."

God sometimes give us surprises?

Dr. Janis' statement floored me. Not that I wasn't already floored, actually bed-ridden. More accurately, gurney-ridden.

Who would have thunk it? An ER doc who actually used the Creator's Name. And, to reassure a patient. Did he notice the cross around my neck? Did he somehow assume? Or, is he really a believer? A doctor who is comfortable sharing his faith, or one who is on the cusp and experimenting with sharing it? Definitely, food for thought.

~

"This might hurt." The radiologist technician turns my foot so my ankle is askew. I do the old biting lip and cheek thing the first time, and she's right. I scream in agony the third, fourth and fifth time.

"I'm so sorry, but the doctor insists on all angles."

It isn't her fault. She is kind, and her dye job intrigues me. I focus on it, then ask her for the number of her hairdresser. I love the big, but subtle, clumps and strands of blonde.

The ride back from radiology is actually fun. Pudgy shows up. Why, I don't know. But, he scoots me back to the ER pushing the gurney at top speed like a NASCAR driver and deposits me in the examining room with a flourish—raised arms, a rat-a-tat-tat on the metal footboard, and a thumbs up. Never mind the grin. That was the fake part.

~

Lolling around in jammies and sweats ain't the worst. The bottoms of the pants are easy to pull over my cast, even with one hand, and the insides of the legs are fuzzy and soft, comforting. I still struggle with all the contraptions Bett rented for me. A motorized wheelchair (so extreme), a three-pronged cane, a walker with wheels that turn and a basket to carry stuff in, and a little fanny pack filled with tissues and a pocket for my cell phone. Really! So much wretched excess when I have no place to go and nothing to do.

Bett means well, but she doesn't realize all these contraptions make me feel more of an invalid. Better if I had to struggle on my own and hobble around grabbing furniture for support. Giving up my independence is a big deal for me, so I try to focus on doing everything I need to without companionship. Sitting is difficult, especially sitting on the john. Going down isn't so hard, but the coming up part is very challenging. I have a little chant I've made up, "One, two, three, heave ho, thee." It helps and provides a bit of levity for my battle-weary soul.

"Honey, I'm coming in." She rushes to grab my wrists just as I'm heaving ho. Pulling at my sweat pants, she exclaims, "Guess I got here just in time. What would you do without me?" Her giggle is charming, usually, but today it's lost in my frustration.

"Bett, I'm not a child, not an invalid." I hear the edge of anger in my voice and regret my response to this woman who is my friend. "Sorry. Not a good day," I offer as explanation.

But, I know my excuse is feeble compared to her display of love and friendship.

"It's okay, Honey. I've wanted to do this for a long time."

Suddenly, the air is filled with tension. The silence is almost suffocating, capturing our thoughts and unspoken words. What did she mean "for a long time"? How long? Why?

I feel my eyes open wide and my eyebrows rise forming a wrinkled frown on my brow. My eyes seek Bett's but find only lowered lids and faintly colored cheeks. She looks embarrassed.

My sweatpants are still around my knees, and Bett's hands grip the waistband with bloodless knuckles. I want desperately to pull up the pant legs, but I sense any movement will break the mystery of the moment. So, I stand still, balancing on my un-cast foot.

A minute passes, and I hear soft breathing from both of our lips. Finally, Bett raises her head. Her face is as white as the bark on a birch tree, and just as craggy looking. Little striated lines are peppered with black dots. Bett's normally foundation-caked face is creased, but without the benefit of makeup. Do I see worry, sadness, regret? I don't know. I only know if I don't change position and relieve my one good foot, I'll collapse.

TWENTY FIVE

I managed to break the spell in the bathroom between Bett and me and pull up the legs on my sweatpants. Neither of us fell over or wept or flamed with embarrassment. We just laughed. One of those hearty "I can't believe how silly we're being" laughs. Giggles, then guffaws, then diverting to giggles again. It was cleansing, at least for me. I think for Bett, too. We ended up embracing in a bear hug after which Bett sped out the bathroom door closing it with a clunk. I didn't see her again until lunch the next day.

"Honey, I made tuna salad for lunch, your favorite. Do you want a sandwich or a tomato stuffed with it?"

First, I am bowled over that Bett made anything. Second, I am scared. Bett doesn't cook, or even non-cook, as in making anything food-wise that doesn't require actual cooking, but qualifies as edible. I hate being suspicious.

"A sandwich would be great." I'm thinking bread will at least buffer the taste and provide some density to help digest the concoction.

"Mayo?" The question startled me. Isn't mayonnaise a major part of tuna salad?

"Sure, okay."

"Mixed in, or on the bread?"

Oh, my, she hasn't even mixed the salad with mayo.

"Both, please."

I bite into my sandwich and feel Bett's eyes scanning my face. I can tell she wants to talk, and not just about the sandwich. "This is good, Bett, very unique flavor, and I love the crunch."

She grins with pleasure, but I notice a slight quivering around her lips. "I tried to remember some of the ingredients The Wildflower Café puts in their tuna. Almonds and dried cranberries. Then I added some of my own ideas."

"So, the wonton noodles were yours? And the arugula?"

"Yep. I love Asian food and thought it would be fun to add them, plus a splash of soy sauce. Good, huh?"

"Verwy," I nod with my mouth full of crunch. Not something I'd want to eat every day, but better than I expected. I think Bett succeeded in incorporating all the food groups in one hearty sandwich. "Thanks for coming to my rescue in the bathroom yesterday. That was sweet of you to care." I neglect to add it was also unnecessary and embarrassing.

Another grin, this time accompanied by moist eyes. I guess Bett doesn't often get to help others, mostly just pays others to help her. I reach to touch the back of her hand. Fortunately, we are sitting near each other and not across from one another at the massive table. She stares for a full thirty seconds at my large hand with clipped nails covering her tiny one with dainty fake nails and gives her tousled curls a shake. Her eyes squeeze shut and a tear escapes. Wiping her knuckles across her cheek, she whispers, "It's time we talked."

"Sure, Bett, what about?"

I'm expecting some horrible revelation, like she has cancer or is financially destitute. But, I don't get to find out because she shakes her curls again in a negative nod and scoots out of the bench clutching a monogrammed napkin. I hear the powder room door slam and the lock click.

Five minutes later while I'm cleaning up our dishes, a small voice drifts from behind the door. "I'm sorry. I'm not ready."

~

I remember the phone call. It still sticks in my craw.

"Hi, dear."

"Betsy, I'm outta here."

"Excuse me."

"As in gone."

I remember plopping down on the cheap cushion adorning the bench that served as our breakfast niche. Breakfast? In thirteen years we'd never shared the meal or the bench. He (sorry, I've stuffed his name down so deep in my psyche I refuse to remember it) rushed off to "meetings" at six a.m. I found out later the "meetings" were with another marketing guru named Stacie—wheat-colored hair that resembled uncooked strands of spaghetti, clothes that must have come from Baby Gap on a body that would have made Victoria's Secret blush, and lips pumped so full of collagen they were about to burst. So much for "till death do us part."

The blue plastic made a woofing sound under my butt. I thought of my son James at ten when he discovered whoopee cushions and placed them under all the chair pads at the Thanksgiving dining table. What a hoot! I wish I could have captured the look on Mom's face and the scowl on Uncle Ernie's, but digital cameras weren't in vogue then.

I remember twisting the coiled phone cord around my thumb. That's how long ago it was, when phones had cords and the cords resembled elongated corkscrews. I know my tongue stuck to the roof of my dry mouth and my words came out garbled.

"Whadda you mean—gone?"

"It's over, Betsy. You and me."

Remember the pregnant pause? This was the original, the biggie. And, to make it authentic, I was pregnant.

Shaking off the toxic memories, I scrub the translucent china salad plate with a wire sponge. Not a good idea. I wonder if Bett will notice the scratches. Guess that's another confession on my list.

~

My life is really a great big "maybe." Maybe my ankle will heal; maybe Bett will explain why she can't explain anything to me; maybe Noel will get better before our wedding date; maybe we really will get married.

Aw—rats! My Sunday School upbringing takes over. I'm reminded of Zacchaeus and the song I sang with twenty other seven-year-old children about the "little man" in the tree. Right now, even though I'm five foot seven, I feel small. I petition the Big Man in the sky to give me hope. Peace and calm wouldn't hurt, either. Answers would be an enormous gift. I know He listens, but I'm getting a bit like Bett, wondering if my paltry needs are at the bottom on His list of "Prayers to Answer Today."

Maybe I should have followed Bett and banged on the powder room door. Or, better yet, joined her.

TWENTY SIX

Talk to your daughter.

The whispery command repeats itself over and over in the cobwebs of my brain. Child number three, Brie, and I usually have a brief chat once a week, but it's very perfunctory. "Hi, how are ya, honey. I'm good, too. Anything new?" That just about covers it. Once upon a time we were closer than enjoined twins.

My other daughter, Julia, the angry one, blamed me for her father's abandonment when she was a teen. She sends me flowers for Mothers Day. But, she's not the one whose number I dial. I'm never sure if I'm amazed or convicted when God puts something on my heart. But, since He just did, I react. Hopefully, in obedience.

I dial and hear the thrum of the phone in the next state, California, the one nestled next to my Arizona. Finally, after ring three, on the cusp of ring four, a weary voice answers. "Brie?" Here I am again stating the obvious.

"Mom?" She does it, too. Confirms my peas in a pod philosophy.

"Brie, what's wrong?" Here I go again making assumptions. But, I know from her voice something is.

"Oh, Mom." I hear choking sobs and grab my own throat. When I realize my pinching it is going to leave an unsightly mark, I remove my hand and rub my ample hip.

I turn into Sergeant Major Mom mode and yell. (My dad used to say when the kids were little I sounded like a drill sergeant the way I yelled at them to get them to obey.) "Brie, stop!" The silence on the other end gives me pause. Did she hang up or simply do as her mother commanded? "Brie?"

"I'm here, Mom." Pause.

"Honey, I love you, and I can tell something is wrong. Please—what is it?"

I hear a big gulping sigh, then a few seconds of silence. I check the little window on my phone. We are still connected.

"May as well tell you." Silence again. But, I'm a patient mother. I wait. "I'm pg. As in pregnant."

"Oh."

"That's all you can say, Mom? Oh?"

I cover the receiver with my free hand to, hopefully, to stifle the catch in my throat. "Gosh, Brie, this is great. A surprise, but wonderful news." Looking back, I can only attribute my response to God's grace. Given freely to all who believe in Him. And, I do.

"You really think so, Mom? Are you ready to be a grandma again? Maybe to a grandchild without a father?"

"Brie, I love you so much I'm ready for anything, any challenge you have." I pause to absorb her words. "What do you mean without a father? Where is Derek? What's happened?" Did I mention I'm a master of conundrum? Once again I silently ask God to bridle my tongue and take away the images swimming in my head.

"Derek left, two weeks ago." She pauses, and I hear breath sucking in. "When I told him I was expecting." The sobs start again, and I feel helpless.

~

I am so tired my joints ache. But, I'm wiping all the surfaces in my tiny guest room, slash, den and pulling the cumbersome wallbed down. It was one of those momentary lapses in sanity, almost a "point of purchase" purchase, as I was leaving the store that builds in closets and dens. I thought, why not? Maybe someday I will need an extra bed, and since I have no guest room, this will be a backup. Good thing God played with my brain that day.

I toss away the damp wiping cloth, noting that the legendary dry Arizona dust has left it unusable for future. After putting fresh sheets and a quilt on the pulled-down bed I turn on the ceiling fan and close the door. I debate about turning on the fan since I'd read an article in the paper this morning saying their only use is to cool the human skin underneath them. The reporter said turn them off if no one is in the room. Still, believing they circulate the stale air, I leave it on. My biggest concern now is picking Brie up at Sky Harbor Airport tomorrow morning at 8 a.m.

Did I forget to mention I moved back to my condo today, again? Sometimes I am so obtuse. Must be my age. Anyway, I schlepped back with hangers of clothes dangling from my fingers. That's when I got the heart call to phone Brie.

Bett wasn't too happy to have me leave. I think she counted on company to abate her loneliness. But, I knew it was time. I think I even got a nudge from Him. Maybe to get home for the phone call with Brie. I think Consuela was happy, though. She squeezed me so hard I almost called Noel for an adjustment. I mean, she's been used to caring for one prima dona, but when I came on the scene, even though I didn't ask for or require anything, she felt obligated. She'd treated me like a queen. But, I sensed she was tired of having two beds to change, two bathrooms to clean, two people to clean up after. Not to mention a 8500 square foot house to take care of. I'm sure she was relieved to see me go.

Speaking of Noel, I need to call him about Brie.

~

I hear a lot of clattering and a mild expletive. He's probably fumbling with the phone next to his hospital bed. I've noticed hospitals seem to have a designated place for the so-called nightstands that hold the rooms' phones. Always back by the patient's shoulders, so said patient, who is probably either in pain or incapacitated, has to push up in the bed and turn halfway around to even reach the dratted thing while it shrills loud enough to wake a comatose person in the next room. This in hospitals whose rooms come equipped with flat screen televisions, DVD players and computer keyboards.

Finally, I hear a grunt and "yeh?"

"Good morning to you, too, Mr. Sunshine."

"Sorry, Betsy. I had trouble reaching the phone." No kidding.

"I do have some good news," he proceeds to tell me without asking how I am. "Doc says I may be going home tomorrow. But, I'm still weak." I hear an exaggerated sigh. "I'll have to take it very easy for a few days till I get my strength back. And finish the medicine," he adds. "Think you can help me out? Maybe with a few meals and a little companionship?"

"Uh, Noel, have you forgotten I'm barely mobile? I want to help you all I can, but driving is still a problem. I'm even trying to figure out how to get to the airport tomorrow."

"The airport!" I cringe at the volume of his voice, forgetting I haven't told him about Brie. I explain hastily, actually babbling, but he gets the gist. Nevertheless, his next remark sounds accusatory, like the whole wretched situation with Brie is my fault. "I thought you said Derek was a great guy. You're proud to have him for a son-in-law, actually another son."

"I was, still am. I just have to support Brie and help her get to the bottom of this mess. She needs her mommy right now, and I'm not about to let her down. I'm sure it's just a little misunderstanding between her and Derek." I hear the tiny crack in my voice and wish I felt more confident. My mind keeps wandering back to that "sins of the fathers" thing, even though What His Name wasn't Derek's father, but Brie's.

Derek has a great dad, the kind who took him fishing and to movies and arcades and church. The kind of dad who made an extra effort to parent his son the right way after Derek's mother died when he was eleven. John was an exemplary role model dad. Far as I know, still is. I used to think maybe he and I might get together, but it wasn't to be after he met the auburn-haired beauty at church. The fifty-something gal with the slender body—the Yoga instructor who could eat half a dozen chocolate chip cookies and never gain an ounce. Ouch! My mind is wandering still, but without a compass.

"Oh." Noel's voice is flat, and I sense disappointment. "Of course. She's family."

"Not just family, Noel. My precious daughter. The very one whose father left me when I was pregnant with her. So, I do know what she's going through, but I don't know the whole story yet." I know it's hard for him to understand since he and Maizie never had children. But, I don't want to say that because I know her barrenness was the one disappointing thing in their marriage. However, it may be the thing that helped them cling together so tightly. Marriage is such a complicated thing.

Truth be known, I was secretly hoping Noel would stay in the hospital a few more days. I know that sounds unfeeling, but it would have been a load off my shoulders to know he would be taken care of with minimal attention needed from me. Now I have two problems to confront—how to help Noel without seeming uncaring, and do I have the courage to drive to the airport with a cast on my leg? I've been experimenting driving to Sprout's Market and the bank and other local places only a few blocks away. I drove home from Bett's in Fountain Hills, a twenty-minute ride on Shea Boulevard during rush hour. But, I haven't tested freeway driving yet. Certainly not early in the morning during high volume time. I'd just have to brave it and pretend Jesus is sitting in the passenger seat like my camp counselor suggested when I was sixteen.

I'm pacing, actually hobbling, around my condo with the portable phone jammed against my ear when my toes that are exposed at the open cast stub the coffee table and my hand lands on a book to catch my balance. My Bible! *Hello, Lord. I am so sorry I'm trying to solve these problems without your help. I need your guidance. What should I do?* I think He just pushed a button in my brain. I'm not exactly crazy about His suggestion, but I must trust His judgment over mine. My tongue starts to work again, maybe faster than my brain. I spout out my crazy idea. Is it God's, or mine?

"Noel, I know the perfect place for you to recuperate." Did I hear a crack in my voice again? A tinge of jealousy? Still, I press on knowing it's the right thing, the perfect answer. "Bett's." There, I said it. I swallow hard waiting for a reply. When none comes immediately, I start the parrot questions. "Noel? Noel?" Maybe he's fallen asleep or dropped the phone. Finally, I hear a hoarse whisper.

"You sure? You'd be all right with that?"

"I—I think so. It might be the best solution for now, and I know Consuela would dote on you," I hasten to add. "Have you ever slept in a velvet-paneled room? With a huge furry cat as your blanket? And, a silver-handled guest toothbrush?" I wonder if my forced attempt at levity has fallen on deaf ears until I hear another whisper.

No. It would be a new experience. You sure?" he questions again, and I can almost see the devilish grin on his face—below the Crayon blue eyes and above the cleft chin.

"Yep. I know she'd love to have you." *I hope I'm right.* "You'd get three delicious squares a day from Consuela, a soft bed and lots of attention. Bett will hover I warn you, but she's lonely. If you felt up to it and had the desire, you could even do laps in the pool. That's a great way to get back your strength." I close my eyes tight and silently pray, but for what – maybe God's will and my acceptance of it? "What do you say?"

"Okay." Suddenly his voice seems stronger, even chirpy happy. "I'm game if you are."

Now, I'm feeling conflicted. I'm not sure if I'm having latent jealousy, or just guilt because I'm not the one who'll take care of Noel and nurse him back to health. I feel torn between the man I love and the child I love.

"Betsy?" His warm voice hums over the phone line. "I know this is a difficult time for you. I understand your devotion to Brie, and I agree you need to be there for her. I'll be fine at Bett's. Probably won't want to leave if all you say is true. But," he hesitates, "I hope I'll have a chance to meet Brie, even be part of her life."

"Noel, I'd never keep her from you. I love you so much. I just feel it's time for me to be a strong parent for her. I've been where she is now. I get the picture, as ugly as it is. After she and I sift through the emotions," I continue to ramble, "we will all get together as a family. I know Brie will love you as much as I do."

When I finally hang up sending slobbery smooches over the phone, I take a deep breath and dial Bett's number. Nothing would ever have prepared me for her answer.

I blew it, Lord. I blew it. How was I to know what Betsy would ask me? I can change my plans. It will be a hassle, and a big expense, but I can afford it. Not to mention the others I'll offend. Please give me guidance. I love to be needed, to be helpful, but this is the most awkward time to rearrange my plans.

Where is that Scripture she loves so much? Jeremiah? Something about the plans you have for me, not my plans, but yours.

TWENTY SEVEN

I guess you could say I was floored. What is that old adage about "never assume because—?" Never mind. As my Auntie May used to say, "Great minds run in the same gutter."

I'm doing the thumb-twiddling thing again and, at the same time, slamming kitchen implements on the counter. (I've gotten really good at multi-tasking.) The metal spatulas don't make the same pinging sound on the new marble countertops as they did on the old Formica ones, but at least there's no chance of chipping. The sound is kind of neat, too. I'm drumming out my version of Dave Brubeck's Take Five and fuming over my egotistical assumption Bett would welcome Noel for caregiving. "How could you be so dumb?" I say with teeth bared glaring into the reflection on the back of the copper bowl? I learned as a teenager forty plus years ago to never assume. Just as I'm slapping myself on my forehead, the phone rings.

"I am such a ditz."

"Bett?" This time I do have to question since I'm not sure about the voice. It sounds like Bett, even showed her name on Caller I.D., but the tiny, soft voice isn't like hers.

I can almost see the tears trickling down her face and rolling over the crevices of her caked makeup. That vision almost undoes me. But, before I, too, start to weep she bursts into joyful laughter. She must have the phone receiver tucked between her shoulder and ear because I hear her hands clapping gleefully, like after we sing a praise song at my church.

"What an opportunity! God is SO good. Noel's room will be ready tomorrow."

"Bett," I try to keep my voice even and modulated. "I don't understand. I thought you had plans to vacation in the Caribbean. I hope you didn't change them for Noel—or me." Truth be known, I hope she did. I feel this sort of leaden weight in my chest. Guilt maybe? Now I start to rationalize to myself. Bett goes to fabulous resorts every year. Surely, this was no big deal, just a diversion for her. No big deal. Yeh, Betsy, when did you ever go to the Caribbean?

Never.

~

I am such a wimp. Bett insists on having "her man" pick Noel up from the hospital and bring him to her opulent house. Turns out "her man" (originally stated as "my man") is her faithful gardener, Roberto. I knew Bett didn't have a chauffeur, but in my stress mode about getting Brie from the airport, and gleeful at not having to nurse Noel, I hadn't given it a thought. Poor Roberto. At least he won't have to deal with Pudgy since there's no reason to traverse the ER, and hopefully he'll meet Nurse Jones. Although I cringe to think what his reaction would be if she pulls the Nurse Ratchit routine on him. Especially since he barely speaks the English language and probably never saw One Flew Over the Cuckoo's Nest. Surely, Nurse Whatever She Calls Herself from time to time will have to be sensitive enough to not impose levity on the poor man.

I stuff these thoughts down into the guilt gully of my gut as I swing from the 101, Pima Freeway, onto the 202 freeway toward Sky Harbor Airport. My right leg is aching from trying to keep my toes hovering on the gas pedal at sixty-five while sitting at a slight angle with the cast left leg stretched uncomfortably under the dash. Scottsdale had installed speed cameras on the Pima Freeway about a year ago and they put a cramp (pun intended) on driving a major stretch between Shea

Boulevard and Tatum. Thankfully, according to dubious statistics, the cameras have cut down on accidents, as well as catching a few weirdos who paid no heed and zoomed by them at 100 plus miles per hour, including several illustrious major sports figures.

Terminal Four's sign looms ahead, and I dip to the right. I am ten minutes early, a first for me at airports, and circle twice. The third time I slow past the Southside exit a chunky woman with frizzy hair leaps toward Sassy. Glory be! Is it, could it be…my Brie?

My first thought, however unmaternal, is *who is that fat girl, and what has Brie done to her hair?*

~

"Momma, he just keeps saying he's sorry, but he's not ready to be a father," Brie whines. She picks rhythmically at the loden green jersey stretched across her bulging belly as if constantly loosening it will make the bulge disappear. It's unbearably hot today, pushing 114 degrees, and I notice dark rings under her arms and trickles of sweat running down her temples. Because of my cumbersome cast I stayed in Sassy while Brie hefted the planet's largest suitcase under Sassy's swing-up back door. I couldn't help but notice the scattering of cruise line stickers adorning it. A reminder that she and Mr. Not Ready to be a Father had some nifty trips in their short marriage. I debate whether the nagging twinge of bitterness I'm feeling is resentment at Derek or jealousy toward both of them for their flamboyant excursions. Maybe Noel-guy will take me on a cruise after we've both healed—and married. Yeh, right. Isn't there a song titled "In Your Dreams?"

I reach toward her knee to give it a squeeze midst her babbling, but she pushes my hand away. "Sorry, Momma, but my knees are so sore and swollen. The baby's taking its toll on my body." She reaches into her saddlebag-sized purse and extracts a bag of M & M candies that she proceeds to shove by handfuls into her mouth. I console myself that she didn't refer to my future grandchild as an "it." Some blessings come in small doses.

I try to recall the Bible verse about gluttony, but since I don't need to refer to it often (honest, I hardly ever eat what I cook), it escapes me. *Just as well, Lord, huh? What's that verse about being judgmental?* Aw, "…stop passing judgment on one another. Instead, make up your mind not to put any stumbling block or obstacle in your brother's way." Somewhere in Romans I think. I thank the Creator for the reminder and swerve around a van displaying a carpet cleaning ad.

Drat! I miss the exit to Shea Boulevard and have to go to the next one. Trying to follow Brie's constant soliloquy, and nod, and give an appropriate "Hmm" occasionally has distracted me. When we finally pull into the parking lot of my condo complex, I hear myself whooshing a giant sigh. Both my legs ache, the one in the cast for obvious reasons and the right one from stretching to reach car pedals. I feel as if I've run a 5K, which I actually did once. Twenty years ago. No comment, please.

"Brie, honey, could you please come around and help me extract my cast?"

Instead of rushing to her mother's side, she stands like a pillar of salt (I know, the image comes to mind again) and says in a plaintive whine, "*This* is where you still live?"

~

When she was fifteen, I sent Brie to charm school.

I figured Cotillion hadn't worked, so we'd try the next step. Certainly not a dance one since she'd never mastered the basic two-step. I remember sitting on the sidelines with dozens of other mothers while Commander Olander and his Mrs. called the instructions from a small stage. All of us moms wore pasted on grins, sort of like the ones you see grade-school kids drawing irreverently on their teachers' photographs in school annuals. I'd glance at Mary Beth Baker and Louisa Mae Smythe and my heart would fill with hate. Not exactly for them, but for the fact they'd produced daughters who were, although still preteen, lithe, slim and sure on their feet. Boys rushed to dance with them, probably because the boys had no clue how to dance themselves. So, they clung as much as decorum allowed and let Rachel Baker and Suzanna Smythe lead. Two girls in elegant dresses, one in shimmering blue and the other in topaz satin.

Once, a large, muscular boy held his hand out to Brie. My first thought was he must be a potential football star, an athlete, much adored and looked up to by his classmates. I found out later, during Brie's sobs, he was the school clown, the dunce two years behind the others. We quit Cotillion the night her so-called-father didn't show up for the father-daughter dance.

Charm school wasn't much better. Mrs. Weaver, the owner's wife who was really Mrs. In Charge, told Brie repeatedly she'd never "find her style." I mean, how much "style" does a fifteen-year-old have? Mostly what's "in" and being sold in the wanna-be boutiques. Oh, where was Bett and her boutiques then?

Did you guess? Charm school was Disaster Number Two.

When Brie started swim team her freshman year in high school things got better. At least she had some pre- and after-school activity to divert her thoughts from boys. As it turned out, with Coach Dempsey's help, she developed a mean butterfly stroke and won a few medals. Plus, her body toned out and she lost a few pounds. Dempsey's encouragement by pushing her to the limits of her abilities garnered her a small scholarship to a local college. Plus a few medals and a trophy. I hope God blessed that man who made all the difference between getting a higher education or not. I will forever be indebted to him screaming and cheering during her high school graduation. He gave the first soft drink toast at her party, and because he came, so did several football and basketball players making Brie's grad party very special. I wish he were here now. How I'd love to thank him again and have him give encouragement to her during this rough time. Sadly, he can't be.

Coach Dempsey died of heart failure three years ago.

~

Brie lugs the gargantuan suitcase up the stairs to the porch and drags it across the carpet to the guest bedroom I'd lovingly prepared. Because of my cast I can't help much. "Uh, honey, you didn't tell me you were *this* pregnant."

"Momma, if I'd told you five months ago, you would've...well, whatever." She shrugs her shoulders dismissing me, whining—still. I stuff down the thought that if she wasn't my daughter I'd have fingers around her throat. What has happened to the gentle, soft-spoken, almost timid girl I raised? Perhaps that small swimming scholarship and the stint as editor of the college paper went to her head. Maybe the newfound confidence from rooming with the girl from England and the one from Shaker Heights, Ohio. Maybe they taught her style, enough so when Derek met her at a sorority function he was intrigued. But, what happened to the teaching, the style? Somewhere, maybe during the past few months of pregnancy, it got lost.

"Brie, I would've been so excited for you. I would've been buying baby goodies in every boutique in Arizona."

She turns abruptly away, making a fuss with putting clothes in the dresser drawer.

~

Dinner is soup and salad. Canned and bagged. I only have so much energy left after the nerve-wracking drive to the airport. I do have talent beyond "salades," but tonight I have no need to impress, or so I think.

It's so hot, and even though the air conditioning is pumped up (or is it down?) to 75, I still feel the moisture on my skin. I decide a chilled soup and light salad is perfect. Until, "This is what a chef serves? Don't you have any meat...and potatoes, Momma?"

My first irreverent thought is how chunky, naw *fat*, Brie is. Remember, I've been pregnant three times. During my pregnancy with James I gained a lot of weight, nearly forty pounds. Devastated by needing over a year to diet and lose them, I was very cautious during my pregnancy with Julia. Twenty-two pounds max.

Allow me to digress. James and Julia were named after famous chefs, even though I wasn't a chef or personal cooking type person then. Must have been something in my genes, or maybe a glimpse into the future. Brie was named after my favorite snack when I was pregnant with her.

"Ahh, meat and potatoes. Not on the menu tonight, Sweetie. I guess I was thinking about how hot it is...(hesitation) how you need to eat light being pregnant."

Oh, Lord, what happened to you helping me keep my big mouth shut?

We don't talk much during dinner. It's hard to converse with mouthfuls of Romaine, and I sense Brie is actually thankful. After helping me rinse off the plates, she bolts to her room. I'm guessing for candy sustenance. Yep, she lands on the sofa with a plop, an exaggerated sigh and a smear of brown around her lips. She reaches for the remote, but I lay my hand on her arm. "Honey, I know you're tired, but don't you think we should talk a bit? Catch up?"

"Not ready." Her face, like polished stone, stares at the blank T.V. screen. Suddenly, she grabs a throw pillow and hugs it close to her swollen breasts, shoulders hunched over and nose buried in the pillow's fringe. I don't want to push her (oh, no?), but sharing her pain is supposed to be why she's here. I'm also miffed she hasn't once asked how I'm feeling, nor thanked me for picking her up at the airport. Especially the ride home. After all, she used to love Mr. Toad's Wild Ride at Disneyland. I chuckle at that thought, and Brie swivels to face me, her watery eyes glaring at my baby blues.

"*What* is so funny? That really hurts, Momma, that you'd find my situation humorous." Her comment knocks me off guard and I have the indecency to guffaw. Not my best Momma Dearest presentation.

"No, no, Brie. Not, hic, laughing at you. Ride, hic, home. Call me Mrs. Toad, hic."

After a few more hiccups interspersed with a more concrete explanation, she gets it. The sneer she's been sporting morphs into a shaky smile. "Oh, Momma, I guess we both needed that laugh," she says as she flings her arms around me. She may be pregnant and fat, but she smells wonderful.

"Estée Lauder Beautiful Intense?" She nods to my wink. "A fav of mine, too." I grin. "Today I'm wearing Jessica." I hold out my wrist for her to sniff. She giggles, and we're on our way. Who'd have thunk a mother-daughter relationship could be repaired by a high-falutin New York perfume company. I roll my eyes upward and silently repeat an old friend's favorite phrase, "God is so good *all the time*."

"Okay, Momma, I'll spill the proverbial beans. Guess

that's why I'm here, huh?"
"You betcha, girl, and it's getting late. Spill."

TWENTY EIGHT

Derek is a wimp.

There are many other less flattering names I'm tempted to call him, but from what Brie tells me, he has no backbone. "No spine," as my Nana used to say. I resist the temptation to phone his dad. That will be reserved for when Brie's in the shower tomorrow morning. How does a man who was raised by a strong military-type father walk out on his pregnant wife? That question and others, such as who is the other woman, will be dissected and pondered the next few days.

I have a good talk with myself telling moi Brie's life isn't over, many women raise children alone (I did), and God can correct any dumb mistake man makes. I'm counting on Him to punch dimwitted Derek in the nose. I have this vision of a huge, mighty hand slamming against Derek's perfectly formed Scandinavian nose and red blood spurting down his chin. Aw, Betsy, not nice!

"Brie," I hesitate. "Now, please don't be mad at me, but maybe Derek's hurting, too."

Her reddened eyes look like those individual pizzas sold in the freezer section that moms buy for their kids. I steel myself for the scream I know is coming. Instead, she crumbles in a heap on the sofa, sobbing, still holding the pillow. Am I insensitive worrying about my expensive throw pillow being smeared with mascara? I remember the cover has a zipper—why I bought it, so it could be dry cleaned. Interesting how the mind jumps around when confronted with stress. I feel like a total loser of a mother, the blue ribbon winner. Mrs. America Underdog, here I am.

"I guess that's a fair question, Momma." She swipes at her eyes with absorbent knuckles. We are making progress. "He was very contrite." She swipes again. "The night he left." This really is a pregnant pause. "Begged me to believe him that Amanda was chasing him, that he'd never done anything wrong. He said she must have been following him, turning up wherever he went—mostly bars."

"You know, even on all those cruises we took, we never drank. Once, eating at the captain's table we were served a glass of wine. Derek took a sip to be sociable, then I did, too. We're basically Diet Coke people, so why was he in bars?"

I need to get my head in gear for that question. It computes, and I answer with my limited experience, mostly from reading novels and watching television. "Uh, I think bartenders, and other patrons, are good listeners. You've watched Seinfeld?" Her head nods. "Maybe not the best example, but I remember Kramer and George going to places where they could spout off and get confirmation about how they felt. Does that make sense?"

Another nod, more lively this time.

"You think he just wanted someone to talk to?"

"Yep. I also think of that show 'where everybody knows your name.' You know the one where Sam the bartender listens to everyone's troubles. Maybe Derek is like the mail carrier guy, or the shrink – needs confirmation about his life."

"Okay, Momma, what do I do—to get Derek back?"

Losing weight comes to mind.

God, please help me.

~

We decide on a strategy.

We both slept soundly getting much needed rests.

Morning Number One: We make a list. All possible reasons for Derek leaving are jotted on the yellow-lined pad.

#1. He is scared, terrified. Why? Financial commitments,

lifelong commitment.

#2. He is in love with another woman. Not a huge possibility since he's never strayed before and still vows he loves Brie.

#3. He's a screwed up, psychological mess. Very possible.

#4. He's a fallen Christian. Not such a stretch since he has fallen and not fulfilled his Christian vows—marriage and otherwise.

We are scanning our list, eyebrows raised dramatically when the phone rings. "Gosh, Noel, your timing is…" I say under my breath, not finishing the thought.

"What did you say, Momma? Something about Noel?"

~

As it turns out it wasn't Noel, but a client asking for salads for a corporate luncheon. I pencil it on my calendar and will email her an order form later. Repeat clients seldom order from my website, although I have a pretty impressive one. Most repeaters prefer to talk to me in person, hash over (perhaps "discuss" is a better word) the event they're catering. Lily Anstol, president of the local board of realtors, wants a luncheon that'll reflect both luxury real estate and the current R.E. market. I'm tempted to suggest topping the salad with nuts (to represent the realtors) and rings of black olives (zeroes, get it?). She keeps emphasizing the word "green." Isn't that the basis for most salads? Perhaps between now and the day of her event next week I'll think of something clever. Maybe I'll make three salads and name one "Market," another "'Interest'ing," and the last "High End" with a lot of rich cheeses sprinkled on.

Lily finally ends the one-sided conversation with, "Trusting you. Know how clever you are." Yeh, so clever I haven't given Noel a thought since Brie arrived. Poor man, my health-challenged "intended." My excuse? I know he's being fussed over by Bett and Consuela. He's sleeping in a velvet-paneled room and using a silver-handled toothbrush. Also, he really isn't *that* sick. Is he?

"Brie, dear, I really should call Noel. He just came home from the hospital yesterday."

"Momma," she whines, "you didn't tell me." Why does it

sound like she's accusing me of keeping some dark secret? "This is your special guy, right?"

"Well, yes." I hear the hesitation in my voice wondering how much I should reveal. Her problems seem more looming than mine and Noel's. Truth-sayer that I am, I blurt it out. Sometimes God uses my motor mouth to advantage. Like now when I see Brie's angry face transform into soft sweetness. If she hadn't been sitting right across from me at the kitchen counter, I'd swear someone had sprayed a nasty substance in her eyes they're blinking so rapidly.

"I'm sorry I've been so self-absorbed," she whispers while dabbing her eyes with a paper napkin. "When can I meet him?"

That is a loaded question.

TWENTY NINE

I arrange through Bett for Brie and me to visit at two. Thank goodness it will be past lunchtime and I won't be expected to provide the meal. I could have called Noel on his cell, but I didn't want to disturb him if he was sleeping. More likely I would have disturbed Snoopy if the huge feline was draped across his legs.

I am such a transparent mother—offering to lend Brie some makeup and helping her select an outfit. Not an easy task since she didn't bring much more than maternity jeans and Derek's old extra-extra-large T-shirts. He's a big boy. We finally settle on a plain black one, sans baseball and football team logos. Her flip-flops will have to do.

Brie has a long, angular face with wide-set smoky eyes she inherited from her father, The Jerk. A few eye drops and a touch of concealer camouflage their redness, mostly. A bit of blush, a zap with my plastic lash curler and a dab of mascara, then a swipe of soft peach lipstick do the job. Her hair is more of a challenge. Perhaps pregnancy hormones have made it more curly than usual. She used to take almost an hour to flatten and straighten it with a special iron, but I've always favored the natural curls. I remember a technique I saw once an Internet site. I was killing time and browsing when I clicked on *Seven New Hairstyles for Summer*. I remember the kinky-curly one because I was so envious, probably as much of the model's heart-shaped face as her hair.

I spritz the mass of curls with water, bend her head forward and set the hand-held hairdryer to low while pushing my fingertips laced with volumizer through the raw umber-colored roots—a retired Crayon color enshrined in the Crayola Hall of Fame in 1990.

I know way too much trivia.

I shush her whining about not wetting already kinky hair. Roots dry, I tip her chin up with a forefinger. "Eeeow! I look like a freak." The bathroom mirror displays an angular face surrounded by kinky curls sticking out at least a foot. I swallow hard and pray.

"Not finished. Calm down. I took a course." Sort of. I wonder if stretching the truth is lying. "Here, hold this." I hand her an oversized plastic butterfly clasp I bought last year in a vain attempt to update my own hairstyle. Except I don't have enough hair for the thing to clasp. The silly thing kept slipping down to my neck.

Standing behind her and grabbing a hunk of hair at both temples, I tug lightly—not too hard or she'll look like she's choking from a bad facelift. Satisfied with the effect, I clasp the bundle with the silver-coated clip. For the almost final touch I coax tendrils with the pointy end of a barber's comb to form a fringe of soft curls all around her face. I spit on a finger and twist a few around it. Lastly, I saturate both my hands with hairspray and squish and squeeze the mass of corkscrew curls forming a shawl around her shoulders. Although I was a teenager in the sixties, our "spit curls" were plastered to our faces, simulating, I think, Elvis's sideburns. Brie's new curls are loose and soft.

"There—stunning," I announce proudly offering her a hand-mirror. "You look like a famous model."

"You think so?" Cautiously she turns around several times holding the mirror at different angles. "Is it too way out for me, being pg and all? I feel rather glamorous."

"Honey, you are glam. You've lost some confidence being pregnant. After we visit Noel, let's go shopping for maternity clothes."

It takes some convincing, but she finally agrees, insisting she has plenty of money to pay for them. *Praises, Lord, 'cause I don't.*

~

Bett's almost preppy appearance nearly knocks me off balance. I make a concerted effort to re-hinge my jaw. Surely, my chin is reaching the base of my neck. She gives me a subtle smirk accompanied by one raised eyebrow. Like, "Don't go there. Pretend I always dress this way."

I gaze from the white button-down collared over-blouse to the tailored black slacks. Then I notice the shoes. Black, square-toed penny loafers. Has she been taking dress lessons from Noel? I wouldn't have been surprised to see Topsiders on her feet. She stretches out a perfectly manicured hand with rounded, white-tipped nails. "You must be the beautiful Brie," she states in a modulated voice. My aren't we refined! "Your mother's told me so much about you." I have not. Well, maybe some. "Come in, dear. Welcome to my humble home," she urges as she opens the almost eight-foot high door with the polished brass handle wider. I want to slap her.

I nudge Brie across the intricate Italian tile floor of the foyer toward the kitchen, my usual bailiwick. Bett gives my shoulder a squeeze and practically shoves me in the direction of the formal living room. This is not an easy task since my cast hampers swift movement. Brie hesitates, not sure whom to follow. Who is Bett trying to impress I wonder…until I see the tip of a brown Topsider peeking out from a leather chaise. The back of the chaise is toward my line of vision and I don't see any flecks of salt and pepper hair above it. For a second I think this is a cruel joke and Bett has propped the Topsiders at the other end to fool me. Not even Bett's sense of humor is that bizarre.

"Noel, sweet man, look who's here to visit," she simpers. Like he doesn't know. I notice Bett hasn't used my name, probably because she isn't sure what version Brie has heard. Or, maybe *she* still isn't sure.

Noel has no such compunction. Any misgivings I had are erased by the sound of his deep voice saying my name. "Betsy, my love" almost does it for me. Momentarily forgetting my plastered leg I race toward him, trip on the edge of a probably authentic Persian rug and land head forward across his knees. "Ouch! Betsy you are the master at dramatic entrances," he quips. What a guy! Still has his sense of humor. "At least your softest parts cushioned your fall." That's enough, Noel. My daughter is present.

Brie and Noel seem to like each other fine, although I sense some reservation in both. He is the epitomy of courtesy and kindness. His gentlemanliness and his gentleness still awe me. He answers Brie's not too probing questions (she's on her best behavior, no whining) about his profession and his health. He compliments her about how radiant she looks without once mentioning her condition. After a few minutes of Noel-Brie exchange, Bett declares tea will be served. I high-thumb her toward the kitchen even though I know Consuela will be serving.

"I'll help you," I say with deliberate firmness. "I insist."

She gets it, although it's clear from the scowl on her face she doesn't like it. Clomping behind her in my cast I steer her toward the walk-in pantry and practically shove her in, ignoring Consuela's shocked expression. I leave the door slightly ajar so Consuela can hear our voices, but not our words. "What," I hiss, "in Sam Hill is going on? Why the charade, the Ivy League clothes, the 'tea will be served' instead of 'anyone want a soft drink?'" It takes every ounce of control not to shake her, especially since I notice she's shaking. Dagnabbit, what have I done?

"I wanted you to be proud of me, classy, instead of looking like an overgrown butterfly. I know you think my outfits are extreme. I caught the expression on your face once, when I was wearing the purple one. Or, one of them. I have several." Her mouth twitches into a sheepish half grin. I just notice the mop of blonde flyaway curls is missing its usual loops. Instead she is wearing an almost sleek hairstyle, mostly waves.

I debate how to reply. I want to tell her I love her no matter what she looks like, that it's the beneath the surface woman I adore as a friend. I decide to do just that, and my honest words produce arms wrapped around me tightly.

"I love you, Betsy. Did I get it right this time? The name, I mean."

~

Brie and I are rehashing the afternoon over Frappuccinos from Starbuck's drive-thru. Mine is half-caf and hers decaf, both lite. Neither of us needs the extra calories. After lifting my cast leg onto the coffee table for support, she settles into the over-stuffed chair kitty-cornered from me. This way we can see each other without turning our heads or staring face on. Cozy.

"I like your friends, Momma. Bett is very elegant (I sense she's leaving out the word 'phony') and," she pauses slapping a hand over her heart, "Mr. Sheppard is *velly, velly* handsome." She's reverts to her childhood slang, a huge grin gracing her face. I feel heat creeping up the sides of my neck. It's embarrassing to blush in front of my daughter, especially about a man.

"Thanks, glad you like them. They're both special to me." I refuse to elaborate. Brie senses this and chatters on. At least she isn't whining.

"You said on the way home that Bett owns a string of boutiques. I think you mentioned most of her designs were flowing, not form-fitting like the outfit she wore today. I, uh, wonder – would any of them look good on me, fit me?" I'm startled by her hopeful voice, bordering on whining. Surely she doesn't want to look like a Bett-wannabe. A pregnant one at that.

"Not sure. Let's try the maternity shops first, okay?" We didn't have time to shop after our Bett-Noel visit. My leg was aching from dragging the cast around Bett's "humble home." What an anomaly. Or was the expression a misnomer? I must bone up on my vocabulary and grammar. Brie seemed exhausted, too, probably from trying to figure out the triangular relationship between Bett, Noel and me.

"Something to look forward to tomorrow since Derek hasn't cut me off financially. Let's go first to Pea in a Pod in Fashion Square."

Oh…my. The girl has done her homework. I agree. "Phtt" on Derek for leaving her. She might as well look as elegant as an expectant mother can in the most expensive maternity clothes available. As long as Derek is paying. Betsy, you are so bad.

We munch on nachos, calories neither of us need, but comfort food we both need. Brie may not make the kinds of salads I make, but she knows her appetizers. Mostly calorie-laden ones, but tonight we don't care. Following the nachos, she finds a can of crab meat in my pantry, some sour cream and cream cheese, shredded cheddar and—you bet—brie. Thawing a round of Hawaiian bread in the microwave and chopping green onions, she concocts a dip she pours into the hollowed out bread and bakes it. I, momentarily, think about my hips when a searing pain shoots down my foreleg under the cast. Who cares, I need this yummy stuff for my broken bones and my bruised psyche. Suddenly, I'm Dr. Freud's trainee.

We pig out. We relax. We share.

Secrets are revealed.

THIRTY

"Bett set you up?"

"You set Derek up?"

"It was a blessing to me."

"It was supposed to be a blessing to us."

Whoa. What Bett did was a little underhanded, but not subversive. What Brie did was…

"Deceptive. That's what you did, Brie. You deceived your husband. Does he know that?"

Again she crumbles into a heap, tears dripping again on my fancy throw pillow. When, if, she leaves, it goes right to Prestige Cleaners.

I try to reach her to comfort her, but my cast leg is stuck on the coffee table. I manage to touch her shoulder with my fingertips and coax her forward. She moves from the chair to the sofa and inches toward me like a reluctant snail. Not happy with what I've just learned, that my daughter lied to her husband, all I can say is, "Oh, honey, come to Momma."

"I know it was wrong, but we'd talked about it even before we got married." She gulps, a sure sign she is feeling guilty. "He said he wanted children right away. Then when his business got so successful," another gulp, "we decided to take advantage of the financial perks and do all the things we wouldn't be able to do after we had children." Gulp. She straightens and wipes her absorbent hands across her eyelids, smearing the mascara I'd applied earlier. "I guess my timing was wrong. And," she sucks in a breath, "deceiving him was, too."

I can't decide if I want to shout, shake her or slap her silly. Instead, I bite the inside of my cheek and taste blood. Maybe I should have been a stronger parent, spanking her with a wooden spoon instead of giving time outs. Tasting the tang of blood in my mouth reminds me of Jesus' blood shed for me, and Brie, and Derek.

"Brie, you can't take back what you've already done. But, you can ask Jesus for forgiveness, and," I pause with all the drama of a soap opera queen, "you can forgive Derek. You pulled a fast one on him. Wonder how you would have felt if he'd done that to you?" A thought suddenly occurs to me. "Does Derek know you deliberately 'forgot' to take your birth control pills?"

~

I am staring at an ashen face. The squeaky "no" that comes out of it confirms what I suspected. *Sorry, God, I can't help my big mouth this time.* "Do you think that's fair?"

Head-shaking, and flinging those kinky curls to and fro, has become a sudden new thing for my Brie. Actually, it is quite attractive, or would be if the situation were different. She's given up whining, substituted wailing. A sound I'm not good with. Still, I try.

"Let's fix that." Hopefully, I exude more confidence than I feel. I do truly believe God can fix anything, even broken hearts. I clasp her hands so tight she can't pull away. "Dear Forgiving Heavenly Father," I begin. Now, why did I insert the 'forgiving'? Making a point, hmm. "I thank you and praise you for always being there to listen to our needs. Tonight we have a special one for Brie and Derek. You know the circumstances, Lord, so I won't go into detail. Please heal both their hearts, bring forgiveness and reconciliation. Guide Brie and Derek back to celebrate their love and the birth of their child—together. Amen." Me, always to the point, even talking with God.

Brie wipes at her eyes again. Gosh, those absorbent hands

are working overtime. So is my mind. I am trying to process the details of this mess. Frankly, I'm disappointed in Brie. Also, in Derek. What happened to communication, talking, spilling the beans, being honest? As usual, questions flit through my heart like an unchecked forest wildfire. When I was pregnant with Brie and Mr. Bigtime Jerk hightailed it, he already knew. Although he hadn't jumped with glee, he'd gone through the motions of holding my hands and kissing me behind my ear (my vulnerable spot—gotta tell Noel about that) and calling his parents to announce the news. Everything he did said he was great with having a child, even excited. Then, he split. Poof!

"How did Derek respond, react, when you told him he was going to be a father?" Time to ask that question.

"His face turned gray, like leftover ash in a fireplace. He said, 'How?' I said, 'Must have missed a pill.' He said, 'How?' again. He was starting to sound like a puppet, and my heart was starting to break." Brie coughed and blew into a tissue from the box I'd shoved near her. "We'd wanted, talked about, children for so long I was sure he'd be happy, even thrilled. I dreamed he'd embrace me, shout with glee and start painting the extra room for a nursery. Guess I was wrong. Dead wrong."

I venture the next question. "Tell me about when he left. Did he sneak out or give an explanation?" I fully expect to hear "snuck."

"He left a note, after we'd talked until three a.m. I was so drained I almost sleepwalked to bed. I didn't hear a thing. Not him packing clothes or leaving. I found the note on the kitchen table the next morning."

"Wanna share? Or, is it too private?" I am dying to know.

Without a word, Brie gets up to retrieve a paper from her purse on the kitchen counter. She hands it to me saying, "Read it out loud, Momma, please."

My Darling Brie,

Your news last night was such a surprise. So unexpected when we'd agreed to plan for children. What happened to those plans, that agreement? I thought that was a silent part of our marriage vows.

You practically confessed to me you had deliberately "forgotten" to take your pills. Maybe it was truly a slipup, but your eyes told me different.

I can't do it now, Brie. I just can't. So many things happening at work, so many obligations. Can't explain.
Please trust me that I will provide for you and the child. I will never let you suffer financially.
I will always love you.
Derek
PS – Don't try to contact me. I will call you when I feel ready to talk.

"I thought maybe it would sound different being read by you. It sounds the same."

My heart almost broke in a zillion pieces. I hadn't contacted Derek's dad as I'd planned this morning. But, tomorrow I would, for sure.

~

Next morning, I decided to tell Brie my plan. It only seems fair. As she drags her sorry self in to breakfast, I greet her with a hug and make my announcement.

"First, I'm calling Derek's father. Then, I'm calling Noel. One for confirmation, the other for advice. Maybe Grandma," I add. I feel rejuvenated and in control. I'm not.

~

"Why are you interfering?"

Noel chastising me is more than I can take, so I hang up. Slam! So much for you, Mr. Courteous, Kind and Gentlemanly. What happened to Mr. Understanding, and especially Mr. Fixit? Oh, forgot you and Maizie never had children, so you have no clue about parent-child relationships, or pregnancies, or spouses who don't communicate. I circumvent my plan and call Bett. I haven't called Derek's dad yet. Too chicken.

"Why don't you and Brie come over for lunch, dear?" No Becka, no Lizbeth, no fake name. Just "dear." I buy into that. She even promises she will provide lunch. Such a mystery.

THIRTY ONE

"Your mother did mention, I assume, men can be such jerks? So obtuse." Bett keeps her eyes cast down as she takes a slurp of Trader Joe's French Onion Soup from her ornate silver spoon. *Coward!*

My spoon clatters to the saucer that's cradling my china bowl. I glare at her and twist the creamy linen napkin on my lap into a corkscrew. Glancing at Brie I notice she simply nods and takes another gulp of the delicious soup. Her mouth is filled with at least half the soaked crouton, and strings of cheese suspend between her lips and the bowl. "Yep," she manages to mutter. Did I fail Teaching Children Etiquette 101? Must have.

"I certainly did not say any such thing, Brie." My voice takes on the drill sergeant quality my dad used to tease me about. "FYI," I continue hoping both Brie and Bett know that abbreviation for For Your Information, "I don't believe Derek is a jerk." (I won't say it out loud, but I'm tempted to say, "Like your father.") I grit my already ground down teeth (the ones my dentist friend Dr. Kumar keeps trying to fit me for a device to wear while I'm sleeping) and practically hiss. "He's scared, he's young, and he's going through job and financial trauma." Ssss. "Give the guy a break."

I stare again at Bett as she makes an attempt to scan the

pots on the racks above the commercial cooktop. No way, Bett girl. I make sure my eyes lock with hers. I glare. Or, did I do that already? I'm frustrated, confused and angry. Not sure with whom. Maybe everyone.

Derek, certainly, for not consulting his earthy father and his Heavenly Father. Maybe he did. I don't know. Bett for making assumptions and imposing them on my daughter. Brie for being subversive, tricking Derek into being a father, and not taking responsibility for her deception. Last, but not least, Mr. Crayon Blue Eyes.

I know it's latent and leftover, but Noel really disappointed me when he pulled the "Why are you interfering?" bit on me. My heart is still trying to climb up to its proper place after that comment. *Dear Lord, I hope I'm not in love with another insensitive jerk. Please, save me from that. Or from my own stupidity, if that's the case.*

Bett nods, head bowed, and whispers, "Sorry." To her credit, she actually apologizes, sort of. Brie continues to slurp.

"Yep, Mom. Will." That's her giving a break, possibly forgiveness, of Derek?

I'm on the verge of throttling them both when a hoarse voice comes over the Intercom. I'd forgotten about that feature of Bett's home since I never used it. Now, it sends me reeling. Noel!

I'd also forgotten about him still being ensconced here in a velvet room. Hopelessly invalid. Yeh, right! Consuela serving him pancakes in bed every morning and Snoopy wheezing and purring at his feet. Not to mention a silver-handled toothbrush.

"Hello," the hoarseness proclaims. "Anything to eat?"

I think momentarily of all those words my former husband, The Jerk, used to use, and I'm sorely tempted to spew them back into our end of the Intercom. Instead, I taste the blood in my mouth from biting my tongue.

"Mom, you okay?" Brie has sucked up the last of the stringy cheese and scraped her bowl. Only bits of onion cling to the sides. Her look of innocence infuriates me more. I grab her hand and pull her up leaving the dirty bowls for Bett, or most likely for Consuela.

"Sorry, Bett, but we hav'ta leave. Thanks for the soup." That's about all I can muster for Bett, the turncoat.

~

My head aches. I resist the urge to take my hands off the steering wheel and press thumbs to my temples. Brie sits statue-like next to me, hands tucked under her protruding belly. I glance in her direction and notice a tiny string of cheese dangling from the corner of her mouth and a lone tear dangling from her chin. Aw, oily onions, what have I done. Overreacted, you idiot. Offended both of them, maybe even Noel when he learns I knew he was there, then barreled out without acknowledging him. Wait a minute! Bett offended me, and she knew she did by making her anti-male comment, and not even looking up like an honest person. Noel offended me with his "Why are you interfering?" remark. One I will never share with Brie.

Brie. The only way Brie offended me was by embarrassing me with her lazy table manners. I admit I was too sensitive about her slurping, gluttonous behavior. After all, the child is pregnant, probably starving constantly. I try to remember what it was like.

When I was pregnant with James, my first, eating seemed to be my only diversion from feeling, and especially looking, like an over-sized beach ball on steroids. Pregnancy wasn't considered cute or attractive in them there days. Maternity clothes were patterned cotton muumuu things that looked like discarded circus tents. Sure, they camouflaged that one was "that way." So, being "disguised" lent itself to eating for two.

Six years later, I was widowed and remarried. Pregnancy with Julia had a bit more hope on the fashion front. Must have had something to do with the hippy era. Maybe also the fact I'd moved and changed docs. Dr. Podinski (did I like him because of his Polish name, or because his home backed up to ours?) encouraged me to eat more healthfully and not gain more than twenty-five pounds. I surprised him, and me, by only gaining twenty-two. Lots of raw carrots. Probably why Julia hates them to this day. Today obstetricians encourage expectant mothers to gain a lot. No holds barred quantity wise what they eat. Still, Julia was a healthy seven pounds, twelve ounces, exactly the same as her brother.

Brie was tiny by comparison, only six point seven. I attribute my minimal weight gain, nineteen pounds, during my pregnancy with her to The Jerk.

"I'm sorry, honey. I over-reacted. Must be a bad day for me." I hope my voice is contrite and apologetic as I turn briefly from my view out the windshield to catch her gaze. I lay fingers on her forearm, but she shifts it dramatically away.

"Mom." She whispers and squeezes her eyes, and another tear trickles out making a trail down her left cheek. "You embarrassed me." Out of my peripheral vision, I see her scrub her arm where I'd touched her. So much for motherly affection.

What, I wonder, happened to the feeling I had when I held her for the first time? The overwhelming love that filled me. I remember touching her all over—running my hand along her chubby legs, kissing her head of down-like hair, smelling her new baby smell. Realizing the only other person in the birthing room was my mother, not Brie's father. The Jerk.

Now, I'm doing it again, punishing her for her father. I swing off Shea Boulevard and turn left onto 100th Street and into a cul-de-sac. Cutting the motor I reach over to hug her.
She shrinks away from me and presses her body against the passenger door.

THIRTY TWO

Plan B. I swing Old Sassy around, not an easy feat as she hovers precariously to the left. Righting herself, I swear she knows what direction to go. Is the old girl reading my mind now?

Pulling back onto Shea, she heads toward the 101 Freeway north. After several pregnant pauses, I ease into the Scottsdale Road exit, then turn into the newest Scottsdale101 shopping venue. Destination Maternity's parking area is packed, except for the handicap spaces. No stretch of the imagination there. Although, many pregnant women are temporarily "handicapped."

Aw, a Cadillac Escalade with a woman whose cell phone is glued to her head pulls out, slowly. I grab her parking space and kill the motor. "Sorry about Sassy's coughing." I turn to Brie hoping for a smile at least. Instead, I am flummoxed. Brie is grinning from ear to ear.

"Momma." She sounds like a talking head announcer on T.V. "Pea in the Pod?" Her misty expression captures mine and almost melts me. Did I mention "almost?" Pea in the Pod is probably the most expensive maternity store in the good old U.S. of A. It's sale items are twice or thrice the price of other maternity stores.

"Can we go in?"

Yep, Hello Brie. That's what we came for.

Instead, I say, "Sure. Let's have some fun."

The expanse of three combined stores and a spa takes up almost an entire block of the new mall. Whole Foods cleverly opened a market here, too, obviously depending on expectant moms to want healthful, maybe organic, "whole" foods. It's no coincidence this new mini-mall is directly across from the largest BabiesRUs store in Arizona. Marketing is primo here.

Brie practically leaps out of Old Sassy landing with a ker-plunk on her thong-attired, swollen feet. I refrain from comment. *Thank you, Jesus, for her change in attitude. But, please, I petition You, help me from spending too much. My bank account is questionable right now.*

I am caught up in perusing the three stores in one, especially the sale racks. Some cute things here. Black clad sales associates approach me asking if I need help. Half, at least, are pregnant. How clever is that – to hire pregnant sales people? Insures confidence.

I hear a squeal off to my right. "Momma. The perfect outfit to bring Derek back."

Is the girl crazy? An "outfit" is not going to bring back a husband she'd lied to.

"What, honey?" I say in my best mommy dearest voice. (Suddenly, Joan Crawford becomes my secret heroine. Well, maybe only my ally.) "You found something?"

I can't believe how stupid I feel. This is the way I used to respond to Brie when I took her shopping at five years old—when because she was into dressing herself (a known phenomena of 3-5 year old preschoolers) I pretended to acquiesce, then stuffed what I wanted to buy in the plastic bag. Or, were the bags all fancy paper then, with raffia handles? Anyway, when we got home, Brie had forgotten all the princess outfits and was thrilled with the more practical clothes.

"The princess calls," I sing out in my most melodic voice. The black clad sales assistant nearest to me gives me a questioning stare. I ignore her and lope toward Brie's dressing room.

It's not a stretch to say I'm flabbergasted, dumbfounded,

amazed, overwhelmed, bowled over. Pulling aside the curtain, I swear I'm looking at Bett, younger by fifty years. Brie seems to glow, as in radiate. True, her hair is darker, not like Bett's streaked and crunched into foil for twenty minutes under a steamer. Her makeup is not as extreme, but the look on her face…well, it's Bett's. That's when I notice the dimple.

"Hey, honey. Never noticed that cute little indentation in your cheek." I pause to inhale, hopefully not too loudly. "You look great!"

Actually, she does. IF Derek ever comes back, IF Derek actually sees her, IF Derek is willing to accept her again—Derek will be bowing on bent knees to beg her forgiveness. That is how beautiful Brie looks.

~

Okay, so I spent a hundred and eighty dollars on one outfit, on sale. It was so worth it to see the expression of pure pleasure on Brie's face. Not to mention her relaxed posture on the way home. She never cupped her protruding belly once. Nor did she bring out the promised credit card to prove she had lots of money. Oh, well.

Yes! I raise my fist toward heaven in my best sports fan gesture of winning. Brie grins and grabs my hand, the right one not on the steering wheel. She squeezes and smiles.

Thank you, Lord. We are at peace. At least for tonight.

THIRTY THREE

Daddy always said you could tell the caliber of people who live in a community by the cars parked there. Probably not a PC attitude nowadays, but he was referring to apartment complexes moons ago when helping me apartment shop after my divorce. We swung through dozens of parking lots in Tempe and Scottsdale, leaving almost all of them post-haste. Case in point. After three frustrating, abortive days viewing dirty pickups with scum on them and cars with dented fenders, he offered a proposition.

Turning toward me, after pulling under a multi-car overhang, he narrowed his eyes and sighed. Daddy is not a "sigher," so I sensed this was important. "Betsy." Sigh again, "I know your finances since you've shared them with me. I know, although Mr. Jerk didn't leave you a lot of leeway, he left some." I almost giggled. Daddy called him Jerk, too. Neither of us wanted to blister our tongues using his given name. "If mom and I could help you with a down payment, what would you think of investing in a small condominium? You'd probably be paying the same in a monthly mortgage as you would in renting an apartment," he rushed on to explain. His thick dark eyebrows, barely starting to wisp with gray, raised dramatically. "That way you'd own something you could later sell. It would be yours."

I remember blubbering and nodding and hugging. The next day we explored eight condo communities, an exhausting feat for me at five months pregnant. We nixed five of them for various reasons—distance from the freeway, remotely located from shopping for groceries, too many stairs, "bad" cars. We focused on three—one in Scottsdale Horizon neighborhood (near two markets, two drug stores, three Starbucks); one that hovered on the edge between Scottsdale and Fountain Hills; and another off Mountain View Drive in the mega-conglomerate community of Scottsdale Ranch (condos, apartments, patio homes, town homes and huge, lakeside homes). The one between Scottsdale and Fountain Hills was mostly filled with boat-like Cadillacs and Lincoln Town Cars. We decided most of those residents were older, based on their selection of autos, and I needed a community that would accept children, especially embrace the one in my belly since the two older children were away at school.

The Scottsdale Horizon one was literally around the corner from a daycare/preschool combo that was highly rated. The cars in its parking lot were a mixture—a few pickups (not dirty), a few Cads, many SUV'S (although we didn't call them by that name twenty-five years ago), and lots of clean two and four-door vehicles of varying ages. It hadn't hurt that while walking the perfectly groomed grounds and the sparkling community pool we'd met Bernice.

Hearing her tell how, as president of the homeowners association, she kept tabs, and how she has a list of people who'd asked her to call them if any condo became available, well that did it. The big bonus was for only fifteen dollars more a month tacked onto my mortgage, I could have an oversized garage. Whoopee! Daddy and I hugged and danced right in front of Bernice who probably wondered about a thirty-something pregnant woman and a fifty-something graying man displaying so much affection.

It all comes back to me, twenty-five years later, when I open the letter in my mailbox from the blankety-blank Home Owners Association to me: It has come to our attention that your vehicle is out of compliance with the stated CC&Rs and Rules and Regulations of the community.

X Unsightly, dirty vehicle

X Out of compliance with R&R #7 (please see page 2)

It is a standard letter, probably the kind sent to other homeowners. But, it irks me. Sets me on edge. I think it offends Old Sassy, too. Especially since she's recently had a bath. I swear she hiccups when I glance in her direction. It's especially offensive since I usually park in my garage, but because of Brie's condition, I have been parking in one of the open spaces. It's easier for her to get out and make headway into the condo.

I stomp into my living room quelling the temptation to shred the missal when I spy Brie reading my Bible. Her head is bowed low over it, her mass of curls sheathing her face like a thick veil. I catch the door behind me just before it slams. Slinking backwards, I try to sneak out to sit on the stoop when I hear "the whine."

"Momma, get back in here. Please." So much for stealthiness.

I mumble. "Sorry, Brie. Didn't want to disturb you."

"Momma. I need you—now. Need your advice." She turns her face toward me just enough for me to see the smeared mascara and the trails of tears across her cheeks. Wiping her hand under one eye, she says, "I've been reading about forgiveness. Proverbs, I think. Can't remember the verse."

I could.

"Brie, it's not in Proverbs, but in Psalms, I think in Psalm 25. 'For the sake of your name, O Lord, forgive my iniquity, though it is great.' Is that the one?" Pressing the notice from the HOA in my left hand, I find my right hand hovering over my heart. Brie replies.

"Yeh."

THIRTY FOUR

The next morning I dig through the pile of papers in my den, the dusty ones on the floor to the left of the desk I'd pushed back to open the wall bed for Brie. Homeowner Rules and Regulations glare back at me in blue 18 point letters. At least the words aren't all in caps. That would really be intimidating. Yep, number seven states some nonsense about "Offensive vehicles." Mostly the dirty part. That galls me. Sassy was bathed to the tune of twenty-eight bucks (for oversized vehicles at the car wash with the grinning yellow sun sign) just two days ago. It cost almost as much as filling her tummy with gas.

Reading at the beginning of the R&Rs I learn the management company the community hired makes a weekly drive-through looking for peeled paint, trash cans not taken in, laundry hanging from balconies (a huge no-no, even though we're all supposed to be trying to be "green") and doggie doo-doo not picked up. My mind wanders to what it might look like if we all hung out laundry. Maybe like a village in Italy? Our community does market itself that it's supposed to have a Mediterranean ambiance because our condos are all painted a Pepto Bismol pink. But, oops, we are in Scottsdale, America, a planned community that must at all times look pristine.

I am furious. I have never received a notice from the

HOA before. This one states I am "subject to fine" if the situation isn't corrected within thirty days.

~

The call came at 8:15.

Brie's Derek. Or, at least, her used-to-be Derek. Accident, head injury, need next of kin.

I'm fuming over my HOA letter when I absently answer the phone. A soft, apologetic voice asks for Brie after remembering to state she is calling from the hospital. I don't think too much about it because HonorHealth has many clinics and seminars pregnant women and couples can sign up for, like What to Expect When You're Pregnant, Natural Nursing, even Daddy Boot Camp. I figure maybe Brie had enrolled in one.

I automatically hand the phone to her while still shuffling through my HOA papers that I've brought to the kitchen table. I hear a gasp. She is leaning back against the sink counter, but starting to slide down. Her face is the color of a plump oyster about to be sucked from its shell. Shoving aside my stack of papers I grab her and flop her into a kitchen chair. I pluck the phone from her trembling hand.

I have to hand the receiver back to her to hear her mumble to explain it to me. After all, I'm not technically next of kin. I hear the news. When the simpering voice explains the situation to me, I also grab a chair. *Help me be strong, Lord. Fill me with your courage.*

Okay, I tell moi, the good part is Derek is asking for Brie. The bad part is his head injury.

~

"No, Momma, no!" Brie flings the tousled curls back and forth like a mop being shaken. A few loose strands hit her cheeks and stick to the tears. I remember how she was as a tot stomping around defiantly before naptime. The best way to calm her down was to promise a treat, for after the nap. That worked at three, but I doubt it will work at twenty-five. Still, I try.

"How about you wear the new, sexy outfit? Seeing you looking so beautiful will give Derek hope and help him recover." Prayer wouldn't hurt, either, but I'm not gonna go there yet.

"What part of no don't you understand, Momma? He left *me*. Now, it's my turn." My body gives a reflexive jump at the sound of the front door slamming. I glance at the indoor-outdoor thermometer my dad gave me and notice it's 104 degrees outside. I doubt if she'll stay on the porch too long.

I spend the next five minutes praying hard for Derek and, somewhat reluctantly, for Brie. I'm glad she's outside so I won't be tempted to slap her. Not that I ever have, but *lead me not into temptation, Lord*. I wonder if I've raised a spoiled brat. Not a big stretch considering I made a lot of concessions for her, raising her alone after The Jerk abandoned us. My heart melts a little remembering the pain I went through when her father left me pregnant and lonely. She's hurting. As much as she's mostly at fault by deceiving Derek, by fibbing (her version), and lying (my version), she's in a vulnerable state—raging hormones, and fat.

I try to visualize Derek's handsome face covered in gauze, head propped on a hard hospital pillow, tubes stuck in his arms. Is he moaning? Can he hear, see? He must have been able to vocalize to give my phone number and Brie's name. Or, was that information tucked in a pocket? Maybe his dad was notified and he told the hospital to call Brie. The massive headache I had yesterday is playing at my temples again. The screen door slams, then the inner wooden door. I push fingers against my temples and close my eyes.

"I want to hate him." The declaration hangs in the air like the odor of fetid fish. She refuses to look at me, but I know her downcast eyes are pleading. I fling a quick prayer to heaven, but I realize this is between them. I also realize if Brie refuses to go see her husband, possibly lying on his deathbed, I still can.

The little information I got from Simpering Voice was that Derek was involved in a car accident. "Not his fault, trying to help someone else," comes back to me, and I say it out loud.

"Just like Derek." I grab my new fake designer purse, keys and Bible and make for the door. "You coming?"

She didn't answer, but she didn't argue.

THIRTY FIVE

My reluctant passenger has trouble pulling the seatbelt across her belly. I refuse to help, but I have this rule: Car doesn't start until everyone is belted.

I fiddle with my keys, check my lipstick in the pull-down mirror on the sun visor and wait to hear a click. Finally, it comes and we roll.

Pudgy face is so startled when he sees me he looks tempted to run to the restroom. Maybe I'm reading too much into it, but he does scoot his chair back and start to make motions to rise. Instead, he rolls his bulbous eyes and makes a popping sound.

"Practicing your aerobic breathing?" I can't help myself. He and I've had way too long a relationship.

"Nell…again?" Pretty obvious he knows both our names, even though he still calls Noel Nell.

"Nope, this time it's my son-in-law, Derek." His look is unbelieving, as if he thinks I'm trying to pull a fast one. "Really, honest." That's the best I can do to convince him. Oh, I could pull Brie forward, but she has become part of the mural on the side wall, blending in with the fantasy castles, maybe hoping to be a pretend-to-be princess.

Pudgy Face leaves the security of his chair and gestures me forward to the sliding doors that lead into the sanctuary reserved only for next of kin, and hospital personnel. Now, I do grab Brie and pull hard. Her clammy hand is like melting ice, and her face is a frozen mask. I worry if she has a psych problem, like a duel personality. But, I realize she's scared, very scared. The father of her baby, her husband, is in ICU, possibly dying.

I say all the expected things. "He needs us. Be strong. God is still a God of miracles."

I didn't expect the glare, the angry, nasty one. Maybe I misinterpreted it. Brie's just frightened.

"I still want to hate him."

Okay, she's said it twice. That's enough for moi. Time to be MIC, mother in command.

"Brie, this is not about you. It's about Derek. Maybe, in the long run about your marriage. But, right now, it's about Derek." I take one of those breathe-in breath-out breaths I was taught long ago in a class I took at the Senior Citizens Center. Trying not to scream, I take her limp wrist and shake her hand, hard. "Loosens the muscles, relaxes them," our instructor Pam used to yell over the music.

Towing her behind me we follow Pudgy Face through the whooshing doors.

~

Derek is lying prone, a sheet pulled around his torso so tight I think "strapped." His head is swathed in so much gauze he looks like a ghost in a cartoon. The obligatory tubes hang from hooks on stems on both sides of his bed. A few end under more gauze in his left arm, and several more under strips of bandages in his right. Nurse Ratchit slips into the room, and I almost lose it. Has God sent an angel, again?

Netta Jones clasps my hands in her small bony ones. "Mizz Betsy, he belong to you?" Her angelic face is a composition of butter melting on toast and sweet tomato preserves. The defining lines are still there, but softened by the butter and jelly combo. Her eyes are the same, yet different. I can't remember what color they were when she took care of Noel, but tonight they have tiny specks of twenty-four carat gold catching the low light. They sparkle, and the flecks dance. I get lost in their uniqueness until Pudgy nudges her and she jumps. "Yes, thank you. You may leave." He shrugs, turns his back and hikes out of the room. I feel a sort of sadness for him. After all, he and I have a history.

"My son-in-law." I make the simple statement and squeeze her hands. I turn toward Brie who is collapsed in the room's only chair, brown vinyl with arms. Her hands are devoid of color from clinging to the arms. Her eyes are closed so tight her eyelashes are laying on her cheeks, maybe even stuck. I know she's in pain, emotional turmoil, but I am over it. I'm mad.

"Stop being a diva, Brie!" My voice is beyond functional having risen five decibels above normal.

THIRTY SIX

I bought new potholders today. I went to the Dollar Store for R & R and found two. I may be the Queen of Green, but I also concoct and cook hot. These are bright yellow terry, and they make me happy. I smile every time I lift them off their hook on the side of the fridge. Today I'm making One Pot Stroganoff, and I need happy.

Brie has been an itch. Can you guess I'm leaving off several choices of consonants at the beginning of the word? I can't decide. After you learn how she's acted, maybe you can.

You already know a little bit about last night, her announcing she wants to hate Derek, then slumping into the chair in his ICU room and gripping its arms. That was just the beginning.

When angel Netta Jones, a.k.a. Nurse Ratchit, tried to take Brie's hands in hers to pray, Brie rolled her eyes and yanked her fingers away. Sweet Netta looked at me confused. I could only shrug. I prayed with her, both for Derek and Brie. I wasn't sure who needed prayer more. Nor am I now.

I love the softness of the potholders, so easy to grip. Not like those rubberized new-fangled ones that slip out of your hand. These remind me of Nurse Jones hands, gentle and pliable. In the end, she saved Brie last night. At least from guilt and remorse. Her sweet nature, and gift of forgiveness, captured Brie's spirit. Finally, hoisting herself off the vinyl chair, she leaned her protuberant belly against Derek's bed and kissed his forehead. I had to contain myself from cheering.

Clasping the potholders in my hands now, I grab the huge metal pot and lift it out of the oven. Steam clouds my eyes and stings them, and I blink furiously. The aroma from the beef, soups and dab of sherry fills my kitchen. And my heart. I remember One Pot Stroganoff was the first meal I served Derek when he and Brie were dating. I made it especially because it was easy and required no attention, just three hours baking. I'd wanted to have time to chat with Derek, get to know him, learn his intentions toward Brie.

I wipe a tear from my cheek with the yellow terry cloth just as Brie lumbers into the room.

"Smells yummy, Momma."

"Thanks. It's Derek's fav." Now, why did I say that? Adding fuel to the feeble fire. Guess it's a gift.

I fuss with adding the sour cream to the broth. Just as I scoop it out over the rice on our plates and set them on the table, she says, "Maybe we should take him some."

Save me, Lord, from passing out.

"Tomorrow, when we visit." It's a statement. Her voice is calm, matter of fact, like visiting Derek is something we do daily, watching him struggle against the restraints, hearing his muffled mumbling, seeing the blink, blink of drips from the plastic tubes into his arms.

"Sure. Let's do that." I bow my head in prayer.

~

Nurse Jones is off today, so we are "greeted" by Nurse Smith. Can you believe it? Two nurses on the same floor with the two most common names in America. Also, two opposites. Nurse Smith is gruff, scowling and puts me on edge. I try the "kill her with kindness" ploy my mother taught me, but it isn't working. She bustles self-importantly around Derek's bed, fussing with the IVs and the sheets, plumping his pillows so much he moans. I'm tempted to grab her wrists and secure them behind her back with surgical tape. If only there was some handy.

We still don't know the whole story about Derek, what happened and how bad his injuries are. I think yesterday we were so grateful he's alive, and Nurse Jones was so reassuring, we hardly thought to ask. Stupid, I know. Goes with the territory, mine at least. I'm still dragging around my cast, worrying about Brie and trying to keep my business going. Not to mention Noel who is topping my list of ingrates.

Bett calls every day, even says she is praying "hard" for Derek. Says Noel is still recuperating "nicely." My responses have been mostly "thank you," and "wonderful." I am too involved in the Derek situation to feel anything but sadness about Noel's and my relationship, if there still is one. I feel like my heart is being picked apart, separated into categories—now, then, later. I'm wallowing in self-pity when a gray-haired, gray-bearded, very handsome man swings open the door to Derek's room. He reminds me of a deep-sea fisherman. Don't know why, maybe I saw an ad, or a bit of a program on the history channel. His eyes have deep wrinkles around them, kindly wrinkles, like when a child pulls a finger through the thick frosting on a cake and can't resist the naughty grin. He has possibly the warmest smile I've ever seen. And, he smells good. Must be some kind of citrus cologne, maybe that unisex Jo Malone one.

I clasp his extended hand and shiver from the threads of electricity going up my arm.

"Ms. Wysinotski? I'm Doctor Duggins." Wow! A doc who checks on patients personally and smiles, and pronounces my name correctly. "Are you cold?" His concern transforms his handsome face into the ideal bedside manner doc, and he leans toward me, searching my eyes. My mouth is plastic, so I shake my head and hope he can hear the rattling. "I know seeing your son this way is devastating," he continues in a melodic voice, "but I really do believe he'll recover." He hesitates. "In time, and with therapy. After all, he was a hero, a Good Samaritan. He must have God on his side."

A hero? Our Derek? In my confusion I almost forget about Brie who is again slumped in the vinyl chair. I gesture toward her mumbling Derek is my son-in-law, married to that lump in the brown chair (no, I really don't say that, but I'm tempted). "I love Derek like a son, Doctor," I say feebly. The good man bends down to Brie's level and takes her limp hands in his. This time she doesn't resist, but stares blankly at him. He's murmuring something I can't understand, but Brie's chin lifts and her eyes perk up. They actually start to sparkle. I edge closer, trying to hear the doctor's words. I catch a few.

"Asked about you." Pause. "Our baby." Pause. "Good man, your Derek."

"Thank you, Doctor. That gives me hope." Did Brie really say that?

Without warning, she hoists her bulky self from the chair and rushes into the bathroom. Pregnancy and sudden revelations can cause urgency, so I grin at Dr. Duggins who winks back at me. "Thank you," I whisper. He nods, just as I feel an overwhelming need to use the facility.

Brie comes out smiling, and I rush in as quickly as I can while dragging my cast. Plunking myself on the throne I start to chuckle, then guffaw into a full-blown spate of laughter. How suggestible we humans, especially we women, are. I remember when Brie was three taking her first ballet classes. We'd been through a week of potty-training, but it wasn't down pat yet. I almost didn't take her to class, but decided since she adored dancing that would be a punishment. She deserved to twirl in her dream-like state of happiness. I pulled her teacher aside before class and explained if Brie gave her some kind of obvious sign it meant she had to go potty. Teacher was very understanding, and halfway through the thirty-five minute class she opened the door and led Brie out for me to take her to the restroom. What neither of us expected was a bevy of miniature divas following Brie who led a brigade of tiny ballerinas to the ladies room. Ten minutes later, nine other little girls in tutus had peed, but not my Brie. She held it in till we got home.

I'm still chuckling as I close the door to the bathroom.

"What's so funny, Mamma?" I just shake my head and drag my cast close to Derek's bed.

~

"It was a freak accident." The doctor explains. "Of course all accidents are freaky, not intended, but this one was unusual." He's sitting on the brown vinyl chair and Brie is perched on Derek's bed. Not a small feat. It took two of us to hoist her up. I'm cast-clumping and pacing.

Dr. Duggins has a tendency to lower his head when he talks, so not every word is clear. But, I think I'm catching most of them between the sounds of the papers he's flipping on his metal clipboard.

This is what I hear: "Pregnant woman, car trouble, stranded at side of freeway, waving with flashlight." There's that pregnant pause again, and a sigh from the doc. "He...he apparently pulled over to help. From what we know, from the Highway Patrol."

More shuffling papers. "A drunk driver slammed into his car and pinned him between it and the woman's." He stops and looks Brie face-to-face. His own face looks pained. Seems like he's aged ten years in the last few minutes. The creases deepen, and his eyes take on cloudiness. Doc clears his throat, loudly. "Badly bruised both his legs and smashed his head against the trunk of the front car." Now, he rushes on as if he has to get it all said quickly. "Legs will heal. Lot of therapy needed. Head, we hope." He flips the clipboard closed. "Minor internal injuries. A blessing." He rises and holds out a hand to Brie, then me. "Call me, anytime. God bless."

THIRTY SEVEN

I remember Brie sobbing and reaching to me, shoving herself off the hospital bed and almost collapsing in a heap on the floor. It happened so fast I couldn't catch her while lurching forward with my cumbersome cast. We somehow caught each other and I flung her toward the vinyl chair.

Perhaps it was our panting and the commotion, but when she landed in the chair with a loud whoosh, we both started to giggle uncontrollably. "Whoopee cushions!" we cried in unison. That was when we heard the "Whoo, whoo," and our faces blanked. Both at once, at each other. The weird sound came again.

"An owl?"

"Not in this room."

"Derek?"

"Derek!"

I don't know how either of us did it, but Brie extracted herself from the chair and I loped across the room. We both arrived at Derek's bedside in tandem. We fought to clasp his hand, but I gave up and patted his knee.

The sounds were garbled and mumbled, and whatever happened on the monitors brought two nurses rushing into his room. The way Nurse Smith shoved me aside made me wonder if she hadn't played linebacker for her college team. Her "Oops," as I almost fell didn't quite count as an apology. Then I remembered, duh, Derek is the patient. I am chopped liver.

Thankfully, Brie had managed to step aside when the thundering herd pounced. Holding her belly she leaned against the window with a huge grin on her face. "He spoke."

Ignoring us, the nurses adjusted dials, and one patted his face until his lips moved. This time the word came out clear. "Brie."

Nurse Number Two, who didn't know the situation, said, "He wants cheese?"

~

They say laughter is the best medicine. I can attest that belly laughing is primo.

"Your tummy still hurt?" I'm holding my sternum, pressing hard with both hands. The tissue clasped in my hand is soggy from laughter tears. Brie holds her nose and waves at me.

"Praise the Lord!"

"Derek spoke."

"Yep, 'whoopee and Brie."

"He said my name."

~

The next few minutes are total confusion.

Derek lifts his hand, his eyes open briefly, and I'm sure I catch a smile on his face.

Brie starts to sob as I shove her next to Derek's bed. Instead of clasping his hand as I'd hoped, she grabs a fist full of a sheet and mangles it. This is not going well, not as I hoped.

"Momma?"

I know she's trying to get my attention and support. But, she is a big girl who must call on her own resources.

"I'm going to the nurses' station to find out more." Am I being a wimp, dweeb, or being strong to let Brie be strong, too?

The nice nurse at the station whose name thankfully isn't either Jones or Smith, gives me an update, pretty much the same as the doctor. But, reassuring.

"Oh, you, or maybe your daughter, got a call from…a

Noel?"

"Really? When?"

"A few minutes ago. He sounded very upset."

Mmm. The ingrate. Is he really worried about Brie and Derek, or me? I decide to ignore it. Let him wonder. I am feeling mean right now.

I drag my cast back to Derek's room. Tapping on the door elicits no response, so I push it open quietly.

Brie is lying next to Derek on his hospital bed. He is rubbing her pregnant belly and sighing.

I freeze.

THIRTY EIGHT

The next few weeks are awful, demanding. Derek has to attend (such a superficial word) physical therapy and occupational therapy, and sadly, speech therapy. He struggles, but Brie is there every day to cheer him on. I actually see her plant kisses on his face. Especially when he takes a few faltering steps in physical therapy, holding onto the railing on either side of him. When he says her name in a twisted, garbled pronunciation with spittle running down his chin, I see tears in her eyes. He reaches for her, one hand clinging to the rail on his right, the other gesturing to touch her chin. She feather-touches his raised hand and gives him a brilliant smile. He blinks, and his mouth half curves on one side. Brie claps her hands like a preschool child singing the "If you're happy and you know it" song. I am blown away. My Brie has turned into a kind and sensitive woman, no longer an angry, betrayed woman. Jesus has His arms around her. His comfort is her cloak.

Yes, I am here, too. Not every day, but most. I do have to make salads, to make an income.

Bett comes once. So does my mother, twice. Their presence seems to buoy him up. He has his own cheering section. Then, on day seven, my dad shows up.

"Derek," Dad shouts. "Get with the program. You are better than this. Have more spunk. Work harder. Do this for Brie. Do this for your baby."

After this diatribe Dad collapses in a chair. I see sweat on his brow, and he wipes an absorbing hand across it.

I worry and ask if he's okay. His hand is firmly on his heart. I can almost hear it beating.

"Yes, fine. Frustrated. Want Brie and Derek to make up and embrace what they have, what God has given them." He looks up at my face and reveals a lot. Maybe too much. More that I can deal with. "Remember their marriage vows? You were there, Betsy."

Yep, I was. Were they?

THIRTY NINE

Three weeks. It's been only three, seven plus days, since Derek started his various therapies. No one can believe it, not even Doc Duggins.

"I...am amazed."

"Why so, Doc? I had you pegged for a believer." I am so bold. What happened to God lashing my tongue?

"I..." he stammers again. "I believe in miracles. I believe God can do anything." He pulls a cotton handkerchief out of his back pocket and swipes at his face, missing his eyes that need swiping the most. Still, the man is obviously stunned. He turns to me with damp eyes. "You, this family, are experiencing a miracle. Do you understand?"

"Yep." I don't mean to sound so pious, but I feel it. I know God is honoring all of our collective prayers for Derek, for us. I bring to mind one of my favorite verses from Zephaniah 3:17. "The Lord your God is with you, He is mighty to save." I say it out loud to the doc. "Sometimes, I insert the word 'heal' for 'save.'" He looks at me with a crooked smile and nods. I guess that's confirmation.

He calls nurses to check Derek's vital signs, then after checking waves them away. Doc fumbles with the pages on his metal clipboard. Flips a few, then goes back to the one on top. Pen poised he scribbles what I assume is his John Hancock on the top page.

"Good to go to rehab." He smiles and leans toward Derek, then turns his face to look directly at Brie. "Probably for a couple of weeks. Then, must come back twice a week, two times a week," he emphasizes while pointing a finger at her. "Imperative. No excuses. K?"

She nods. Then gets her gall up. "How long do you think? Weeks, months?"

"No telling. Depends on determination. Depends on faith. Only God knows, but He will guide you." He tilts his head to one side and smiles again. "God bless you with your baby. Boy or girl?"

Brie looks at him stupefied. "Don't know. Too scared to ask."

"Whatever it is, it is blessed with the family you have. But," he says, grinning, "You might want to find out whether to buy pink or blue booties. A perk your mother didn't have in her time." He grins again and bounces out the door closing it quietly.

FORTY

Derek has a walker. One of those things with wheels and a cute little purse thing to put stuff in. The only thing I think he keeps in it is a few tissues to wipe his brow when he gets sweaty from trying too hard. It's not as fancy as the one Bett rented for me, more practical.

"How's he doing?" Bett's call is out of the blue. Is she really caring and concerned, or is she being polite? Out of obligation.

"He's doing great. His attitude is terrific, and he and Brie are lovey dovey. You?"

"I'm okay, all right. Still dealing with my secret."

Does she want me to ask, to prod her to reveal it? Instead, I say, "So sorry, Bett. Pray about it. God will give you the answer." I only have so much energy. Right, God?

I hang up the phone and say a mini prayer for Bett. I know she deserves more, but I'm tired, burned out. Pooped.

~

Two months.

Derek is walking without a walker, no crutches, only a cane. It truly is a God-thing. Not sure if it's an actual miracle, but I think back often to John 5:8 when Jesus told the invalid man to pick up his bed and walk.

God's mysteries are still mysteries to me. I have plenty of faith, right Lord? But maybe I need a faith adjustment. Believing is one thing, but…seeing? Like seeing Derek walk and hearing him pronounce words intelligibly, if not always with perfect pronunciation. When he fumbles, he grins sheepishly. At least he doesn't stammer like that talk radio host.

I try to do the "Rest in the Lord" thing. I've never been good at staying still. But, I try. In my hideous brown velour recliner (belonged to The Jerk), I find a small modicum of peace. My cataloging mind flips through all the events of the last few months. Bett telling me she has a secret she is reluctant to share. My condo blowing up. Brie revealing her deception to Derek about how she became pregnant. Noel acting like an idiot—not getting a flu shot, making snide remarks about my mother/daughter relationship with Brie. Bett saying stupid things about men in general. Derek getting mangled on the freeway. Okay, those are the highlights of the negative memories.

I get out my devotional journal and start scribbling. A lot of shrinks, especially that famous female one on the radio, suggest making lists of all the good things in your life. Here goes.

*Bett has accepted the Lord as her savior. Wow! A biggie. I still worry she doesn't exactly understand what that means. But, between Him and her, she will figure it out.

*Noel's "problem" is history. At least I hope so since he asked me to marry him. Did I forget to tell you about that, the proposal? Well, it's our secret. I can tell you it was a day after that Monica woman called and accused me of…what did she say? Anyway, I'll give a hint. Diamond ring (big one!) in paper coffee cup at Mitch's. Almost choked on it.

*Derek driving to reunite with Brie, then having the accident. This one is mixed. But, what a great man to stop and help someone else in trouble. Especially a pregnant woman. This is a testament to Brie and his love for her.

*My condo getting fixed. Pretty much a biggie for me so I don't have to intrude on Bett anymore for sleeping arrangements. Although, I admit I miss Snoopy.

*Derek healing so quickly. He and Brie making up, him accepting "the baby." What more can I say. (Not a question.)

*I heard from scared, reluctant, napkin-folding hostess Nancy. She has started reading the Bible and attending church. What a gift!

I am so tired my toes are aching. I set the journal aside and close my lids. Sleep overcomes me, and weird dreams invade. Noel is bouncing a child on his lap. Wait, it morphs into Brie, then becomes Nancy. He helps her fold napkins. Suddenly, Derek is dancing with Bett, twirling her around in a flapper dress. Bett grabs my dad by the cheeks and kisses him. Mother and I watch the scenario. "That's so cute," she says. Consuela puts a choke hold on Bett and slaps her cheek, and I smash a slice of cheesecake in Noel's face, shoving it up his aquiline nose.

I shake my head awake, but the dreams linger. In my half-awake, half-asleep state I beg. Please, God. Why, God, do I have to go through this? Couldn't I have a deep, dreamless sleep just for once?

Lowering the foot rest on the ugly recliner I manage to heft my sorry self out of it.

FORTY ONE

Nose wax?

That seems weird. Yet, it's what Brie suggests. Is my hair growing out of my nostrils like old men have clumps of hair growing out of their ears? I do feel old, but *that* old? Yikes.

She tries hard to be diplomatic. "Momma, did you notice those little wisps that peek out of your nose? Just a tiny bit. But, enough that a few catch on your makeup?"

"So?" I look in the mirror and wrinkle the nose in question. "Obvious, huh?"

Brie nods, her curls bouncing above her ears. "Not attractive, Momma. Not sexy." She pauses. "You do have a very important occasion coming up. Right?" Her face succumbs to one of those "know it all" grins. Okay, she has a handle on it. She is my new wedding coordinator, otherwise referred to as official wedding planner. Do I have to pay her?

Hope not. If one considers a third marriage, a third wedding important. Heck, I sure do. I hope Noel does, too. I also hope Brie will have good advice and not charge much. After all, I shoved her onto Derek's hospital bed; now, she's shoving me into wedding plans.

Blessedly, remembering the extravagant outfit she purchased

on my credit card at Destination Maternity, the girl does have good taste. Maybe she can help me chose a gown; one appropriate to my age and *stature*. Now, that's a nice, generic word.

She blushes a bit, light strawberry. She must be reserving crimson cheeks for her assessment of my thighs.

I nod, and sniff, then press the offending olfactory appendage against the bathroom mirror. I hold up my 7x magnifying mirror and don't see the straggly nose hairs. Maybe I don't have on the right glasses, the reading glasses. Do I need to read my nose hairs? I stick a pinkie finger in one nostril and feel them. Lots of them. Maybe Brie is right. If nothing else they annoy me, now that I've been introduced to them. I make a decision.

"Call your waxer." I am referring to the one she went to before marrying Derek, before leaving Scottsdale, before she started sporting the big bump. Isn't that what all the famous and wannabe famous actresses call their pregnancies? The bump.

My appointment is for tomorrow. Will it hurt? That's my biggest concern, other than the exorbitant cost. I used to get my legs and underarms waxed in my forties. Cost an arm and a leg, pun intended. But, Falor, my waxer, assured me that when I went through the "Big Change in the Sky," as she called it, I would no longer need her services. She was right. I thought I was free of her solicitous administrations, her blowing on the tongue depressor globbed with wax to cool it. I thought I was over making a choice between hot wax and rose wax.

I pull Old Sassy into a parking spot and breathe hard. Brie is with me, clasping my hand hard. "This is not a death knell, Mamma. It's a good thing. You will be so pleased," she smiles, but her lips quiver.

Jamie, the attractive blonde with the nose diamond and a great smile, checks me in. "Welcome to Aura Salon," she says in a melodic voice. "Ashleigh's almost ready for you. Have a seat in the Spa while you're waiting, and help yourself to water from the fridge."

The spa lighting is dim, kind of spooky. I know it's supposed to be relaxing, but I prefer to see my surroundings. A tall, slim, strawberry blonde with flowing tresses appears to greet us. Brie has to help heft me out of the super deep sofa. Guess she's been sitting on the edge, or Ashleigh would be hefting both of us.

Ashleigh, waxer in charge, is sweet and adorable, and unfortunately only thirty-plus. Perfect body, perfect smile, perfect attitude. There's nothing I don't like about her. She is genuine. Very real. Makes me comfortable.

I heave myself onto the waxing table, feet elevated at least twelve inches above my head. Whoa. Starting to get dizzy. Must be my low blood pressure.

Ashleigh places two cool hands with long fingers on my brow.

"You all right, Ms. Wysinotski?" She got my name right! Girl is okay. I nod as best I can from my upside down position.

"Eyebrows first," she announces barely above a whisper.

Two minutes later. "All done, want to see?" She holds a magnified mirror on a tilt over my eyes.

"Really? I didn't even feel anything. Well, barely." It takes me a few seconds to focus. I'm not used to looking at my face upside down. "Wow! No scragglies. Nice, neat, well-shaped brows."

"I took away some of the shaggy thickness. Now you look five years younger." She smiles, and I believe it is genuine, but it's a bit hard to tell upside down.

"Momma, it's a huge dif. You look fab." Brie has been watching this whole process and fidgeting on the room's only chair while clutching my purse. "It really does make your face look younger, more alert."

Alert I can use, so I grin. Then the adorable Ashleigh makes her second announcement, slightly louder this time.

"Mrs. Wysinotski," she begins.

"Ashleigh, dear, please call me Betsy. Although you haven't struggled with it, there is no need for you to have to remember my complicated surname. Betsy is just fine." I blink my eyes under my new brows and smile. My face even feels different, lighter, more smiley. Why, oh, why did I keep The Jerk's last name? Especially such a hard one to pronounce and remember.

"Press on, Ashleigh. I want to leave here a new glowing-faced woman."

"All right. But, I need to inform you this might be a bit painful the first time. Nose hairs are harder to extract, and noses are sensitive." She looks upside down into my eyes under my newly groomed brows. "You want to go for it?"

I do, and I tell her so. I hear her fiddling in her bowl of wax and she says, "Here goes. Just relax."

I close my eyes, use my shrink's relaxing technique and sigh. Whoa! Imagine a golf ball being thrust up your nostril. A moderately hot one with a popsicle stick stuck in it.

Actually, it doesn't hurt at all with Ashleigh's delicate cool fingers massaging the side of my nose. Until… "Ready?"

"Sure."

She grabs the stick and yanks quickly, then presses lightly on the nostril with those cool fingers. "You okay? We got a lot of ugly hairs out of there. Wanna see?"

Not on your life. "No thanks. I trust you."

"Now for the left nostril." She proceeds, but at least I have an idea of what to expect. Maybe it's better if I don't. I think I'd rather go through childbirth again, even at my age. But, it would be counter-productive, or maybe non-productive, to have one hairy nostril and one clean one. I close my eyes so tight I'm seeing stars. I feel the ripping tug.

"Got 'em!" she exclaims. "Wow, Mrs. Wys…Betsy, you are a great client."

She hands me a tissue for the tears streaming out of my eyes. I dab. Start to sit up until she tells me to relax, again.

"Just have to pluck a few errant hairs with the tweezers that the wax didn't get."

Those hurt almost more than the waxing, but I wince and endure.

Once again, the mirror is held to my face. I admit I am amazed at how clean my nostrils look. Did I not see those straggly hairs there before, or did I just ignore them?

Ashleigh lightly massages my face with some Aloe cream, so cooling. I am ready to roll, if only I can get up without swooning and passing out.

Brie and Ashleigh each take a hand and hoist me. I sit for a few minutes until life comes back in focus.

"You did great, Momma." Brie's made-up cat grin makes me feel great.

"I do feel like a new woman, younger. Thanks for encouraging me, Brie. Needed it."

"I'm glad you finally took some advice from me." She clears

her throat dramatically. "Now for the smile."

FORTY TWO

I am wondering what Brie has up her sleeve next. Smile could mean lipstick, teeth or Botox lips. Not that, please. I hate injections of any kind, although I did succumb to the flu shot. But shots in my lips? No!

"Don't panic, Momma." She must see the expression of horror on my contorted face. I glance in Old Sassy's rear view mirror and bare my teeth. Straight. Not bad for a coffee drinker, gum chewer, former smoker. Lips a bit thin, but normal looking. Thank goodness something on my body is thin.

I approach Walgreen's and Brie says, "Pull in here."

As we enter the store, she takes my elbow and steers me to the toothpaste aisle. She pulls several boxes off the shelves and studies the directions on each. What? I can't read for myself?

"This one," she claims waving it in the air.

"What is it?"

"Strips. Easy to use. Only problem," she says grinning, "is you can't talk for at least half an hour…twice a day."

"Oh."

"Or eat."

"Not at all?"

"No, silly Momma. No eating while strips are in place."

"Oh." Something has taken away my power of speech. Unusual for me. Instead of speaking I raise my new eyebrows high. This produces excitement in Brie.

"Wow, Momma, your face sure looks good. Final touches coming up. Starting tonight."

I'm glad she's happy and having fun with my new and improved visage, but I wonder if cranky Noel will even notice. "Brie, don't you dare say a word about this to Noel, or Bett. Let's see if they notice on their own, 'kay?"

"Works for me. It will be fun to surprise them."

I worry, though. What if neither notices my new appearance, my new younger face? I decide I'm tough, I can take it. Can't I?

"Have we done enough makeover for today? Please? I'm tired."

"Well, Momma, I did have one more thing planned. Guess it could wait for tomorrow." She rubs her now almost enormous belly as we approach the Walgreen's cash register. The lady behind the counter turns the box of dental strips over a few times and smiles.

"These really work?" I'm not sure if it's a question or a statement. Then I realize her smile is all stained teeth between her lips. Guess it was a question.

"I hope so," I say as I whip out my credit card.

"Let me know. I might try them." I hope she does. I hope they are miracle strips. My bold mouth overcomes me.

"I bet you get a discount working here. Maybe you should go ahead and buy some. I'm sure the store has a good return policy."

"Good idea. Maybe I will." She closes her mouth into a tight smile that covers her teeth and rings up the purchase. I hope I didn't offend her. Maybe I encouraged her.

When Brie and I reach home, we rush into my air conditioned condo in sticky clothes and fan ourselves by grabbing the fronts of our blouses and flapping them in and out toward our sweaty bodies. We laugh and hug and almost stick together. "We are Velcro," she giggles.

"Gotta eat," I announce. "Makeovers make me hungry."

I am pulling greens out of the fridge by the bundles. Arugala, red-leaf lettuce, kale, spinach. Yum. "You wash while I start a chicken breast to poaching in the micro."

She moans and turns on the faucet. Brie is not the most domestic woman I know. In fact, Bett is a few percentages better.

"I guess I'd better start learning how to do this cooking stuff to impress Derek," she groans.

"Or maybe to eat healthy?" I say raising those new eyebrows.

"Yeah, that, too."

"Watch how I do this," I insist. I place the skinless breast in a glass meatloaf pan, pour a bit of skinny wine over it, plus about a fourth cup of water. I could use all water, or citrus juice, but the alcohol in the low-cal wine boils away, and gives the chicken a great flavor.

"What's that?" she asks as I start to sprinkle on herbs and spices.

"First one is bouquet garni, a combo of celery, thyme, bay leaf, parsley and marjoram. Then heavy on the dill weed, garlic powder and onion powder. Last is seasoned salt and seasoned pepper."

"You don't measure?" She cocks her head. "I thought good cooks followed recipes."

"Nope. Really good cooks are creative, just wing it." I think I've shocked her because the cocked head starts to nod. "You done washing and drying the greens?"

"I have to dry them, too? I shook them off."

I pat them with paper towels and put her in charge of tearing them into bite size pieces. She wants to use a knife, but I explain that cutting bruises the tender leaves. When she groans again I say, "Look, Brie. I didn't complain about the makeover, so please don't complain about tearing lettuce." I wink. She winks back.

"Now is the fun part." I dump the pieces from the bowl into the basket of my salad spinner.

She pulls the cord, and whir! The greens spin around dropping residue water from the pieces into the cavity of the spinner. "That," she claims, "is so cool. Where'd you get this?"

"Uh, I've had it a long time. Nice, huh?" I refrain from telling her it was a wedding gift from my college roommate, Dee, when I married her father, The Jerk. Dee brought it all the way from Florida almost forty years ago. In those days she was able to carry a wrapped present on the plane and stow it in overhead. The bow wasn't even crushed. The Jerk looked at it like "what a dumb gift." But, Dee, who loved to cook, knew I did also. We had made a lot of salads during our college years, mostly to watch our weight.

Still, decades later the spinner has been a godsend in my business.

"I want one," Brie says with authority.

"You can't buy them like this anymore with the cord to pull. They now have a knob you have to turn. More effort. Takes all the fun out of spinning."

"Maybe I can find one on EBay. If not, I still want whatever is made now."

She watches me toss the greens with black olive slices, pine nuts, cherry toms and thin slices of red onion. I sense she's making a mental list of ingredients. I find a dressing in the fridge I bought at Sam's Club the other day. This is not the time for a homemade dressing lesson. I'm hungry, and so is she.

I hand her the bottle. "Pour this very lightly over the greens. Not too much. We can always add more." She complies, carefully, and I toss again and taste a small leaf. She does, too. "Yum. Perfect, Momma."

The microwave binged a few minutes ago, so I take out the fragrant chicken and slice it thin on a cutting board. We each serve our own greens on the plates I put in the freezer earlier. "Take some chicken slices and lay them on top," I direct. She does and actually fans them out appealingly. I'm impressed. "Now for the grated Parmesan cheese. Sprinkle some over your salad, and we are good to go."

We perch at my new kitchen table tucked neatly into benches under a window. It's not as opulent as Bett's, but it's nice and cozy. Joining hands we both pray silently. I am so grateful that God has given my daughter back, and her husband back to her. He always comes through. If only I had more faith.

We finish our salad dinner and scrape the plates clean, forks singing over them. Neither of us wants dessert, an unnecessary indulgence.

"Okay, Momma. I haven't forgotten. Go brush your teeth and rinse out your mouth. It's strip time!

"Last stop is Kay's. But, I'm reserving that for a few days before your wedding. And after your cast is off," she mumbles.

"Who is Kay?"

"It's a surprise. You will love this one. Promise."

FORTY THREE

I feel like a freak. I'm sure you've seen online photos of chimpanzees with their big mouths grinning in hilarity. Like they are making fun of we humans. That's the way I feel, and I'm sure I look the part.

I wonder what Dr. Kumar my dentist would say. She would probably be glad I was doing something proactive for my teeth. She did give me a sample box of strips about a year ago. They collected dust on my counter until I threw them away after I looked at the expiration date. I should probably fess up to Renuka (that's her given name) next time I'm in her office. It's too bad my Bible study moved from Wednesdays to Tuesdays. Wednesdays are her only days off, and she attended with me. I was blessed to find a Christian dentist, one who belongs to a Christian dental association. Maybe I will call her tomorrow and ask her opinion about Brie's choice of strips. Confession is good for the soul, and probably for the teeth, too.

Brie has me ensconced in The Jerk's brown reclining chair, although she doesn't know it was her father's since he abandoned her and me before she was born. I am trying to relax with my mouth open and a pasted grin on my face. How phony is that? The operative word is trying.

My eyes are closed and I start to repeat The Lord's Prayer, a technique for falling asleep that my prayer partner Jean recommends. Maybe if I can fall asleep, it would help. Then, if I do, my mouth might close and the whole ordeal will be a waste. Or, my jaw will drop slack, and I will snore. Oh, please not that, Lord. So embarrassing, even in front of my daughter.

What to do? Read. I grab a Joyce Meyer devotional and flip it open. How did I happen to come across the one about pride, especially selfish pride? Just as I settle in, a buzzer sounds, and Brie informs me my thirty minutes for tonight are over. That wasn't so bad. I think of that song from Annie. "You're never fully dressed without a smile." Yep, that's gonna be me. The new smile lady.

~

I have no clients today, unfortunately. My bank account is teetering on low, very low. I debate putting an ad in the paper, or on social media. That could be scary, though. I prefer word of mouth so I can trust where the referrals come from. Bett used to send me a lot of clients, but I guess she's busy taking care of my fiancé, the man I haven't had contact with for days.

I remind myself it's early fall in Arizona, the second hottest time of year here. Many Arizonans have split for cooler climes, mostly California. I don't blame them. If I had the funds, I would, too. Soon Snowbirds will return to their second homes and want to entertain. Fall and early winter are the best times for me. I know that, so why do I stress?

Brie is filing her nails when I get a phone call. The number looks familiar, but it's not in my safe list. I decide to risk it and answer. "Who?" I can't believe it. Nancy Faraday, reluctant, scared, new hostess Nancy from Memorial Day.

The conversation from my end varies from "What?," "Really?," "I'm so glad." to "I sure can. Give me the details and the menu." I hesitate a second. "Okay if I bring my daughter? She's about your age."

"Who was that?" Brie looks at me suspiciously. Shouldn't she be visiting Derek? Well, I can't run their marriage, but I'd like to. Then I remember he is temporarily in a physical rehab facility, an effort on his part to get intense physical therapy and up the ante so he can help take care of the baby when it's born. Returning to work at his engineer job wouldn't hurt either.

"That was Nancy, a former client. A lovely young, newly

married, woman." I stopped explaining. How could I explain that Nancy has become close to my heart? Would Brie understand the affection I have for her?

"What did she want? A salade?" Brie pronounces it sarcastically in her boggled French.

I sigh and try to put aside her snideness. Take a deep breath, Betsy. "Yes, and no. She is throwing a surprise party for her husband and wants me to prepare all the food." I stop to think about what Nancy said. "She is a little green in hospitality, though. She's starting with me as food prepper, but she has no theme and no decorations in mind."

"So, you are the caterer? Aren't most caterers hired by event coordinators?"

"I guess so. Maybe I should try to do the whole thing. Maybe you could help me."

"Me?"

"You used to throw great parties when you were just a teen. Great themes, great decorations." I raise my new eyebrows and zero in on her.

She ignores my flattery. "What's the occasion? Birthday?"

"Not sure. I will call back and ask. What do you say?"

I can hardly hear Nancy's voice, barely a whisper. I can tell she's walking outside because of the crickets chirping in the background.

"Can't say much now, Betsy. Just a party to honor him on the day we met. Call it an 'I love you' party. Ideas?"

I tell her I have an event coordinator in mind, and promise to get back to her after Brie and I brainstorm.

~

We have so much fun reminiscing.

"Remember the Girls Night Out party? And the Madonna party when you all sang Material Girl and I videotaped it? How about the…"

Finally, we get serious.

"Brie, we have to be very careful not to make this seem like a teen dream party. Nancy's husband is a big time pillar of the community, a benefactor, an important guy. This can't be a silly party. Maybe a serious, slightly silly, party. You understand?"

She nods, and just as we start to brainstorm, my cell rings.

Drat!

I pick it up and before I can say a word, "Betsy!" the voice booms. "You ignoring me?"

"Why would I do that, Noel? You don't need me. You are getting pampered by Bett and Consuela."

"Who? Oh, the housekeeper. She quit." Now, that's a revelation.

"Really? Why?"

"Not sure. Maybe thought Bett asked too much of her, for me." I hear his sigh on the other end of the phone. "I don't demand or need much. Just want some special perks, and my Betsy girl."

The man is insufferable. Have I hooked up with another jerk?

My hand holding the phone is shaking. If Noel had been here, I would have tossed the phone at his face. I forgot I had the cell on speaker.

In a flash the phone is grabbed from my trembling hand. Brie is screaming into it.

"Now listen here, Noel. You stop playing games with my mother. And, tell Bett too. Also" she adds for emphasis. She sucks in a breath, grabs the phone so tight her hand is shaking. Then she starts prancing around. I stand stunned, like Lot's wife.

Brie marches through the living room, goes in the bathroom and slams the door. I saunter over to the door and press my ear against it. Nada. I can hear nothing. Drat!

When she emerges she slams my phone on the counter. "I set everything straight." She says with a smirk on her face.

FORTY FOUR

Ice on my head.

Do I still have a fiancé, or have I been abandoned again?

"Gotta go, Momma. Getting Derek from the PT rehab." She slams the door. I guess that means she is taking my car. I hope Old Sassy doesn't mind a lead foot.

I am melting into the disgusting brown chair when I hear it.

Door opens. Brie back already?

Soft, steady footsteps approach. Should I be scared? Brie always forgets to look doors, so maybe this is an unlikely intruder, like in mystery novels. Naw, I'm not on anyone's hit list. Yet.

I decide to lay low, ignore the footsteps, pretend not to hear.

I feel a soft kiss on my forehead. Feels nice. Oops. "Who's here?"

"Me, Betsy. Noel."

"My reluctant fiancé?" I fling the bag of ice off my head to the floor. I open my eyes wide under the new brows.

Noel's reaction is not what I expected. "What have you done with your face? Where is Betsy's face?"

A chuckle starts deep in my throat. Then I start to giggle, and it mushrooms into a guffaw. I am shaking in the brown chair, heaving with hilarity. He noticed!

Then the old Betsy takes over.

"Why didn't you come sooner? What took you so long?

Having too much fun and attention at Bett's?"

"I...I wasn't sure you wanted me. Yes, I have been pampered at Bett's. But, I miss our special relationship. And, I miss holding you in my arms. I am such a jerk."

"Don't call yourself that. Don't! Ever." I struggle up out of the chair and my cast catches on the throw rug. I begin to fling forward, just as Noel grabs me. His strong arms are wrapped around me, and I look up into crayon blue eyes that focus on my face. I feel secure, loved. Until...

"What *did* you do to your face, Betsy?"

"You don't like it?" If he doesn't I will grow the shaggy eyebrows back, and the nose hairs. I will stain my teeth again.

He holds me away from him with his hands on my shoulders. For a better look? "Wow. I love it. It's a new you. But," he looks directly into my eyes with his crayon blue ones, "I loved you just the way you were. Still," he hesitates, "you look brilliant, younger. Will I be marrying a younger woman? A trophy wife?"

~

"I dreamt about you."

"Me?" Nancy's pretty face breaks into a wide smile.

"Yes. You were folding napkins."

I chuckle, she giggles.

"You taught me how." She turns toward Brie who is shifting to get comfortable on what I guess is an expensive chaise lounge from Horchow, or maybe Ballard Designs. One of those mail order places that only sell outstandingly lavish outdoor furniture. "Your mom taught me a lot," she states. "But, mostly, she gave me confidence."

Brie seems to be processing that. I know because her face wrinkles.

"You are so lucky, Brie. No, you are *blessed* to have Betsy for a mom."

Okay, Nancy. I really appreciate the accolades, but stop the mushy stuff. You will make Brie jealous. But, it would be nice to hear those comments from my Brie.

Brie squirms, then lights up unexpectedly. "She is a wonderful mom, Nancy."

I have to steady myself to keep from tipping over the patio chair I'm sitting on across from Nancy at the glass table. TY, Lord!

"Thanks, both of you. Now, let's continue and plan this party."

I let Brie take the lead since she is now the official event coordinator, if Nancy hires her.

We bat ideas around and Brie asks a lot of questions. "Tell us exactly where Lester and you met. What was the occasion? Party, blind date? Special place?"

Nancy sighs and closes her beautiful almond eyes. "It was at a friend's wedding. We were both bored and separately walked out to the hotel lake. Just wandering. Escaping I guess. We could hear the music a bit, playing old tunes. Some I didn't recognize, but Lester did. He's a few years older than I am. I remember he said, "Hi, I'm Lester, fifth wheel at this party." His eyes captured mine, and he said, "You look sad. Beautiful, but sad." I wanted to deny that, the sad part. But, it was true. I had just broken up from a long relationship that was going nowhere, and I felt lonely. Even sad. I made an effort to smile at him and held out my hand. 'I'm Nancy. Another extra wheel.' I said.

"'Recognize that tune?'" he asked.

"I had no clue."

"It's Love Comes Around. An old melody." He whispered. He held out his hands and we danced, there in the moonlight shimmering on the lake. We danced on grass, my high heels sticking into the ground. Finally, we just swayed. Close. It was magical.

"We went for coffee, abandoning the speeches and cake-cutting. And," she paused, "the rest is history, as they say."

All three of us had tears in our eyes. I picked up my pen to make notes, but Nancy interrupted.

"It was the best, most wonderful night of my life. I want to memorialize it. I want to honor him, us."

FORTY FIVE

Derek is in the guest room bed recovering from intense physical therapy that left him drained. Brie and I are lounging in my small living room.

"Shouldn't you be with him?"

"Nope. He's sound asleep, snoring like a baby. He needs his rest."

"So, how are we going to plan this party?"

Brie holds her nose and says, "It stinks."

"B…but…"

"I know. We have to do it. But, what? It's so nebulous, vague, unclear what she wants." She presses her fingers to her forehead and wrinkles her nose. "I don't get it. Why doesn't she do a birthday or anniversary party? Something more concrete that has a specific meaning."

"Nancy's sort of scattered. She means well, but she isn't very organized, even in her thoughts."

"You think?"

I raise my new eyebrows and nod my head. I've never had this problem before. Most clients are specific, know exactly what they want, give me a detailed menu. Nancy's wishes are a mystery, obviously even to her. I guess we will have to make up her mind for her.

We mull over all she shared with us, the meeting of two

lonelies, the lake, the dance on the grass during someone else's wedding reception. The coffee date after.

"That's it!"

"What? Coffee?"

"Yes. We have a coffee bar with unique unusual coffees."

"Sounds boring."

"Not if we make it special."

"Like how?"

"It will have various flavored coffees, plus a strong imported one, maybe from Costa Rica, one of the coffee capitals of the world. We'll also have a really good French Decaf for people like me." I see a slight nod, but I'm sure I still see a quizzical expression.

"What about people who like to drink?" Brie squeezes her eyes, maybe remembering events she and Derek attended. "Lots of big wigs in the corporate world want a martini or rum and coke, or scotch. Won't those people think it's a boring party? Maybe even leave early."

"Mmm. I remember at the barbeque she had big metal buckets filled with ice that held beer and wine. I didn't pay much attention because I was flipping burgers." (I am refraining from telling Brie about the ones that landed on Noel's shoes. Another time.) I don't recall Nancy or Lester drinking, but I wasn't paying much attention to what was in their hands.

"How about a self-serve mini-bar of the kinds of alcohol that can be added to coffee? Like Irish Whiskey. Isn't there another?"

"I dunno." Brie shrugs. "I haven't drunk since our wedding, and I certainly can't now that I'm expecting."

Suddenly, she pops up, well forward, not up, from her position on the sofa. "Isn't there some kind of fake champagne? For non-alcoholic celebrations."

The next day I go to Total Wine. The wine connoisseur guides me to some impressive looking bottles, pretty fancy. He assures me no one will know because the labels look so authentic, like the alcohol-based stuff.

I realize I never asked Nancy. Maybe she'd prefer the real stuff. I call her, semi-reluctantly.

"Oh, I forgot to tell you," she says. "We don't drink. I've never liked the stuff, doesn't agree with me. Tummy aches, headaches. Lester is AA, Alcoholics Anonymous. But," she assures me, "it doesn't bother either of us if others imbibe.

"Maybe if we put a definite end time of the party on the invitation? Would that help, give people a clue? So we don't have lingerers who've drunk too much?"

She's getting there to being the perfect hostess. "Great idea, Nancy. We can even say on the invite that a toast to the two of you will be at a certain time. Most people leave right after a toast. Sound okay?"

"Great. Those who want to stay a bit longer can sit and sip coffee."

I go back to planning the food. All appetizers and hors d'ourves. Keep it light and keep it simple – my motto. At least for this party. I start to list ideas to share with Brie, but seeing them makes me so hungry I fix a salad for us both. Derek got Wildflower Café Wild Mushroom Soup, his favorite, that Brie ran to get in Old Sassy. Things are looking up.

Derek is healing, working hard to become fully active. Brie is being a good wife, somewhat solicitous, but kind and attentive. I have a major client. The only hitch in the gitalong is Noel.

FORTY SIX

I am so tempted to call him Jerk Number Two.

It's true, he didn't leave me pregnant, like his predecessor over two decades ago. But, he has sloughed me off for Bett's administrations. When I stayed at Bett's after the fire in my condo, I loved being there…for a few days. Then I got bored and lonely and raring to go back to my life.

Seems not so with Noel. The man loves to be pampered, succumbs to it, wallows in it. I can't do this for him. I am not the solicitous doormat type. He knows that. I don't scrape or bow.

At least not to any man, only God. Well, maybe a little bit to my mother. And, once in a while, a tiny bit to Bett because she always seems so flustered and troubled. I did to Brie, but let's call that acquiescing. She is, after all, going to give me another grandchild.

My event planning partner interrupts my wandering thoughts.

"Momma, I got it!" A Cheshire grin splits her face with obvious pride, and she doesn't even know Snoopy. "You," she points at me with a wiggling finger, "you are the salad lady. So, let's do a salad bar. But, not just any salad bar, a unique one."

I close my eyes and raise my chin. It helps me to concentrate. "You mean with lots of unusual ingredients? Sort of like that Fresh Tomatoes restaurant?" She nods, and the grin actually gets wider.

"Yep. Pastas and protein and lots of fun toppings. And," she continues, as she tilts her head for emphasis, "people who are holding a salad plate find it difficult to hold a glass at the same time. I realize we will have to have tables, some, with chairs, but if there aren't enough to seat everyone, some will have to stand. Those that are seated," she goes on, "will be busy chatting, and those standing will have to put down their glasses in order to eat."

"Are you sure you were never involved in PTA?" That's where I learned to have meetings in small rooms so when all the seats were taken others had to stand. Made the meetings look filled to the brim; better than loads of empty seats. Also, it crammed people together so they had to introduce themselves. "Never mind. In five years you will be."

We make food lists. Potato salad (although not pasta, it's filling and absorbent—of alcohol), pasta shell salad, no long stringy pasta—too hard to incorporate in a salad.

"We should have Aunt Lottie's chicken salad, too. It's yummy on greens."

"Absolutely. And Sprout's cranberry bread, and those wild rice crackers from Sam's Club. I think they're called RiceWorks? Any Wildflower bread is a winner, too. Some guests might want to make a sandwich." She puts down her pen and chews on the end of it like she gnawed on a pencil when she was a kid. "Do you think my crab appetizer in the round bread is right? Or, not?"

My mouth salivates at the mention of it. "I think it's a nice addition, but it would need to be on a warming tray. The Party People rental company can provide one, plus a deep container filled with ice for the chicken salad. A little fish, a little chicken will be a nice touch."

We agree on unusual veggies and fruits that usually aren't part of a salad bar. "Let's do kalamata olives, kiwi slices, apple wedges, artichokes, berries—lots, all different kinds. And lots of different cheeses for toppings, not just croutons, so old school." Brie keeps making a list, and her head is bobbing.

"No croutons. But, tomorrow," she says, "we go to Fresh Tomatoes, even Fry's Signature Market, and check out the salad bars for ideas. Okay?"

I agree and feel more comfortable with our plan. I feel obligated to call Fancy Nancy, as I've taken to calling her in my head. We do need her blessing before we put too much into this menu plan.

"Oh, Betsy!" I can almost see the grin on her lovely face. I can definitely hear it. "Brie is so clever. Wish I'd thought of that. But, that's why I have you two." I now hear the wheels spinning in her scattered brain. "What about dressings? Have you gotten that far?"

"Not yet, but we will." I hang up and start the brainstorming with Brie again.

I put my fingers on my laptop to google unique salad dressings when my cell rings. Drat, it's Jerk Number Two wannabe. "Yes, Noel. What is it?" Do I sound curt enough?

"Betsy, Baby, anything wrong?"

I am not good at lying. Mutiny, maybe. The fifth commandment comes to mind again.

I repeat. "What do you want, Noel?" I'm grinding my teeth so hard I can almost feel my gums. "Make it quick, I'm busy."

"Busy doing what?"

Is the man dense or stubborn? Either way, he is driving me nuts.

"Noel, you are older than I am. Surely, you've heard the expression 'None of your beeswax." Now I feel contrite. That was pretty nasty of me. He hangs up.

I go back to my list of ingredients for the salad bar. Low and behold, the annoying cell phone rings again. I am tempted to click that little button on the top that silences it, but since it's Noel I succumb and press 'accept.' The soles of my Merrill sandals are beating a rhythm on the tile floor. I love these sandals, have them in three colors, so comfy, worth the expense.

"What is that sound I hear? Sounds like a slap-slap."

"It's me beating down the devil." I clench my teeth again. "What do you want? I'm in a very important meeting right now."

"Why'd you answer your phone?"

"Noel," I try hard to be civil. "Go back to whatever you were doing. I can't talk now. Please understand. We will talk tomorrow. Have a good night." I slam down the phone and put it on silent.

"Now, Brie, what were we doing?"

The expression on her face is almost contorted. It is definitely filled with questions.

"Momma, was that Noel? Were you mean to him?"

"Not mean, just angry." I take a deep breath, then blow it out loudly. "The man is dense, sometimes annoying, won't let up with the questions." The expression on her face is now puzzled, filled with *her* questions.

"B...but, you love him, right?" She fiddles with the pen she is using to write the list. "Maybe you should be more accepting? More tolerant? That's what you told me to do with Derek, Momma."

Gosh, darn and whatever. She is right. If Noel and I have any future together. I suck in my breath, grit my teeth again and call him back.

"Sorry, Noel." It is taking a few years off my life to say that. "Guess I was hasty, so involved in my latest project." He asks, I explain.

"Yes, Nancy is a sweetheart. She and Lester are old friends, used to be patients of mine. Surely you remember the Memorial Day party you cooked for them?"

How could I forget the hamburger that landed on his Topsider? "I remember, too well. You were so kind about my faux pas with the meat gracing your shoe." I clear my throat. A subversive way to buy time. Or, admit being a jerk myself.

Brie gives me a glare. When I don't respond she hefts herself out of her chair, wallows over to me and gives me a swift, light kick on my right shin.

"Ow!" I give her my nastiest scowl and stick out my tongue.

"Betsy. You okay?" Noel says. His voice sounds worried. I hope.

"Yes, fine. Well, sort of, maybe." A faint chuckle escapes my lips. "What does one do with a know-it-all daughter and an errant suitor?" I hear only silence on the other end. Or, can one actually hear silence. Like that old if a tree is falling in the woods thing? Or, when a leaf drops off a tree, is there any way to hear it? Dumb comparison, I know. Still, I wonder.

Can I really hear the wheels spinning in Noel's brain? It's not that hard when you love someone. You have a connection, even a brain connection. Surely, a heart connection.

Finally, he says good-bye. This time I do turn off my phone and put it in a drawer. I move to my trusty laptop and google Unique Salad Dressings. Brie asks why I don't use my phone, so much easier she claims.

"Do you notice, daughter dear, the eyeglasses I just perched on my nose?" She grins and nods, a combo that's becoming a habit with her. "That's why. I need big screen text, and someday you will, too," I say smugly.

"Wow, Brie, this is fun." She leans over my shoulder and points to the list of unique dressings.

"Try that one."

"Maple Vinaigrette? It has maple syrup in it. Weird for a salad dressing."

"So? Think of all the fruit we're serving. Let's whip some up and try it."

"How about the sesame dressing? That sounds good, too."

"Let's try them both. Pick one more."

I pick citronette dressing. It sounds light and sunshiny. Brie jots a list of ingredients for all three.

We check the cupboards, the pantry and the fridge. Blessedly, we have all the ingredients needed for each dressing. I am not in the mood to run to the market. Actually, I'm not in the mood to do almost anything. But, cooking is my fun, and experimenting is even more fun. We get to work.

Derek staggers into the small kitchen using his cane. He's still not good at this and bumps into the bar counter. "What are you two concocting?"

"Perfect word, Derek. That's exactly what we're doing. Have a seat and watch the maestros at work."

Brie lifts her hand in a semi-wave to him and blows him a kiss. She goes back to whipping maple syrup into canola oil. "It's not blending well," she says. "What if we try it with a light olive oil?"

"Okay. Play with it, but be sure to jot down what you did."

This is so much fun. I've always hated grating citrus fruit, but for this experiment—Naw. Fortunately, I have picked oranges and lemons from the trees in the common areas of our community. No way will I pay sixty-nine cents for a supermarket lemon when I can scoop them up by the bagsful for nothing. Only in a pinch would I use the kind of rind that comes in a little spice container. I even squeeze the lemons to extract the juice the recipe requires. Fresh is always better.

"Ouch!" Derek is rubbing his eye. Guess I got too vigorous with the lemon squeezing.

"Sorry. Didn't realize the juice would travel that far."

He nods. I suppose that means I'm forgiven. "Wanna be our dressing taster?" I figure he's a man, and men are more cowardly about new flavors. Women usually like to try new things, hardly complain even if they don't like them much. I remember Brie's brother, James, picking through tuna casserole and asking what those little round green things were. My theory is, if Derek has opinions about the dressings, they are either a go, or need more revision.

I place three tiny appetizer plates in front of him and a plastic bottle of spring water. I dip a piece of Romaine in each dressing and place them on the plates. "Take a bite. Savor it and then take a big sip of water between it and the next bite."

He agrees and spits out his first bite. Aw, oh. The maple dressing. But, to be sure, I replace the lettuce with a slice of apple. "Try it on this," I say. He does, and nods and grins. Does he have the same auto gesture Brie has? Or, maybe it's a tic.

"Really good on fruit. Makes all the diff." He asks for more.

"Nope. Gotta try the other two first." I can be so hardcore.

It seems he has mixed feelings, or tastes, about the others. He likes them okay, but one needs more salt and the other needs more "zip." I add salt and zip in the form of cayenne pepper, and he grins and nods. This grinning and nodding is getting to me. I know he has a voice.

Brie and I make adjustments to the recipes, enough to make them our own. Now, we just have to take samples to Fancy Nancy for approval.

~

It's almost noon. Nancy finally opens the door to my persistent bell-ringing and knocking. She has smeared mascara around her eyes and blinks rapidly. I grab her in a hug. "What's wrong?"

She clings to me, but only shakes her head. When she finally lets go I notice she has no ring on her finger. That scares me.

Brie grabs my arm. "Maybe we should come back another time, Momma."

"No! She needs us…now."

I steer Nancy to the opulent butter-leather sofa in her living room and plunk her down. She grabs the afghan on its arm and throws it across her chest. Her face is a blank canvas, and she is staring into the space beyond. Suddenly, tears cascade like Niagara Falls down her lovely, but pale, cheeks. She makes no sound, but her shoulders heave.

"He left me."

It is a simple statement, but filled with pain and unbelief. I, of course, ask the stupid question.

"Why?"

She, of course, states the age-old, obvious answer. "I don't know."

FORTY SEVEN

"Noel, I need your help!" I have left Nancy with Brie holding her and locked myself in another fancy powder room. "Noel! Get your rear in gear. Answer the phone."

Yes, I'm shouting which makes no sense on a cell phone unless the receiving one is deliberately on speaker. I just keep hoping as I press redial a zillion times that he will hear whatever musical announcement he has programmed to signify his phone is ringing. It doesn't help that I've automatically turned the bathroom fan on, and I can hardly hear the ringer on the other end.

It's been at least ten minutes since I left Nancy with Brie. Guilt is consuming me. Then, I remember, Brie has experience in the husband leaving the wife scenario. Maybe I did the right thing. I tip-toe into the designer living room and hold my breath. Brie and Nancy are sitting side by side and holding hands, and…quietly talking.

"Tell me again," Brie says matter of factly. "It helps to repeat it, to go over it." She should know. Nancy looks down at Brie's belly and nods.

"Guess you have some experience in this," she states. Brie grins slightly and nods. A repeat performance. I suppose I should be used to it by now.

"He…he." Nancy gulps sucking down tears.

~

Brie hoists herself into Old Sassy. I guess I should have helped her, but my mind is in a whirl twirling up to the glistening stars, stars seldom seen in an Arizona night. Usually the moon is gleaming and shining, holding court. Tonight, it is blurred a bit by either a recalcitrant cloud or mist. That, according to the weather gurus, means possible rain. How I wish. Tomorrow morning, just in case, I will dig out those cute rain boots I bought on sale last summer at Kohl's.

"Momma," Brie whines, "are you getting in?"

"Oops, sorry. I was counting the stars." I climb in, turn the key and nothing. Not even a sputter. I try again three times. "Sassy's not feeling well tonight," I say to Brie.

"Have you looked at the gas gauge, Momma?"

Oops, again. Yep, the little light is on.

She stares at me with a half trusting, half mean expression. "I guess I forgot."

Brie shakes her head like one does when trying to make sense of a fool.

"What now?" she says. "There's no gas station close to walk to."

"No, but there's Noel." This is exactly what I've been waiting for, a reason to get Noel out of Bett's for an emergency situation. It's time he moved his sorry rear and came to my rescue.

Thirty minutes later he pulls up in his "other car," the Mercedes S65AMG.

OMG!

~

"Fancy meeting you here. Hello, Brie." He steps slowly out of his car leaving the door open. Maybe to make a quick get-away?

"Hi, Noel. Guess we're in trouble. I hope you can help. I need to get back to Derek." Brie can sound so little girlish when she wants to get a favor.

I suppose I taught her that. Feminine wiles. I use them myself. And, I'm kind of proud of it. It's a gift.

"Noel, you have no idea how grateful I am that you came. We were really stuck here." I pause to bat my lashes beneath my new brows. "I hope we didn't get you out of your sick bed." I bat again. "We didn't know who else to call, and I knew you'd be concerned. Bett, too." I search his puzzled face. Did I overdo it too much?

Still, he showed up, and I am really grateful.

Oops, I forgot to hug him. I throw myself against his chest and collide with a gas can he is holding in front of it. "Betsy," he says with a snort, "you are still the master of unusual entrances. Very dramatic."

"Now, can we get to the problem and solve it?" He pushes me away like some fly that's landed on his sleeve. I stumble and end up in Brie's arms, almost tumbling her, too.

"Noel," she screams, "what are you doing? Why are you treating my mother this way?"

To his credit his ears turn radish red, and he mumbles, "Sorry." Like that's an apology?

He ambles to Old Sassy with gas can in hand and bangs on her little door that is supposed to open to reveal the hole in which to put in the nozzle to fill the tank. Uh, oh. Sassy's little door does not cooperate. I get a metal nail file out of my voluminous purse and try to pry it. No deal.

"Momma," Brie chirps, "have you turned the key on?"

I'm sure she knows, as I do, one should never turn on the car when trying to fill with gasoline. Still, I jump back in the driver's seat and turn the key. Voila!

After the reluctant little door opens, I turn off the key. Guess I learned something new about Old Sassy. Even a trick from Brie.

Noel slaps the side of the car and says, "Get in. Try it."

I do. It starts. I jump out to give him a kiss, but he is already back in his shiny Mercedes, engine started and easing forward out of Nancy and Lester's long circular driveway. The coward.

The runaway? The scaredy-cat? The ingrate? My mind is tumbling to find the right adjective to describe his appalling behavior.

"Momma, let's go. I am worried about Derek." Brie brings me back to the present as she hefts herself into the passenger seat pulling up by the handy little grip above the passenger door. Thank goodness she is worrying about her husband. Obviously, she has more sensitivity than I've given her credit for. I remind myself she's a good kid and has matured immensely in the last month. I need to honor that.

I reach across and squeeze her hand, but first thing on my mind is filling my gas tank. So important, necessary. Wouldn't you think?

"No, Momma. Take me home first, please."

After I zoom into the condo complex and give Brie three seconds to jump out of Sassy, I speed away to the closest gas station. Now, if only my credit card will work.

FORTY EIGHT

The supermarket gas station, the one where you can use your preferred customer card gas points, is crowded. I get in line behind a BMW SUV. It's huge tank intimidates Sassy. I can tell because she's starting to sputter and cough. Well, maybe because she's bordering on empty. Poor baby must be hungry. Finally, it's my turn. I pull up to the pump and jump out with my credit card in hand and collide with a woman in a green sweater. (Yes, a sweater in late summer in Arizona. In 104 degree heat in the evening. Must be a snowbird.)

"Sorry," she proclaims. "I must be on the wrong side." She gestures to another car in another aisle. "I thought you had to pull the hose all the way around. Not used to this station." She is referring to how one can pull the long hose around one's car if the car gas tank is on the side opposite from the filling tank.

"That's okay. I guess you misunderstood. The hoses are long so you can pull them all the way around your car if you need to." I smile at her ineptitude, and she nods.

I max my card out at $3.37 a gallon, even with the fuel point discounts. Sassy slurps up a lot. Realizing I need to use the rest room, as well as buy more salad greens, I steer Sassy to a parking spot near the market entrance. I tug on the restroom door to leave as it gets shoved in my face with force. It's the same green sweater woman. She grins. "Wanna dance?" she says with a twinkle in her eye.

"Let's hum a tune," I say grinning. "Thanks for your sense of humor," I yell back to her as she enters and I exit. She makes an abrupt one-eighty and clasps my elbow before the door closes. "My name is Muriel. It's so nice to meet you—"

I fill in the blank. "Betsy."

To my surprise, maybe consternation, she throws her arms around me in a hug. I am a bit bewildered, but should I be alarmed? Is she one of "those" people who have to hug everyone in sight, or is she just being nice because of our earlier gas station situation? Or, is she lonely? I am about to find out.

"Forgive me, Betsy. I know I am overly forward. But, you were so kind at the gas station, and…I've been so lonely since I moved here." Her eyes are moist and her lips tremble. "Forgive me," she repeats.

A lot goes through my mind very quickly. She could be a scam artist hoping to make a connection to steal all my earthly goods. Or, she might truly be lonely and need a friend. Hebrews 13:2 comes to mind. "Do not forget to show hospitality to strangers, for by so doing some people have shown hospitality to angels without knowing it." I decide the Holy Spirit has put Muriel on my heart, and possibly in my life.

I am about to find out.

~

I park Sassy in an open space in my condo's parking lot and gesture to Muriel to park in another open spot. We climb out of our respective vehicles, and she rushes to hug me again. I notice she smells good, possibly Jessica McClintock, my old favorite. For the first time I really notice her attire. I've never been big on labels, but some are obvious, even to plebeian moi.

She is wearing a Ralph Lauren sweater set, (yes, in green), and a pair of cut-offs that are probably from Chico's. I also notice her car. A newish Lexus in black. Very trendy, understated. Her short blondish-grayish hair is styled in a bob, and her earrings are either real, or fake diamond studs. She is not lacking possessions, obviously not poor. Just poor in the human department according to her.

I clasp her elbow and steer her toward my front door. "You sure about this?" she says. "We've only known each other twenty minutes."

I nod. "Taking a chance." I notice she's wearing one of those new cross necklaces where the cross lies sideways. I've been wanting one, but haven't gotten around to searching for it. "You a Christian?" I boldly ask. One of my favorite authors says God wants us to be bold. Well, I'm certainly not timid, but I'm not sure He meant to be bold this way.

"Yes, sure am. I sensed you were, too, from the advertisement on your van." Her grin shows teeth white as dandelion fluff against blood red lips. Startling contrast, but nice. "I suppose," she ruminates as I open the door, "anyone could call their salads heavenly. But, I decided to trust my instincts."

"Momma, who're you talking to?" Brie waddles out of the bedroom, her face all screwed up with concern. "Who's this? Who are you?" Good old diplomatic Brie.

"I'm Muriel, your mother's new friend." The lady in green extends a manicured hand to Brie who looks at it suspiciously, then finally grasps it in a squeeze. Maybe a little too hard I decide as I notice Muriel's eyebrows rise dramatically.

"This is my daughter, Brie," I offer. "Like the cheese." I can't resist a chuckle even though Brie hates it when I add that codicil to introductions. She glares at me, piercing my eyes with invisible daggers.

"Sit down, Muriel." I gesture to the sofa and plunk myself in an adjacent chair and tuck one foot under my ample derriere. "Brie, before you sit down, would you please get Muriel and me a glass of iced tea? There's a pitcher in the fridge." Now I feel the invisible daggers in the back of my head. I don't care. It's payback time for all the money I spent on maternity duds.

Brie practically slams two filled glasses on the coffee table. Two napkins flutter next to each. Muriel and I each have to reach midair to catch them. Brie is being a snot. I'm embarrassed. Even though she's twenty-five years old, I am tempted to treat her like a naughty toddler. Again, I think that maybe I didn't punish her enough when she was one. If I did, it didn't sink in and compute through the years.

"Brie." I turn full-face to her. "I know you aren't feeling terrific. I know you're uncomfortable, so maybe you should hang out with Derek while Muriel and I get to know each other." I want to say, "You rude little snippet, get out!" Now, that would be bold.

Turning back to my new friend I explain. "Derek is Brie's husband who is resting in the guest bedroom. He had a tragic accident and is still recovering." Muriel's eyebrows shoot up again over super-sized eyes. I know it's cliché to think pizza pie proportions, but Muriel's eyes do get very large. Chocolate covered donuts might be a better description.

"Wha...what happened? If you don't mind my asking?"

I just love it when people use proper grammar. Most of us would say "me asking." Even me, I. Drat!

"Muriel, before I answer, with Brie's permission of course, would you mind telling me what you do, or did, for a living?" I smile my sweetest, hoping to put her at ease. It's gotta be English teacher, author, even possibly etiquette guru. Gotta be.

She smiles back, and I sense her warming up. I just don't expect the surprise.

"I am, was, still am, a licensed physical therapist. But not," she adds, "in this state." She goes on. "I've also done a lot of extra stuff part-time. Like hospice, caregiver, cleaning person and server. Guess I'm a Jill of all trades. But, my training is in PT." Her mouth forms a narrow slit, and she makes an attempt to smile while folding her hands together on her lap. Are they trembling? I think so, slightly.

"Why'd you stop, give it up?" Diplomatic Brie, again.

"Life circumstances. I didn't 'give it up,' but needed to make a change." Do I see tears pooling in her eyes?

"Muriel is not here to be interrogated. I invited her as a friend." My turn to fling the invisible daggers at Brie. But, I'm not sure they are all that invisible.

"Sorry. I guess I was a little nosy." Brie brings her own glass of iced tea in and flops overdramatically in the other chair. She is still clutching the tall, slender glass, and the sweat from it is dripping down her forearm. She sets the glass down and wipes her arm on Derek's over-sized tee shirt that spreads across her expanding belly. "Can you still do it? Physical therapy, I mean?"

"Of course I can. I did it for thirty years. Haven't forgotten a thing. I just don't have a license to do it in Arizona, yet. Why do you ask?"

Brie shifts as much as she can while holding her two hands

underneath her belly for support. "I was thinking since you're here, *as Momma's new friend*," I almost get up and slap her for the belittling tone of her voice, "maybe you could help my husband." She focuses on Muriel's face in a confrontational way I'm not comfortable with. "What's your specialty? I understand PTs usually have one, like backs or legs or necks. You got one?" Lordy, is this the child of mine who got A pluses in English? I chalk up her lack of grammar to pregnancy.

Muriel unclasps her hands and rests them on her legs. She nods and smiles one of those quiet smiles that come from confidence. "I work with multiple injuries, mostly from car accidents and major traumas. Sort of like teaching the affected people to be whole and fully functioning again.

Without fear," she adds.

Brie literally leaps out of her chair. I don't remember her doing that so fast even when she was two. I think she's going to crush Muriel when she wraps her arms around the woman, and her big belly lands on Muriel's lap.

"Oh, my gosh. Oh! Can you help my husband?" Brie babbles on about what a wonderful man he is, how he is in this predicament because he tried to help someone else, how much he's healed, but how much more he needs to heal.

Muriel very gently pushes Brie off of her and places her hands on my daughter's shoulders. "Maybe I can," she says noncommittally. "Let's see."

~

The next few days are a Mr. Toad's Wild Ride. Sorry, Walt, but it applies here. Muriel has numerous consultations, notebook in hand, with Derek. She sees him more than Brie does. Fortunately, I have a sofa-sleeper in my living room, and Muriel hunkers down there. She does have an apartment nearby, so she can go home to shower and change clothes. But, she is so dedicated to Derek she tries to stay at my house as much as possible so she will be on spot when he awakens and can be guiding him, actually hovering by him, throughout the day. She refuses to take any compensation. Apparently, as her story comes out in small dribs, she has plenty of financial security, only needs friendship security. She sure has that now.

Brie calls her "hero," and Derek calls her "my angel." I call her "friend." A good one, one God led me to.

When Derek is resting or sleeping, Muriel gets into the planning of Nancy's possible party, the one that might be ditched because of Lester. It seems Muriel in her former life hosted numerous parties, high-faluting ones for professional politicians and athletes and other important people. She also has a gift for empathy and asks if she could meet with Fancy Nancy. I am thrilled to pass on what has now become a burden to me. Nancy is so open to any counsel she can get, not just because of the party snafu, but because of her marriage. We set it up.

~

It's a gloomy Monday, overcast and muggy, a unique scenario for Arizona. I have trouble focusing on my devotions. I have nine, yes nine, devotional books I read every morning. Each one gives me hope and pumps me up for the day. Joyce Meyer is my favorite, but The Daily Bread and Julie Clinton and Oswald Chambers complete it. Sometimes, though, old Oswald is a bit too philosophical. For me, at least. I keep the shutters across the sliding door wide open so I can see the sky and the palm trees poking up above the houses across from mine. They look regal, reaching up to touch Heaven and catch God's eyes, hoping for a blessing. I finish my coffee laced heavily with the new Italian creamer. Shoving the books on my special shelf for morning devotionals, I tromp to the shower. I will catch up on my prayers there.

Nancy calls at seven. I guess even young people get up early in Arizona because of the heat.

"Who IS this person you want me to meet with? Why should I?" The poor woman is such a stress case since Lester left. I should have been more in touch. Guilt consumes me.

"Nancy!" I almost yell, then lower my voice. "She has been through what you are going through. She is a certified counselor." I didn't add in another state, nor what kind. Whatever. Nancy just needs help and assurance from wherever and whomever she can get it. She calms down, we arrange a time.

Muriel and I pull up to the imposing house. She doesn't seem affected by it, but it still overwhelms me. Maybe she had a house like this one, in her other life. She leads the way and rings the brass bell. I have déjà vu when Noel did that at Bett's, and I have a moment of panic. Did he really say, "You must be Bett's best kept secret."? Did I really swoon over Crayon blue eyes? Where is Noel now? The ingrate. The sometimes, only when convenient, only when not sick, lover. I shove the 'what happened' down my gut and try to concentrate on Nancy and Muriel. That is my mission for today. Fortunately, I seldom have salad orders on Mondays.

~

Nancy opens the door in wrinkled sweats and dirty fuzzy slippers. Her formerly luxurious hair is in tangles and loops and straggly strands. Not just around her beautiful face, but sticking out from her head like an egg beater had invaded her.

"Oh, dear," is all I can mumble. I glance at Muriel, whose face is set in stone like one of the famous presidents on Mt. Rushmore. I can never remember all their names, but the most stern one comes to mind. Muriel is a trooper. She pushes past Nancy into the expansive living room and plops down on the nine foot sofa. "Nancy, sweets, come here." And, to my amazement, Nancy does and collapses into Muriel's arms nestling her head against the older woman's bosom.

FORTY NINE

"Where are we, Betsy? Is this Paradise Valley?" Muriel tugs on the car shoulder belt so she can turn sideways to see out the window better.

"No. We're still in Scottsdale, just North Scottsdale."

She makes a comment about the huge homes. "I agree they're colossal. At least some of them. I wouldn't want to live up here, though."

"Why not?"

"Obviously, I can't afford to. But, I like living close to the hospital and grocery stores and the library. Also, the fire department."

"I see." She grins and I clap her hands for the second I take them off the steering wheel.

"How do you think it went with Nancy?" she asks.

"I haven't decided whether to dub you miracle worker or angel. Both fit. You sure have the touch with that lady."

"I'm neither. Just an empathetic old lady. Maybe she was just ripe to let loose and trust."

We're toodling south on a long stretch of Scottsdale Road. We had been at Fancy Nancy's for over two hours. Muriel had taken the situation in hand. After sobbing Nancy told her pathetic story, and Muriel firmly told her to jump in the shower and put on her prettiest and sexiest dress. Maybe an ankle length and strapless sundress. Bare feet, no sandals.

"And, put some jewelry on. Do you have any toe rings? Ankle bracelets? Big dangly earrings? Especially something 'he' gave you."

Nancy nodded, wiped her eyes with her absorbent hand and disappeared.

I had said, "You are one tough cookie. What's next?"

"Lester is." She grinned like a naughty ten-year-old with her hand in the proverbial cookie jar.

A half hour later, Nancy shyly came back. Her hair was damp from the shower, but she had on a flowing, flowered strapless sundress in bright colors that swirled around her ankles. Three toe rings, a chunky turquoise necklace and big earrings that swung when she walked, as well as stacks of bright bracelets that clanked and completed the ensemble.

Muriel took one look and, like a kindly drill sergeant, issued more orders. I thought she was a bit bossy. "Go back, put some concealer under your eyes on those bags, some light blush on your cheeks, mascara and tinted lip gloss. And, dry your hair to a gleam.

Before you go, tell me Lester's cell number."

Nancy's eyes widened in terror. "Oh, please don't call him, please. This is so embarrassing."

"Don't worry, dear. I am not going to call him. Someone else is." That impish grin appeared on Muriel's face again. "A dear friend of his is."

~

I was still a little miffed, but Muriel's ploy worked. After my phone call to Noel, he called Lester. I wish I had been privy to the conversation because I imagined Bett bubbling in the background with choice comments. I still don't know what Noel said to Lester, and I'm pretty sure I don't ever want to.

Muriel and I had hunkered down in Sassy around the corner. Hopefully, out of sight, but still being able to see activity going into Nancy's house. Around the corner is a misnomer. Nancy and Lester live on over an acre, so there is no real corner. But, I found a copse just before the entrance to their long, circular driveway. I backed Sassy into it in case we needed a quick getaway. I think with the covering of pines, we were not very visible. We saw Noel's Mercedes zooming up the drive, then ten minutes later

Lester's Porsche. We hear car doors slam, then noticed a slit of light when the big double front doors of the estate opened. I decided to refer to it as an estate because that's what it is. Not a house, and unfortunately then, not really a home.

Twenty minutes after Lester pulled up, Noel pranced out. I wanted to smack the foolish grin on his face, but I was glad he was smiling. Whatever Muriel suggested had apparently worked. At least for that moment. Maybe she could work some magic for Noel and me.

FIFTY

"Hunk."

Did I hear her right? "Who?"

"Your guy." Muriel runs her tongue over her bottom lip. I can't say she is licking her lips, but close. "He looks delicious. For an older guy." She fixes me with a confused stare.

"I guess he's yours?" Was that a question or a statement?

"He's supposed to be. That enough information for you?" I admit I am undone, floored, and a lot of words I bite my tongue with to stop spewing from my mouth. I am angry, to the core. I step on Sassy's gas pedal and zoom out of the copse. No longer hidden. I don't care. I almost slam into Noel's fancy black Mercedes positioned sideways across the end of the drive.

"What the...?"

"He's obviously trying to stop you," Muriel says coolly. Her hands lay calmly on her lap. Do I hate her, or hate him? Right now I just plain hate.

As I slam, yes slam, on the brakes, my hands are shaking like I am holding a vibrator. Not that I've ever held one, but I can imagine. I grip Sassy's steering wheel with all my might. I am calm now, until...Noel taps on my car window.

I try to manually roll down the window. Can't, so open the door a slit, then grit my teeth and hold my breath and bite my tongue like Miss Alice my kids' preschool teacher taught me to do in stressful situations.

"Betsy," he says in his condescending voice, "you okay? What's going on?"

I stare and stick out my tongue. It's all I can do not to spew venom. So, I use the old tried and true. "Nothing."

~

Noel tugs open the door and spreads his arms, ready to hug me I think, until he sees Muriel. He takes a step back and smiles, his cutesy, flirty smile. The one he graced me with that day at Bett's when I opened the door.

"Well, now, who is this? Who is your l—lady—friend?"

If Muriel, who I now hate, wasn't there, I would slap him. Hard. I'm sure the stuttering "L–L" was the start of the word lovely, or lady, or both. Had to be, because it's so Noel. I am almost expecting him to say, "You must be Betsy's best kept secret." Fortunately, for his safety, he doesn't.

Muriel graciously reaches across me and offers her hand. "Hi. Name's Muriel. I'm the one who had the idea to call you to talk to Lester." She readjusts herself in her seat and asks the pregnant question. "What did you say to him?"

I can't figure this woman out. She seems so genuine, so caring. Still, she called Noel a hunk. Guess he is for his age. Maybe she is so upfront she calls it like it is. Is she flirting with him? Is he with her? My headache is starting again when I hear her laugh. Boisterously. I look at Muriel, then at Noel. Both are holding their bellies. Must be some joke.

"Can I get in on this?" I know my new face is all wrinkled up, and my new brows are almost kissing each other above my nose. I don't care. Brie would have a fit for my contorting my face this way. Still, I need to know before my heart starts leaking blood down the front of my blouse.

They laugh some more, and Muriel lays her hand on my arm giving it a slight squeeze. Noel turns away from the car door and sneezes. Three times. He does that when he's nervous. I just pray he isn't going to throw up. Surely, history won't repeat itself.

I am flummoxed. I don't know what to say, or do. So, I wait for the cacophony to abate. I close my eyes and silently count to ten. Just when I'm about to start over, Noel touches my arm.

"Betsy," he says with tears of laughter still dripping out of his

Crayon blue eyes, "Muriel and I go way back." I hand him a tissue from the glove compartment. He pauses to wipe and collect himself, and I am about to kick him in the shin.

"As in how?" I'm not sure I want to know, but I feel compelled to ask. Is Muriel an ex? Girlfriend, patient, lover?

"She is Roland's wife, er, ex-wife. Should I say former?" Now he looks contrite, apologetically at Muriel. What in Sam's hill of beans is going on?

"Excuse me." I hear my piercing voice, but don't care. "Who is Roland? How do you know each other?"

~

We decide to convene to my humble living room. I call ahead and ask Brie to *please* make a big pot of coffee and get out mugs and flavored creamers. "You'll understand why when we get there," I said in answer to her persistent questions.

I need to understand, too, but I shove my questions down my gullet. The truth would come out. Patience is, as I've mentioned before, not my strongest gift. But, no sense, no common sense at least, over-reacting until I learn more from the two people who "go way back." I'm hoping it's as far back as high school. That would be redeeming. And make me feel less of a fool.

The first thing that hits me when we walk in is no smell of brewing coffee. "Brie, honey, did you forget to put the coffee on?" My voice sounds more shrill than I intended, and I do the tongue-biting thing again. After all, she's not a servant or hired help. But, she should … I won't go there.

I suggest Noel and Muriel sit down, and I go to the kitchen to prepare the coffee myself. I measure, pour water, push the button. The old coffee pot wheezes and burbles. I see mugs sitting out and realize there are five of them. Brie and Derek joining us?

I am just about to pour the brew when I hear Brie's piercing voice from the other room.

"Noel," she practically screams, "what is going on? What kind of game are you playing with my mother? And, why are you and Muriel holding hands?"

I am entering the living room with two very hot mugs of coffee when I see what Brie sees. One mug sloshes, the one in my weaker left hand. I manage to place both on stone absorbent coasters I keep on the coffee table. For just such an occasion as this—entertaining old love birds holding hands, one of which is my fiancé.

All I can focus on is two hands clasped, more like hands entwined, as in a steamy novel. "We had a very special relationship," I hear Noel whisper. Muriel nods and a tear dribbles down her cheek.

Noel notices me and looks up. He seems confused, and the blue eyes are no longer sky blue but stormy indigo. He doesn't look embarrassed or ashamed which relieves me.

I let out a huge sigh and say in a low voice, "Wanna share, Noel?"

He leaps up and wraps me in his strong chiropractor arms. The hug almost cracks my back. Pop! Felt good. After nibbling my ear and almost swallowing my fake diamond stud, he pulls away and speaks.

"Muriel," he says gesturing to her on the sofa as if I don't know who she is or where she's sitting, "was Maizie's dearest friend. She held one of Maizie's hands, and I the other, when she died." He does the pregnant pause thing and wipes under one eye with an absorbent hand. His free hand has one of mine in a death-like grip. Will I need a cast?

"I...I don't understand? Why did you not recognize each other, and who is Roland?" I have so many questions, but I limit them to the basic ones. Brie is standing behind the sofa with a cloudy visage. Ah, oh, storm brewing. Elbows askew, her fists push into the sides of her waist and seem to push her belly out more. I worry she might explode on two fronts, face and belly.

"Well," she says and drags it out dramatically. "Can you answer my mother?"

Whew, Brie, give the man time to compose himself. I watch as he slowly turns to face her. My arms pop goose bumps and my fingers atrophy. I pray he gives a good answer.

"It's very simple, Brie." His voice is strong and deep, and his lips quiver into an edgy smile. "We haven't seen each other for five years. Last time I saw Muriel I knew her as Ann. Last time she saw me, I had a mustache and goatee. And very black hair." Noel pauses and grins. "In fact, she," he points at Muriel, "had brown hair." Frowning at Brie, he says, "Does that explain it?"

FIFTY ONE

"Oh."

"Oh."

Did Brie and I echo each other? She goes first.

"I *guess* I understand, sort of, now." But, her eyes are slits and elbows still askew. Then she asks the big question, and I cringe in despair. "How did Maizie die?"

"Brie!"

Noel cringes, too, then stands up tall and pulls back his hunk shoulders. His eyes narrow and focus on Brie who is now starting to physically shrink, but not in her belly. Just her stature. His voice almost booms, yet I know he is trying to control anger and sorrow mixed together. "She had an inoperable brain tumor."

"Oh." Brie is becoming monosyllable, and shorter.

"It took her months to die."

This time Brie nods and drops her fists dangling from her waists. They hang there like forgotten lumps of wet clay. "I…I guess I shouldn't have asked. It was rude of me." She slinks out of the room, and I hear a muffled sob.

We, who are left, all look at each other with blank faces. I shake my head hoping to fling out the mess of the last hour. Noel sighs loudly and plunks unceremoniously on the couch. Muriel wrings her delicate hands and lowers her head. Someone has to say something, soon. Guess who. I clear my throat and before I can get a word out, Brie reappears.

She lumbers toward Noel and deposits her body between him and Muriel. Voice cracking, she says, "I am so sorry. I was out of line. Please forgive."

Muriel and Noel each grab one of her hands and squeeze. Their smiles reassure her, and she smiles back. Whew! I hope this drama is over.

Just now Derek hobbles in sans cane and grabbing at furniture.

~

"Derek, you okay?" Noel asks. "What's been going on?" His handsome face exudes concern, and he scans the rest of us seeking answers.

"Hi, Noel." Then, "Hi, M'am." Whoa, and he wasn't even in the military.

Brie squeezes his arm, maybe a little too hard. "We just found out Muriel is Noel's old friend."

Still clueless, diplomatic Derek nods and stretches out his good hand. Noel grabs it and says, "Good to see how well you're doing."

Muriel clasps it with both of hers. "I'm so proud of you, Mr. Hero. You are making great progress."

Derek grins, and the tension is relieved.

~

Coffee all around really helps, both refills and new cups. There is something about java, even with all that caffeine, that stimulates friendship. Noel and Muriel, formerly Ann, share a bit about Maizie. Their reminiscences are soft and kind and don't devastate us. I sense it's very healthy for both of them. I reflect on what a small world it is, and how amazing God is linking us together.

Tonight Muriel decides to go home to her own apartment. Derek's progress is much better. Noel offers to chauffeur her to her car parked at the other end of the condo lot. My feelings are mixed. They do have a history.

The windows of his Mercedes are heavily tinted, but I notice two heads together, and I sense laughter. Oh, dear. What is that phrase Mom told me years ago? Let go, let God.

I need to trust. In God, in Noel, in Muriel and myself. Can I?

I excuse myself and retreat to my room. My intention is to pray. I need guidance, and I definitely need peace. My head is swirling with Brie's insensitive question, with Noel and Muriel scooting off together in his "other car," with Derek's suddenly good progress thanks to Muriel. Was she truly an unexpected angel? I want to believe that. I don't believe God makes mistakes, nor does He put strangers in our lives, however unexpectedly, unless they are put there to bless us.

Ancient guilt pops up in my brain. I will never forget. I was three months pregnant with Brie, living with the other kids in a big house, but basically alone. It was almost midnight when the doorbell rang. I peeked out the glass hole to see an elderly woman. She was very disturbed, almost crying.

"What do you want?" I yelled.

"I'm lost," she said in a weepy voice. "I just need to find my way out of this community. Please help me."

I was so conflicted, especially since I knew if one just kept following the street I lived on it would lead to the exit. I was actually scared. I had two children sleeping, and I was pregnant. Our community had recently been warned about break-ins, and I wondered why she chose my house to seek help.

"I am sorry," I yelled back. "I can't help. This door is double-locked." Stupid excuse. "But, if you keep driving down this street, it will eventually take you to an exit. God bless."

I turned off the porch light that I had turned on when the bell rang. I felt so bad that I still remember it to this day over twenty-six years later. I know God said we may unexpectedly entertain angels. But, I simply could not risk my children. I still pray for that woman. Hopefully, she got out of our community safely.

Enough reminiscing, Betsy. I shake my body to get back into the present. Which question should I tackle first?

I chose the Noel and Muriel one. I call him.

"Hi. You home?"

"Yep. Just dropped Muriel off to her car. Anything wrong?"

"Just wanted to hear your voice." Duh, Betsy, couldn't you come up with something more original?

"So, about you and Muriel, and your history together." Pregnant pause, again.

"Yes, Betsy, we do have a history, as you call it. But, it is truly only a friendship." He pauses to blow out a breath. "Because of Maizie's death. Her dying."

Can I feel more guilty? What is next in our relationship? I am such a dweeb. I settle on that adjective.

"I guess I'm feeling insecure, Noel. About our relationship," I add. Am I doing this right?

I clasp my worn Bible to my heart after looking up James 1:6 who cautions us to not doubt, or we will be like a wave of the sea, tossed and driven by the wind. I do not want to be a double-minded woman. I want to feel secure, loved by God, and loved by Noel. Is that unrealistic?

"Betsy. You still there?"

"Sure am. You on board?" Another stupid comment, Betsy. Where, oh, where, is my brain? Maybe somewhere in my aching heart.

"For what?"

"For our relationship."

"Aren't we still getting married next month?"

Men are so obtuse. I vacillate on how to respond. Ignore his stupid comment, or act innocent. I opt for being naïve.

"Oh, we are? You remembered?"

"Of course. It's on my calendar."

That's it? A date marked on his calendar? Like a meeting? I slam down the phone with the biggest bang I can muster. Maybe he is Jerk Number Two. I hope not. I go back to my Bible for consolation and guidance. I twist the big sparkling ring on my finger. Did I forget to mention that?

Brie made a big deal of it. So did Muriel when she noticed it. I blurted, "Hey, I have been married twice. Never with a ring like this. But, it IS beautiful, isn't it." They both looked at me like I am an idiot. Muriel twisted a large diamond on her finger, and Brie touched the one Derek had given her. Neither was as large as the one Noel had graced me with.

Muriel's marriage had ended in sadness, but Brie's was still in limbo. Also Nancy's.

I am giddy with excitement. Noel called me with the idea he and Muriel came up with. I want to be a part of it. I hope Betsy won't mind.

FIFTY TWO

I start to question myself. I know I love Noel, but am I doing the right thing, especially at my age, by marrying him? Actually, by getting married again? I ponder Mom's words, "Love is a gift at any age."

I know she is right. When I was a kid, she used to say, "I am always right. I am a mom. I took a vow when you were born."

Yea, Mom! But, I am a mom now, too. So, what should I do?

I do the most practical thing. I call Mom.

When she answers, "What's up now, Bitsy?" I know I should have texted her to warn her.

"Not sure about marrying again."

"But, neither of your marriages, nor their failures, were your fault," she says with Dr. Mom authority. She is probably a better shrink than Dad, just doesn't get paid for it. Except in love.

We talk about how I love Noel, how he loves me, how financially secure he will make me. Now, I mention the negatives. His acceptance, but lack of genuine love for Brie; his relationship with Muriel; his matter of fact mention about putting our wedding date on his calendar! That was the worst.

We tackle each of my concerns, logically. Mom is logical, very methodical. She ticks them off one by one just fine, until…the calendar one.

"Betsy, it's the way men think. You should know that by now.

Your father is the same way. He marks his personal calendar with things like hearts and exclamation marks for our anniversary and my birthday. Even Mother's Day that is already designated in the little square on his calendar.

"For Noel to tell you is his way of affirming that it is special and important to him. He's a guy. He is telling you it's a special event."

~

I have been chastised, lovingly, by the wisest woman I know. Time to call Noel back and apologize for slamming the phone down.

"What is it now, Betsy?" His turn to sound aggravated, even angry.

I suck in a deep breath and sob.

His immediate response is, "What's wrong? Did something awful happen? To Brie, to you?"

"No, no." I am secretly pleased he thought of Brie first. "Noel, I am scared."

~

It's said confession is good for the soul. It's also said that love has no bounds.

Noel changes his voice from aggravated to a deep, melodically purr. "I will be right over," he says and hangs up the phone.

I stare at the receiver in my hand. Did he just say that? Before I can swipe more blush on my cheeks, I hear the doorbell. I yell, "I'll get it," to Brie and Derek. No response. Hopefully, they are cuddling and discussing baby names.

Noel bursts in the door, which is always unlocked thanks to Brie's forgetfulness, and wraps those big chiropractic arms around me. He hugs me tight and says, "Sit down, Betsy. We need to talk and get a few things straight."

I listen to his soliloquy about love a second time around, about love in the senior years of our lives, about love in general. He should be on stage at the Scottsdale Performing Arts Center.

Stupidly, I ask. "Noel, you ever performed on stage? In a production of some sort?"

"Did any of what I said reach your heart, Betsy?" His eyes look sad.

I fumble with the wadded tissue in my hands and nod. God gave me the special gift of Noel. Actually, Bett did, too, since she introduced us.

"I guess I am insecure." I pause to let that thought sink in to both of our brains. "You are tall, handsome, eloquent looking and successful. I am overweight, over-burdened with family problems. I am just a personal chef with a small business.

"I would never, ever, want you to think I love you for the security you can give me. Never."

"Betsy, I know you can make it on your own. You have now for many years. But, I want to give this to you. Besides, I love holding you. I love the physical you. You are soft and comforting and fit just right into my arms.

"Does that explain why I love you?"

What a guy. Why did I ever question? Thanks, Mom, for reassuring me.

~

After a major cuddle time, during which Brie and Derek, thankfully, did not interrupt, we talk wedding plans. About time, since I'd only discussed them with Bett.

We decide on a small, intimate wedding with only family and dear friends. Bett had insisted on taking care of the invitations if we would give her a list. She also insisted they would be hand addressed by her personal calligrapher. Only Bett would have one of those.

"Can we trust her? To choose the invitations and make sure they are mailed on time? Bett isn't real good with time," I add nervously.

Noel nods. "I think so. She is a successful business woman with boutiques in three states. As for having her own calligrapher," he continues, "she probably has the person address invitations to her sales events and parties. She does a lot of parties in her stores to attract new customers and bring in returning ones." He has a funny, smug grin on his handsome face.

"What?"

"Nothing, Betsy. Just thinking Bett will give us a great party."

"Humph. I feel like I've lost control of my own wedding." I tell him about the cake disaster that occurred when that nasty Monica called. Just like a man, he says "It's just a cake."

I hold my tongue and taste blood. Men!

"Betsy, please let Bett do this for you, for us. She really wants to, and," he grins, again, "I trust her."

Okay. I will, too, I tell him. Another 'Let go, let God' moment. Besides, I am in a tizzy about Fancy Nancy's surprise party for Lester. Why on God's green earth did I agree to have it so close to our wedding date? Lack in judgment, for sure.

Noel hugs, squeezes and slobbers me with kisses. Finally, he leaves. I do my best modulated yelling to Brie who staggers out of the guest bedroom and looks at me quizzically.

"We have to finalize preparations and ordering, finish all plans, for Nancy's party. And," I mention in a panic, "I need a wedding dress!"

Brie grabs my fingertips and starts to twirl me around the kitchen. What now?

"Momma!" She is grinning, almost like Noel. "Bett wants to design your dress. She even showed me her drawing. Don't worry. It will be beautiful and becoming and so you!"

"Really? I will have a Bett original? Wow!" Then, I start to worry. I know my dreams flit like butterflies, but I don't want to look like an overweight one on my wedding day. My third wedding day. I know Bett loves me. I know I need to trust her. So, I do.

We get cracking, finalizing the food list. I leave ordering the extra tables and chairs and patio umbrellas and table cloths and *white* napkins to Nancy. She insists on white. She has used the same Party People vendors several times, so her credit card is on file. I suggest she asks for the napkins to be pre-folded in some attractive design. She agrees; the vendor agrees, for extra money. Whew, got past that trauma!

Brie and I go grocery shopping. It's Thursday, and the party is Saturday. The veggies and fruits will keep in my fridge, and we will prepare some tomorrow, and the rest Saturday morning. I check with Nancy. Yes, she has had her personal assistant (glory, be!) send invitations two weeks ago, and she has had numerous replies. The party is coming together on all fronts.

I only worry about one thing. I don't think Brie and I, just the two of us, are enough help in the setup and serving department. But, I have an idea, and I call Trader Joe's.

Yes, if we buy a certain amount of the food from them, they will provide people in Hawaiian shirts to set up and serve, for an hourly fee. Oops! We bought almost all the food from Fry's market. I try to come up with something we still need that we haven't purchased yet.

"How about baskets of flowers?" I ask the manager. "Little nibbles, too. Like your wonderful almonds and cashews? Would that work?" He agrees, and we are ready to roll!

I had forgotten about the Chinese lantern lights, but Nancy hadn't. Her back yard was aglow with them hovering over the tables and food. I knew she had it in her. She is now the perfect hostess. In my book, anyway.

The salad bar is set out beautifully. The tables sport white linen cloths and white napkins in the shape of cranes. Four men and a woman in Hawaiian shirts are serving salads and pouring drinks. All Brie and I have to do is oversee and supervise.

Thanks to all the help, cleanup is a breeze. Nancy hugs us both so hard I feel my back crack. But, the best is that Lester took her in his arms and danced to their special song. Everyone cheered and sang along. Brie and I are out of there by eleven.

FIFTY THREE

Two weeks! Just two, until Noel and I say our vows. Scary.

I decide to call Bett. For updates, and tell her how grateful I am about her doing the invitations.

"You're kidding, right?" I hear the anxiety in her voice. "I wanted to do this for you and Noel." I can almost see the makeup crinkling around her eyes. "Don't you trust me?" Then I visualize the tear drops.

"Of course, I do, Bett. This is so much what you are doing, so over the edge." I pause to catch my breath. "You sure you want to do this?"

"I already have. After all, the wedding is only two weeks from now." She pauses, perhaps to catch a breath or wipe a tear? "I deliberately waited to send out invitations. To locals. I did send the ones to your family in California two weeks ago." Another pregnant pause. Yikes, what is going on? "I have only received a reply from Julia, but not from James. You and your son have an okay relationship?" I think I hear a tissue being pulled from a square box.

"Yes, James and I are great. He's a very busy IT guy, but his wife, Sandra, is extremely socially adept. You sure you sent to the right address?"

"Yes, sure. You gave me the list."

"Don't worry, Bett. I will call them."

Suddenly, I have become my own wedding coordinator. Isn't that what wedding gurus are supposed to do, call the people who haven't responded and ask why? Where is Jill S. when I need her? She did such a super job when I hired her for Julia's and James', and Brie's very expensive weddings. Brie's was over the top in every way—financially, eloquent, mostly financially. But, Brie is my baby, and Derek is my second son now, at least.

I look at the list I gave Bett. Is Derek's dad on it? Check? My son and daughter and families? Check. Oh, Muriel? Check. How about Nurse Jones, or was it Nurse Smith? Confusing, but check. Fancy Nancy and Lester? Check. Mom and Dad? Check. Coffee house Mitch? Check. I can't think of anyone else. Of course, Consuela, but she would be there anyway since the wedding will take place at Bett's and she has agreed to return, at least for the wedding.

I should have gotten an invitation. So should Noel. For keepsake, at least. I run to the gatehouse to collect my errant mail that I haven't picked up in several days. There it is!

Butterflies! Bett decided on butterflies. It is stunning. Of course, embossed with raised lettering. A lovely butterfly graces it.

Ms. Elizabeth Alice Emma Wysinotski
And
Dr. Noel Daniel Sheppard
Request your presence at their
Marriage Ceremony

Blah, blah.

It's beautiful. I love the butterfly. It's a theme.

Noel's middle name is Daniel? Like in the Bible? Am I the lion in the den?

~

"Bett, it's lovely! But, why the butterfly? How did you know I love them?"

"Because, sweet girl, you flit around like one." She giggles softly. "I'm so glad you like it."

"Like doesn't say it, Bett. I adore it. Noel is right, you are so creative." I hesitate, but I need to ask. "What else do you have up your sleeve? Brie is so excited about your designing my wedding dress. I'm sure I will need a fitting, so it can't be too much of a secret. Right?"

"Wrong!" comes the answer accompanied by another giggle. "Maybe, possibly, the day before your nuptials. I do want you to be excited about it, but I don't want you to fuss over every little thing. For instance," she continues, "I will take some measurements tomorrow. You can be free for about an hour, can't you? I have a wonderful on-site alteration seamstress in my local boutique."

"But, the wedding is only two weeks away." Surely Bett has thought about that. What if the dress is too long, or too short, or worse, too tight. I don't want to look like a blimp.

"Not to worry, Betsy. I've known you all…these past few years." I wonder why she has hesitated. She goes on. "I know your style, at least when I've seen you in street clothes, and not in that silly chef uniform." She pauses, again. "Forgot to ask about what you want to wear on your head."

I am too old for a tiara, and certainly too formerly married for a veil. What should I request? Maybe a flower or two? My wonderful stylist Francine who indulges my weekly extravagance with a Friday shampoo and blow dry will style my hair. She has this new tool that forms masses of curls. She is also very talented at styling, even French braids. Naw, not my style. She will design the ultimate hair style for me. After all, her business in Salon Boutique is called The Concept of Hair. She will also style Brie's hair, and Bett's, even Mom's. Oh, dear. What on earth will she do with Brie's mass of curls?

Not to worry I tell myself. Francine is a Master Stylist whose specialties are cut and color. She does perfect work.

I discuss head gear with Bett who poo-poos the single flower idea. "I will come up with something perfect, something special," she declares. "Trust me."

We chat about the ceremony and the refreshments to be served at the small reception. I know Bett has excellent taste, and I really don't care about hors d'ourves. They aren't my specialty. Salads are. But, the reception will be brief with no time for salad.

Mr. Crayon Blue Eyes and I will leave post haste to catch a flight to Hawaii. I've never been, and I am so excited, and worried. Yes, worried. About wearing a bathing suit. I even went to Dillard's and tried on the expensive ones with the tummy and derriere inserts that promise to take off ten pounds. I was so discouraged I went on to Nordstrom's. Finally, Brie dragged me to a specialty shop. How she, who is from California, knows about these places in Scottsdale is a mystery. Winifred, the sales associate with the old-fashioned name, took one look at me and pulled a suit off the rack.

"This," she said, "will be perfect for you. Tucks the tummy, pulls in the butt, lifts the girls and looks sleek."

It is black with a diagonal sash sort of stripe and high cut leg openings. Who would have thought? Also, a very low cut back. Winifred was right. I still would love to lose fifteen or twenty pounds, but this suit does the trick. I am so thrilled I hug her, and she doesn't even blush. She must be used to that kind of enthusiasm from post-menopausal, overweight women. The suit is packed in my carry-on luggage, just in case the big suitcase gets lost.

I tell Bett about the bathing suit, and she hoots. "Yea for you! You will look beautiful."

I am still worried about the wedding cake, the one I wanted to make myself, but it collapsed. "What are your plans for the cake, Bett?" I swallow hard waiting for her answer.

"It's all taken care of, Betsy, all arranged." I can almost see the smug smile on her face. Trust is a big issue with me, but at this point in time, I need it.

I want this wedding, my third, and definitely last, to be more than special. It is also Noel's second wedding, and I know his with Maizie was very special. It actually did last 'until death do us part'.

Bett says she has also designed Brie's matron of honor gown, and Mom's mother of the bride attire. That woman has been busy.

"What will Noel wear?" I ask. I hope not a tux or tails. Something in between.

"He is all outfitted," she says. "Don't worry. He will look handsome."

I am sure he will, even in jeans and a tee shirt.

"Who is standing up for Noel?" I had never thought to ask him this. He has no children, no male relatives that I know of. So, I ask Bett since she seems to be the fountain of information about my wedding.

"It's a last minute thing with him. He hasn't decided yet whom to ask. Usually, Noel is very decisive, but he's vacillating. At this point, I think, and this must be very confidential," she sucks in a breath I can hear over the phone, "it is between Derek and Mitch, the coffee guy, and possibly Lester, Nancy's husband." She sucks in another breath. "Maybe even Muriel?"

Yikes! What the heck? No, not Muriel, please. I am okay with her now as a friend, but I don't want memories of Maizie invading our wedding. Derek would be wonderful, and even Mitch would be great. He and his coffee house played a great role in our romance. I could even accept Puffy Face from the hospital, or even the hunk EMT guy. They both have some history with us. But, not Muriel. At least not with me. Oops, other than with Derek.

Doesn't he have a good colleague friend? Someone who supported him during Maizie's illness, or a mentor from chiropractic school?

I say goodbye to Bett after confirming Dad will walk me down the garden path in her extensive back yard. I take some solace knowing her roses are blooming and the setting will be beautiful.

The only thing we haven't discussed is bouquets, mine and Brie's. I think I need Mom to take over from here.

~

"I am so glad you asked, Bitsy." I can hear Mom pulling a tissue from the silver box next to the phone. "I didn't want to interfere, but I have been concerned. Bett can sometimes be a little over the top with her ideas and plans."

"Mom, you are so right. You will never interfere. I should have asked you to plan this from the get go, but you planned two other weddings of mine, so I didn't want to overburden you." I pause for a breath. "I, too, worry about Bett. She can get overly enthusiastic, maybe a bit crazy."

"Don't worry, dear. I will take care of it. Bett and I go back a long way."

They do? Never thought about that. I know they are friends, but for how long? I thank Mom and hang up.

I feel so much better after having talked with Mom. She has a logical head on her shoulders. I forgot to ask her about favors for the guests, so I call her back.

"Little details, Mom. What about favors for guests? What about a photographer?" I pause with a really big question. "Is the butterfly theme too femmie? For Noel, I mean." I hear another tissue being pulled from the box. "I worry it's too cutesy for a grown man. What do you think?"

I imagine the tissue being crumpled. I wait patiently for her response.

"Yes, Bitsy, I've worried about that, too. Bett seems so determined, so excited. I have a call into her voicemail to ask that very question. Don't worry, please. I will handle it." She hangs up, and I feel much better. I trust Mom completely.

It is going to be okay, actually not just okay. It will be wonderful. I need to remember I am marrying a man who loves me, and I love him. That is all that is important.

~

Brie rushes into the kitchen and hugs me, hard.

"Don't worry, Momma, everything is going to be wonderful. About the wedding, I mean." And, she laughs.

"But," I say, "I stress when I have no control."

"For once, could you please relax, and trust? The decorations and all the other stuff is just fluff. The important thing is your vows." She squeezes my hands. Ouch, Brie! "I am sure whatever Bett has planned will be lovely." She lets go of my fingers, and I feel blood flowing through my arms again.

"Okay. Since you know so much, has anyone contacted the pastor who is going to marry us?"

"Uh, Momma. The pastor at your church isn't available. But," she continues with enthusiasm, "we have a great backup. I think you will be pleased."

"What? Who?"

Brie hesitates too long for my comfort.

"Mitch!"

I roll my eyes and swallow hard. Actually, I almost gag. Mitch, the coffee house proprietor? He is not a pastor or minister, certainly not ordained. This cannot be right.

"In fact, Momma, he is legal to do weddings. He took some online certification. He is okay. Really. And," She pauses with emphasis, "he is thrilled to be bonding you two together."

~

Everything seems to be wrong. Mitch is a very nice guy, actually a former patient, now friend, of Noel's. Noel sends me a link in an email that shows Mitch is certified. Maybe not exactly ordained, but like a judge, he can perform marriage ceremonies.

Okay. So, what will he wear? I don't care about GQ fancy, but I do care about tasteful attire. Mitch's daily attire is usually a rumpled tee shirt and khaki cargo pants and leather flip flops. I groan and call Noel.

I tell him my concerns, and he cheerfully replies, "Don't worry, my love. I have already chosen Mitch's outfit for him." He waits for my response, then hearing none continues. "What say you about a blue button-down shirt, dark gray trousers, a lightweight linen blazer and a pair of my Topsiders. Polished!" he adds.

Linen wrinkles. Doesn't he know that? Guess he hasn't thought of that, so I say it aloud, firmly. "Linen wrinkles."

"Well, he won't have it on for long. Besides, wrinkles are in." I can almost see him grinning. Mr. Up On All the Latest Male Styles.

"What about a tie?" I want Mitch to look proper and, yes, legal, to marry us. "And, clean-shaven? Haircut? No ring in his ear?" It never bothered me when the sixty-something man was serving coffee, but it worries me now. After all, there will be photos with him. I cut Noel off.

Oh, dear, another worry. Photos by whom? I yell for Brie and call Bett.

Brie gives me the don't worry hug, the one I gave to her the week before her marriage to Derek. Bett answers with, "What now?"

I explain my concerns about a photographer. At Noel's and my ages, I don't care that much about a videographer, but I do want timeless photos. Good ones that show our happiness.

"Betsy," she sighs so loud I move the phone away from my ear. "Please, don't be a bridezilla at your age." She waits to see if that offensive remark sinks in. It does, but I remain silent. Ignoring my lack of response, she carries on. Suddenly, I realize she used my name properly. I chalk that up as progress.

"I have engaged the professional photographer who takes all the runway photos of my models when I have a fashion show. He is great. Perhaps a bit flamboyant, do you get my drift?" she asks innocently.

"That's okay," I reply while gritting my teeth. I, stupidly, never arranged for one, but I hope my very traditional family will be accepting and smile brightly when he tells us to wet our lips and turn sideways.

Mom calls to tell me she has found butterfly flowers on an internet search. Two exotic kinds that actually look like miniature butterflies. She was worried she wouldn't be able to get The White Ginger Lily, from Cuba and the Blue Wings raised in Africa. Then, she remembered her friend, Marg, who owns North Scottsdale Floral. Marg not only came through, but was very excited. She called a vendor in Miami and one in Los Angeles. The Miami one came up with the Cuban flowers, and the LA one is providing the others. I can't wait to see them, and I am grateful I am not paying the bill for this extravagance. Marg has excellent taste, so I know my bouquet and Brie's will be gorgeous, as will Mom's and Bett's corsages. Mom says Noel will have a boutonniere to match my bouquet, and Derek, who Noel finally asked to be Best Man, will have one to match Brie's bouquet.

Did I forget to say that Brie will be my only attendant? I would have had Julia, too, but she declined graciously. Too much being so far away, as well as bringing kids to the ceremony. Noel doesn't know my son, James, so that wouldn't have worked to ask him to stand up for Noel. James is pleased for us, and I have sent him lots of updates about Noel.

Derek is the best choice. He and Noel have gotten to know each other, mostly through Brie, and because of Muriel's physical therapy with Derek. I do wonder about Lester, though. Seems as if he and Noel go back a long way. Still, I am pleased he asked Derek. Good choice, Noel.

At almost the last minute I decide to ask my five-year-old granddaughter, Chelsea, Julia's child, to be a flower girl. All of the other grandchildren are too old, but Chelsea is adorable and very confident. So, I think she will add something special to the wedding. Children always do.

Julia finally puts aside her anger over her father, The Jerk, who abandoned her. She agrees and is pleased, as any mother would be, to have her daughter in a wedding. But she is concerned about a dress for Chelsea. I call Bett.

"Aw, how sweet," she says. "Have Julia send me her size, plus measurements. And, her shoe size, please." She explains the children's boutique next to hers in Scottsdale is owned by a good friend. Chelsea will have a gown. Post haste. This time she calls me Bethy. Oh, well.

I call Noel. "Y-you never answered about the tie for Mitch, and the haircut and beard trim."

"Bitsy, calm down." He calls me by my mother's nickname for me. "All is well, all is in control. Not your control, Bits." I hold the phone away from my ear and seriously contemplate slamming it down. Then, I remember God never stutters. He reminds me He is in control. Carry on, Betsy!

~

I wiggle my toes and form little circles with my ankle. The warm water swirling around them feels heavenly. It's three days before my wedding, and I'm finally meeting the famous Kay, proprietor of Paulene's Nails.

Dr. Janis' office called last week to schedule a final X-ray and possibly remove the cast from my leg. I was a bit surprised to learn he had an actual office; I'd thought ER docs seldom did. I hobbled into a dark cubby hole and flopped into a worn wooden chair. I remember gripping its scratched arms, closing my eyes and praying, hard. How I'd feared hobbling down the aisle on my wedding day!

The good doc's thin lips formed an even thinner smile. "Leg is healed. Go to Outpatient down the hall," he gestured behind him, "they will remove your boot." Boot is the euphemism for the cumbersome annoyance that had burdened me for six weeks.

Now, even though my left leg is less pudgy than the right, and is a bit weaker, I am basking in a massage chair during a pedicure. The renowned Kay is giving me a gel manicure while the talented Tammy massages my feet. Bliss, pure bliss!

"Diamonds?" Kay asks.

"What?" I struggle to understand in my almost slumbering state.

She opens a tiny round, flat, plastic container and shakes it sideways to display minute rhinestones in every rainbow color. "You want clear diamonds or blue? You are getting married, so you must sparkle," she insists in her sweet Asian accent. "You want flower?"

"Can you do a butterfly?"

She jumps up and click clacks on four inch sandals to the

front counter where examples of designs are displayed on fake nails stuck on wooden picks. Holding out two to show me, I gasp. So beautiful.

"Can you really do that?" Of course she can. She giggles. I hope I haven't offended her.

"We will just do thumbs and ring fingers." She winks. "Maybe toes."

"I don't want it to take away from my diamond, so maybe we should just do thumbs."

"No, no. Diamonds will make ring sparkle even more. Show it off."

Tammy nods her agreement, and Kay's husband Duc (pronounced Duke) stops to agree. "Will look beautiful, Miss Betsy. Special for your wedding."

Brie bounces up from her pedicure massage chair, feet dripping. "Mama, do it!" She apologizes to Tom who was about to dry her legs and massage them. He grins. So much confirmation.

I love that Kay calls the rhinestones diamonds. We choose clear and pale blue ones for my butterflies. I am going to sparkle. Will Mr. Blue Eyes notice?

"I wonder if my groom (it's so exciting to call him that) will even notice." I look expectantly at Kay, Duc and Tammy who have gathered around me.

Duc nods and gives me a lopsided grin. "He will," he says. "He loves you."

Tammy has started to massage my legs with a yellow sugar scrub; Kay is massaging my hands and arms with a warm yummy-smelling lotion. I am in Nirvana. Please, God, may there be mani-pedis in heaven.

"Miss Betsy, Miss Betsy." Duc is lightly touching my fingers. "You gonna be able to drive home?"

I shake my head and yawn. Grinning, I look over at Brie who is sound asleep in Tom's pedicure chair. I may have to, but I was counting on Brie to be my designated driver.

I am so excited I can hardly contain myself. I almost put my dress on inside out. I feel like the mother of the bride. I've thought of every detail for this wedding for two people I love dearly.

The hors d'ourves look scrumptious, and the pink lemonade is glistening in the enormous punch bowl. The servers in their Hawaiian shirts are a nice touch, thanks to Nancy for suggesting them. She and Lester have been a huge help with details. She must have taken lessons on how to fold napkins.

I hope they like the cake. I made sure Cakes Galore alternated the layers between chocolate and lemon, just as Betsy wants. But, the top is special. I will freeze it and give it to them to eat on their first anniversary. Fondant butterflies do freeze, don't they?

I hope I've done the right thing giving Betsy the letter immediately before her wedding. I've waited so long. I couldn't wait any more. I pray Harriet understands.

Thank you, Lord, for being my best friend. I adore You. I am so blessed you gave me Betsy and she led me to You.

EPILOGUE

The Big Day

I hear music. Beautiful Frank Sinatra songs play softly over muted loudspeakers in Bett's garden. I have butterflies flitting in my stomach, and on my toes and fingers. I glimpsed an incredible wedding cake when I came earlier to the garden. Butterflies cascading down the layers, and two butterflies kissing on top. Sweet Bett, so extravagant. Everything, from the tables to the lanterns to the bouquet I am holding, is butterflies. Mom found flowers that actually look like butterflies, although she ordered them from far and wide with Marg's help. Their delicate petals form tiny wings. Mine are white Ginger Lilies, Brie's deep blue ones from South Africa match her gown…and Noel's Crayon blue eyes. Too perfect!

Mom and Brie fuss with my dress, Bett's special creation.

The dress is not a traditional wedding gown, rather a vision of billowing, flowing silk. It is a soft, almost silver that compliments my recently tinted hair, a Francine specialty, as well as her idea to scoop my curls up in a rhinestone-glittering butterfly clip. My nuptial hairstyle is elegant, and my wedding dress is Bett extraordinaire. It hides my hips and my tummy and makes me feel and look beautiful. I love it!

Brie's Matron of Honor gown is also flowing to subtly camouflage her pregnancy, now advanced. Little Chelsea's gown, that just arrived yesterday, looks adorable on her. The wide, blue satin sash is perfect for a perfect child. She is holding a white rose-studded basket filled with white silk rose petals. I know she will probably fling them, instead of tossing them delicately. But, I don't care.

This is my big day.

Actually, my third 'big day.' I think of Clyde, my first husband who died suddenly in a car crash. Sweet man, father of James. Didn't leave me much, except memories. I think about The Jerk who abandoned me when I was pregnant with Brie and Julia was barely a teen. Didn't even leave me good memories. Then, I think of Noel, the man I am about to wed.

I start to question. Why me? Do I remind him of Maizie? Was she plump? Noel is Cary Grant handsome. He could get any number of women a lot younger than I. Yes, he has had some issues, mostly with flu symptoms and performance problems. But, we have worked those out. Mostly, Noel is trustworthy. He is a Christian; he doesn't lie, even to save his face. He cuddles wonderfully. He loves my kids, my grandkids and my grandchild to be.

I hear the organ music start. How did Bett do that? There is no organ in her back yard.

Mom says, while adjusting my skirt for the umpteenth time, "Aren't you going to open the envelope?"

She hands me a thick square envelope, the one I'd handed back to her a few minutes ago. I guess I had better loosen the flap. Mom and Brie step back and fold their hands in front of them, almost prayer-like.

Dearest Betsy,

I never know when is the right time to share, but I feel you should read this before you embark on your wonderful journey with Noel. Please share it with him, too.

Betsy, yes, I know your name well, and have known it for many years. You are my niece.

Many years ago, I guess fifty-eight or so, my brother, Joel, came to me to tell me his girlfriend was having a child. The girlfriend died in childbirth. Joel begged me to adopt the child. He was only eighteen and very confused. But, he was mature enough to realize he had an obligation to his child. He wanted a secure, loving life for her. He called her Elizabeth after our maternal grandmother.

I agreed on Joel's deathbed to adopt you. (He was very weak from many health problems. I held his hand when he died and made a promise.)

I realized later I could not raise a child alone when I was just starting a business. My friend Harriett, with whom I'd roomed at college, had recently married and found out she was unable to conceive. They desperately wanted children. So, I appealed to Harriett. She and her husband Daryl were very receptive. They were, still are, the perfect couple to love you.

We made all the legal arrangements; not difficult, since both your birth mother and father were deceased, and I was appointed guardian. When you were less than a year old, you became Elizabeth Lindstrom. Now, in a few minutes, you will become Mrs. Noel Sheppard.

God bless you, Betsy. I love you.

Aunt Bett

By the way, Noel is adopted, too. Ask him.

~

I feel tears pooling in my eyes. I should have guessed, maybe almost did. Still, the truth is a bit of a shock.

I hear organ music again and realize Bett actually has a real organ with a real organist playing the traditional wedding march. For me. For Noel.

Dad offers his arm and beams at me. Gosh, how can a father go through this scenario three times and still be happy? I really am blessed.

Chelsea flings rose petals along the white runner-covered aisle. Mom came through with that. Abundant pots of flowers line the moss-covered sides that Bett created with the help of Roberto, her faithful and talented gardener. Mitch looks very presentable in his fashionably wrinkled sport coat. Mom, having been escorted by Derek to her Mother of the Bride seat, is glowing.

Noel looks handsome, but uncomfortable, squirming in his attire. I love the striped navy and gray trousers and the midnight blue jacket that matches his smoldering Crayon blue eyes.

What! He is wearing a bolo tie? So is Derek. Just to get my goat? I swallow hard, then I laugh. How many women laugh going down the aisle on their wedding day?

He winks, and he and Derek both pull off the bolos to reveal real four-in-hand neckwear. They stuff the offenders in their pockets, and his wide smile reassures me. I hope we won't be spending the evening in the hospital.

Brie whispers in my ear before she takes her first step on the aisle.

"We are having a girl, and we are naming her Bettina Elizabeth, Betsy for short." She squeezes my hand, smiles and steps forward.

The End

Aunt Lorrie's Chicken Salad

Aunt Lorrie insists one must use only Kirkland (Costco brand) chicken that comes in a six pack. She also insists on Maille mustard which can be purchased at Safeway and WalMart.

3 cans chicken, drained
1/2 large sweet onion finely diced
3 ribs of celery, finely diced
1/2 to 3/4 cup mayo (to taste)
3 to 4 tablespoons of Maille old style stone ground mustard.

Mix all ingredients
Makes about 4-5 cups of chicken salad.

Brie's Baked in Bread Crab Appetizer

1 Hawaiian round bread, hollowed out and insides saved and cubed
1 envelope dry Knorr Cream of Leek Soup
1 cup mayo (not low fat)
1 cup sour cream (not low fat)
1 can crab meat drained (canned shrimp can be substituted, but not as good)
5-6 finely chopped green onions
1 can water chestnuts chopped fine
1 package frozen chopped spinach drained and all water squeezed out
8-12 oz. shredded cheddar cheese (to taste – more is better)
Dash Worcestershire sauce and Soy sauce
Blend all well in bowl and pour into hollowed out bread. Loosely wrap bread in foil. Bake in 325 to 350

degree oven for about 10-15 minutes until starting to bubble. Toast cubes of bread in foil in oven or toaster oven to crisp.

Serve with bread cubes around bread filled with dip and lots of long toothpicks. Enjoy!

BUTTERFLY DREAMS

Dear Reader ~

Thank you so much for spending time in the kitchen with Betsy and me in Butterfly Dreams. I hope you had as much fun as I did when Bett made the tuna salad, sans mayo and with soy sauce.

And what about that horrible phone call from belligerent Monica? How did she get Betsy's number? I haven't figured that out yet, either. Did Noel have an affair with her, or is he telling the truth that he didn't?

If you've read my next book, A Winning Recipe, you have learned about making sparks in the kitchen and Lance using mystery meat in his meatloaf. Have you figured out what it was? I haven't. Wasn't he too cute in Kate's mother's apron? I bet even Sandy the dog rolled her eyes.

Hopefully, in A Winning Recipe you also learned how to solve a mystery. Not a huge, earth-shattering one, but one that hurts hearts and has the potential to destroy love. Dead roses anyone?

I look forward to spending more time with Bett and Betsy and Brie in Butterfly Dreams as their lives take unique turns. Dear Bett just can't resist playing matchmaker. Gosh, will Derek and Noel hang in there and be adoring husbands, or will they feel too much pressure from the women? And, what about Mitch, the sometime wedding officiant? Does he ever find love? Is Fancy Nancy and Lester's love secure now, or will they have another trauma, maybe one that involves white napkins?

I am excited about the sequel to A Winning Recipe to find out about Kate's friend Val and Kate's brother Rob's romance, if there is one. And, sweet Sandy, Kate's Golden Retriever. Will she have a child to love in that empty bedroom? And, what about Kate's dad? Will he find love again with Mrs. Kinsey the widow from the mission trip? Remember, the next mission trip to China will be Kate and Lance's honeymoon. That could be exciting, or just interesting.

I would love to have your thoughts on these. None of these books have been completed yet, just begun, so there is potential for reader suggestions. Let me know what you would like to have happen in a Butterfly Dreams sequel (remember, Bett plays matchmaker again) and A Winning Recipe sequel. My characters, Bett, Betsy, Brie, Noel, Derek and Muriel in Butterfly Dreams, and Kate and Lance from A Winning Recipe would love to have your suggestions.

Don't forget as Betsy's mother Harriett says in Butterfly Dreams, "Love is a gift at any age."

Email me at **bengstrom@hotmail.com** (be sure to put the word BOOK in the subject line). Touch base with me at my website **www.bonnieengstrom.com** where you can link to my email, and visit my Facebook pagehttps://www.facebook.com/bonnieengstromauthor?fref=ts . You can also write to me at 8776 E. Shea Blvd., 106-528, Scottsdale, AZ 85260.

ABOUT THE AUTHOR

BONNIE ENGSTROM, is a free-lance writer and former newspaper columnist. Also, wife, mom and 'NEW' grandmother. She lives in Southern California with, Dave, her psychologist husband of forty years, and Jake the Dawg, a Miniature Pinscher.
She holds a B.A. in English from the University of Southern California, has studied creative writing at the University of Pittsburgh, is a member of the Orange County Christian Writers Fellowship, American Christian Fiction Writers and a participant at the Mount Hermon Christian Writers Conference.
Bonnie's favorite genres are romances, mysteries and 'fun' animal stories. She tries to live her life by the Bible verse,
Hebrews 10:24
"Think of ways to encourage one another to outbursts of love and good deeds."

She loves to hear from friends and readers at her website: www.bonnieengstrom.com.

Other Books by Bonnie:
Recipes for Romance
Her Culinary Catch
A Winning Recipe
A Cup of Love

The Candy Cane Girls series
Her Candy Cane Christmas
Her Valentine Promise
Her Wild Ride

www.ingramcontent.com/pod-product-compliance
Lightning Source LLC
LaVergne TN
LVHW011945060526
838201LV00061B/4214